Rebecca held on to the arm that circled her...

...and tried to quell the doubts rushing to fill her thoughts. She felt the sensuous pressure of Don Rigo Aviles's hard thighs behind hers as he straddled the horse, and it occured to her that she could have been found by some ugly, offensive brute instead of this attractive, charismatic man.

The chill air ruffled her hair, but she was warm now beneath the layers of her clothing, and it didn't have nearly as much to do with this serape she'd been given as it did with the man who held her. What sort of man, she wondered, picked up a strange woman in the middle of nowhere and carried her by horseback to his home? The same sort of man, she was sure, who could warm a woman's body with even the most impersonal touch.

She was either very lucky, she decided, or riding toward the worst sort of danger—a danger that might well be found in the arms that held her close.

Dear Reader,

From a most traditional marriage of convenience to a futuristic matchmaking robot, from a dusty dude ranch to glistening Pearl Harbor, from international adventure to an inner struggle with disturbing memories, this month's sensational Silhouette **Special Edition** authors pull out all the stops to honor your quest for a range of deeply satisfying novels of living and loving in today's world.

Those of you who've written in requesting that Ginna Gray tell dashing David Blaine's story, and those of you who waved the flag for Debbie Macomber's "Navy" novels, please take note that your patience is finally being rewarded with *Once in a Lifetime* and *Navy Brat*. For the rest of you, now's the time to discover what all the excitement is about! Naturally, each novel stands solidly alone as, you might say, an extra special Silhouette **Special Edition**.

Don't miss the other special offerings in store for you: four more wonderful novels by talented, talked about writers Nikki Benjamin, Arlene James, Bevlyn Marshall and Christina Dair. Each author brings you a memorable novel packed with stirring emotions and the riches of love: in the tradition of Silhouette **Special Edition**, romance to believe in . . . and to remember.

From all the authors and editors of Silhouette **Special Edition**,

Warmest wishes.

ARLENE JAMES
A Rumor of Love

Silhouette Special Edition

Published by Silhouette Books New York

America's Publisher of Contemporary Romance

SILHOUETTE BOOKS
300 East 42nd St., New York, N.Y. 10017

A RUMOR OF LOVE

ISBN: 0-373-09664-X

First Silhouette Books printing April 1991

Printed in the U.S.A.

Books by Arlene James

Silhouette Romance

City Girl #141
No Easy Conquest #235
Two of a Kind #253
A Meeting of Hearts #327
An Obvious Virtue #384
Now or Never #404
Reason Enough #421
The Right Moves #446
Strange Bedfellows #471
The Private Garden #495
The Boy Next Door #518
Under a Desert Sky #559
A Delicate Balance #578
The Discerning Heart #614
Dream of a Lifetime #661
Finally Home #687
A Perfect Gentleman #705
Family Man #728
A Man of His Word #770

Silhouette Special Edition

A Rumor of Love #664

ARLENE JAMES

grew up in Oklahoma and has lived all over the South. In 1976, she married "the most romantic man in the world." The author enjoys traveling with her husband, but writing has always been her chief pastime.

CALIFORNIA

ARIZONA

Tijuana
Mexicali
Ensenada

BAJA CALIFORNIA

Gulf of California
(Sea of Cortéz)

MEXICO

El Rosario

U.S.—Mexico Border

Guerrero Negro
Rancho de Dos Fuentes
San Ignacio

San Benito

Santa Rosalía

BAJA CALIFORNIA SUR

Pacific Ocean

N

La Paz

THE BAJA PENINSULA

Underlined places are fictitious.

Chapter One

The first sputter of the engine brought Rebecca back to reality. She'd only been driving about an hour, but already the narrow ribbon of road and the vast, empty, dry vista had lulled her into a kind of trance. It was more than the desert, of course, more than the unbroken, tumbledown range of mountains to the east. The past week had taken a terrible toll on her. The shabby little hotel in Guerrero Negro at which she'd spent the night had proven especially noisy, but it hardly mattered. The noise had made her irritable, but it was uncertainty that had kept her awake.

This was a Mexico she hadn't expected. Away from the beaches and the tourist areas, the Baja Peninsula was nothing more than a long, narrow desert with a crooked spine of bare, rocky mountains populated by a few hardy Mexicans, fewer and hardier Indians, and the occasional eccentric American. It was nothing at all like bustling, bawdy Tijuana or even picturesque Ensenada. It was barren and bereft. She hadn't expected to feel so alone out here, so apart. In one way, it made the journey harder, in another, more focused, for she carried with her the constant knowledge that without Matthew, she was truly alone.

She was still angry about the circumstances that had sent her on this eight-hundred-mile journey. Her father had died when she was thirteen. Her mother had then married his former business partner, who had turned out to be petty and greedy and cruel, before drinking herself into an early grave. As a result, Rebecca had seen her brother hounded and belittled and finally driven out of the country by trumped-up charges of embezzlement and theft, his rightful position in the family business handed to a smug, undeserving stepbrother and her home usurped by their enemies. Moreover, she had seen her own dream of exonerating Matt come to naught. Then, only a week ago, she had given in to pressure and settled for getting the charges dropped. In return, she had surrendered the final family interest in the business. Harper and Albertson, Inc. was now simply Albertson Industries. And unless she could find Matthew, it would all be for nothing.

Perversely, as if mocking her, her car's engine knocked, clattered and died, locking the steering wheel. Rebecca groaned as the battered little station wagon rolled to a lopsided stop, one front wheel coming to rest several inches beyond the pavement, and she put her hands to her head. This could not be happening to her. She could not be stranded in this bleak, forbidding desert.

Desperately, she pumped the accelerator and twisted the ignition key. The engine sputtered, then clanked and died. She laid her forehead against the bumpy steering wheel, pleading silently with the vehicle. After a moment, she took a long breath and raised her head to look around her. As far as she could see was—nothing, *nada,* zip. With fresh desperation, she tried the key again and again and again, until finally the battery ground down and the starter gave out, yielding nothing more than a small muted click at the turn of the key. She'd have to walk.

All right. She'd walked before. She was in shape. There had to be something close by, probably just over the horizon. But in which direction? Bucking up somewhat, she fished the map out of the cluttered side pocket fixed to the door and unfolded it, smoothing out the stiff creases. It wasn't difficult to locate the Vizcaíno Desert or the many lagoons along the shore of the Pacific Ocean, and there, just below the border between the two Bajas, was Guerrero Negro—and not another blessed thing until San Ignacio, some one hundred miles to the southeast at the base of the mountain known as Sierra San Francisco. Her heart thumping anxiously, she glanced at her watch and calculated her distance from Guerrero Negro. Good Lord, help was fifty miles away in either direction!

Fighting down panic, she told herself she'd just sit and wait until someone came along. This was Mexico Highway I, after all, the only paved road that ran the length of the peninsula. Someone would come. Eventually. Just because she hadn't met another vehicle since leaving Guerrero Negro didn't mean the road wasn't routinely traveled. This was the route of the famous Baja 1000, after all, or at least it was every fourth year. She bit her lip, trying to decide if this was the year, then realized she was being foolish. She rolled down both front windows and leaned back, forcing herself to relax. It was early in the day yet. Someone was bound to come along soon.

By noon it was sweltering inside the still car. Rebecca fanned herself with the folded map and sipped water from the plastic gallon jug she had placed on the floor on the passenger side, comforting herself with the knowledge that two more jugs rested safely just behind the seat. She'd bought them for three American dollars each in Cataviña and refilled them for the same price in Guerrero Negro. She had food left, too, so it was just a matter of coping with the heat. She tied her hair back with a scarf, rolled up the legs of her shorts and unbuttoned the top four buttons of her sleeveless shirt. By 1:00 p.m., she'd unbuttoned the shirt all the way, and by two, she'd folded the tail up and tucked it under the band of her bra. By half-past four, she'd drunk three-fourths of a gallon of water; yet her throat felt dry and she hadn't developed the slightest urge to urinate. She began to wonder if she might actually die out here.

Slowly, the afternoon passed into early evening with its blessedly lower temperatures. Rebecca got out of the car to stretch her legs. She felt weak and lethargic, but the situation didn't seem quite so bleak as it had at midafternoon. She walked a bit and took a good look around her, squinting into the distance when she'd catalogued all the rocks and tiny cacti in the immediate vicinity. It seemed to her that she could see the curving, prickly, elongated limbs of a boojum tree to the west, but after glancing at the sere mountains to the east, she could no longer make out the ghostly shape. When she came to a snaky track in the sand, she went back to the car and sat for a while in its shade, tossing pebbles at a lump on the ground until she actually hit it and it moved, disappearing down a tiny hole in the ground. She was wrong about there being nothing out here, just nothing recognizable. She got back into the car, shivering slightly as she pondered just what sort of creature that might have been. Soon she was shivering a lot, the cold, black night having settled around her.

The windows went back up, and she put on a pair of jeans and a long-sleeved shirt. She wanted to sleep, but she was afraid that a car might come along and she would miss it, so she ate, instead, beef jerky and canned pork-'n'-beans. Afterward, she tried singing, but all the songs she could remember were mournful, so she gave that up and occupied her mind with thoughts of her brother, Matthew, and how it would be once they were together again.

Poor Matt, still in hiding even though there was nothing to hide from now. But then, he didn't know that. How could he? He'd left in the dead of night more than a year earlier in the company of the family maid, a Mexican immigrant named Anita Martinez, who had promised him refuge in the home of her grandfather in San Benito near Mulegé, deep within the Mexican state of Baja California Sur near the Golfo de California, which many Mexicans still called the Sea of Cortés. Anita had always been fond of Matthew, but the two had so little in common: Matthew had once told Rebecca that Anita couldn't read, while he had graduated with honors from Southern Cal, and yet it had been Anita who had offered him hope when Grange and Louis had first leveled their outrageous charges.

Rebecca supposed she should be grateful for Anita's help, though at the time she had wanted Matt to stay and defend himself against the Albertsons' lies. When he had not, she had sworn to prove him innocent, and in the first few months after Matthew and Anita had fled, Rebecca had held on to that intent with all the stubborn will she could muster. She had even had herself transferred to the accounting department of the family business so she could go over the financial records, but she had found nothing to exonerate her brother. Grange Albertson and his insipid son were just too smart.

Now, fourteen months after she'd watched Matthew and Anita drive away, her stepfather and stepbrother had won. Grange and Louis now held all the private stock issued by the company. No doubt that had been their goal from the beginning, but Rebecca no longer cared. What mattered was that Matt was free from prosecution. In return for the surrender of her meager holdings, Grange had dropped the charges. Perhaps now she and Matthew could have some sort of life together, albeit a penurious one. Matthew wouldn't mind the loss of the stock. He knew too well that the Harpers could not coexist peacefully with the Albertsons, not in the same company and not in the same family. Besides, he had sold his own stock in the family company some time earlier in order to fund one of his obscure investments. Unfortunately, that investment hadn't paid off. But one day he would be back in the money again. Matthew was too brilliant to be a failure, and now he would have his chance to prove it.

Rebecca wondered if Anita would be happy to return to the United States. She secretly hoped that Anita would choose to remain with her family in San Benito, but Rebecca knew that might not be the case. It didn't matter as long as she and her brother were reunited, as long as she was alone no more.

The truth was that Rebecca had been alone too much of her life with only Matthew, seven years her senior, to occasionally pat her head and call her "babykins." She'd been invisible to her parents. They'd had the child they'd wanted, a son, and never had intended to have another. She had been an accident, "one too many double martinis," as her mother had been fond of saying, and somehow they'd simply never made room for her in their lives. Matthew hadn't had it any easier being the favorite. He'd told her often how stressful it was to be expected always to excel, to have the hopes of one's parents pinned squarely to one's chest, and there was the guilt of knowing that his little sister suffered by living in his shadow. How often had he told her how gladly he'd have changed places with her? It was all so unfair.

Their father had intended Matthew to inherit his position within the company, and had he done so, Matthew would have taken care of Rebecca for the rest of her life. He'd promised to many times. But Matthew had been too young when their father had died. Only a sophomore in college, he simply had not been ready to assume the co-chairmanship of the board. Then about the time he'd graduated, their mother had suddenly married Grange Albertson, and it had soon become apparent that Grange didn't think too highly of his late partner's son. In Grange's mind, Matthew simply couldn't measure up to Louis, who had started with the company the same year Matt had entered college and, therefore, had a four-year headstart.

Matthew had seen the hopelessness of his position, of course. Who could blame him for not applying himself as determinedly as he might have if only Grange had given him the benefit of the doubt? In the end, Grange had succeeded in ruining Matthew even in the eyes of his once-adoring mother, and, no doubt in a drunken haze, she had signed over to Grange the vast holdings with which the father of her children had endowed her. Now Grange had it all. Even the shares Matthew had sold to a family friend, Grange had somehow managed to obtain. He had won. But Matthew was free. Rebecca had driven more than half the length of the Baja Peninsula, nearly seven hundred miles from Los Angeles, in order to bring Matt home, and she would, too—provided she didn't die out here in this godforsaken wilderness.

Despite the cold, she slept, only to jerk awake in those black hours before the dawn. Something had awakened her, a sound, a feeling, something. Barely moving, she peered into the darkness in front of her, then to the right, seeing only blackness where road and desert ought to be. Then, relaxing a bit, she slowly turned her head to the left and screamed at the sight of a dirty brown face pressed avidly to the glass. For an instant, she could neither think nor breathe, but then the face jerked back, and she shot across the seat, hands slapping at locks already depressed. She cowered on the passenger side, one foot still dangling off the driver's seat, ears alert for any sound, until finally she began to feel alone.

Slowly, every muscle poised for a flight to nowhere, she rose and peered through the glass that had given her the apparition, for already she was thinking of it as a nightmare. What else could it have been? The window framed only a black desert. She let out a pent-up breath and slowly eased back to her original place and settled down, shivering again. She willed herself to relax, to believe that what she had glimpsed was nothing more than a leftover image of a bad dream, but no rationalization could produce relaxation. She had slept all she would that night, and so much the better, for she ought to remain alert for any genuine sound or sight that might come to her.

What came to her first, after what seemed like hours, were loud, hollow hoofbeats. She sat upright, tense as a watch spring, and the hoofbeats abruptly halted. Rebecca held her breath, shivering in the cold, and stared through the window on her right. Something moved against the blackness below the western horizon, telegraphing an impression of great size. Her mind instantly recalled that hideous face, and she pressed a hand to her mouth, staring hard into the night. She seemed to make out the shape of a large animal...a horse with a man on its back. A man. Help. Thank God!

Fear gave way instantly to euphoria. Impulsively, she yanked open the door and leapt out, only dimly aware of the faint glow of light from the car's interior.

"*¡Madre de Dios!*" came a voice from the darkness. Another voice sounded from a greater distance, and the nearer one answered it.

"English!" Rebecca called. "*¡Americana!* Does one of you speak English? *¿Habla inglés, por favor?*" The one nearest her clicked his tongue and brought his mount on across the pavement, its hooves sounding loudly in the broad silence. Suddenly, she was frightened again. The skin prickled on the back of her neck as the rider drew near the car. She put her back to the car's interior and pulled the door close as the horse moved onto the sand and swung toward her. The rider loomed above, silent, mysterious. She could not get that face in the window out of her mind, and even though the present one was not it—too long and narrow beneath the wide brim of a battered hat—she felt the same urge to bolt. Instead, she squared her shoulders, gulped and found her voice, searching her memory for some helpful phrase from Spanish class.

"Uh. *¿Cómo está—?* No. Umm ... *¿Habla inglés, por favor?*"

"No," came the succinct reply. *"No inglés."*

Rebecca's spirits plummeted. "Listen," she began desperately, "I'm stranded, see? Do you understand *stranded? ¿Comprende* 'stranded'?" The only reply that she got was a disinterested snort from the horse. "Damn."

The rider called out to whoever was following and was answered not by one voice but by two. It occurred to Rebecca, too late, that these were not the best of odds. What if they chose to harm rather than help her? She could fight off one if she must, but more than that? She was trying to think what to do, how to escape, when the clatter of hooves on the pavement announced the arrival of still more "help." The new arrivals wasted no time joining their companion, each reining in on one side of him. They were three in all, with what seemed a herd of colts milling behind them. The one nearest was quite tall, and likewise his mount seemed larger, while the farthest was so small he appeared childlike, his steed more of a misshapen pony than a real horse. For some reason, that made her feel better. Bandits didn't take their youngsters along. Or did they?

The tall one dismounted, his slow, deliberate movements accompanied by the comfortable creak of leather, the blow and shuffle of horses and a few indefinable pings. He walked forward, trailed by his mount, and stepped past Rebecca to peer into the rear side window of the small station wagon, reins in his hand. Abruptly, a large white head swung at her, pointed ears twitching, brown-and-pink muzzle snuffling.

"G-get away!"

The tall one tugged sharply on the ends of the reins and the head bobbed and withdrew, only to return a moment later, draped loyally over the broad shoulder of its master, his own face partially obscured by the wrinkled brim of a conventional straw cowboy hat. Rebecca stared at the strong chin, blackened by the stubble of a growth of beard, and mentally measured him against herself. He was tall, this rider in the night. She figured the top of her head would come just under his chin, making him six-three or six-four, not the size fellow she could fend off. Disconsolately, she let her gaze wander down the front of his faded denim jacket. It was buttoned tight against the chill, reminding her of her own discomfort, and she shivered, hands clutching the top rim of the car door.

The first one, still astride his horse, said something low and rumbling in Spanish, and the tall man replied sharply without ever looking away from Rebecca. She straightened, knowing that their talk was of her, determined not to show her fear. Talk continued for several minutes, some of it clearly argumentative, until the tall man raised his hand and angrily chopped off the flow of words. The horses blew and shifted while he rubbed his chin pensively with a brown, long-fingered hand, the nails blunted and pink. Rebecca watched him think, steeling herself for whatever was to come. Would he strike her? Grab her? She thought of Matthew and wondered if she would ever see him again. The man lifted his hand and she cringed, realizing belatedly that he was only lifting off his hat.

"Woman," said a thickly accented voice, "wha' de hell are you doing here?"

Rebecca nearly collapsed. The sound of English, even thickly accented and poorly pronounced, was an immense relief in itself.

"Y-you speak English! But the other man—"

"He do no' speak eet. On'y me."

She didn't care if it was the horse, so long as she could make herself understood. "Thank God one of you does! I'm looking for my brother, but the car broke down, so I waited—"

"You look for your brother?" he interrupted, and she nodded. He chuckled and shook his dark head, inky hair swishing about his collar. "I am sorry, *señorita.* Your brother ees no' een dis place."

She stared at him, confounded. "I know that!"

"Eef you know dat, *señorita,* den why did you come to dis place?"

"That's what I'm trying to explain," she said slowly. "I am looking for my brother."

"Your brother is no' here," he insisted. "An' eet ees crazy for you to be here een de deser' alone!"

"Yes, I agree, but—"

"No 'but,' *señorita,*" he said. "You mus' come wit us."

Rebecca blinked at him. Go with them? Surely he was joking. She put on a reasonable smile, enriched her voice with patience. She would make him understand.

"It's just that the car is broken down," she said evenly. "*¿Comprende* 'broken down'? It won't go." She reached inside and patted the steering wheel, then made a putt-putting sound and moved her hand along at a steady pace. She stopped and smiled. "If you could make it go again, I could find my brother and you could..." She waved her hand absently.

The wide grin beneath his narrow black mustache gave her hope. She took measure of his face again in the faint light. He was actually quite a handsome man, with patrician features somewhat obscured by his dirty beard. The thin, stylized mustache wasn't bad, though, and neither was his hair. Loose, black curls framed a high, broad forehead, across which cut straight black eyebrows. His nose was neither too long nor too short, and his mouth, though a trifle thin, was well-sculpted beneath the precisely manicured curve of his mustache. She couldn't see the eyes, shadowed as they were in their sockets. Altogether it was a pleasing, intelligent face, although set along somewhat stubborn lines at the moment.

"We go here," he said, pointing with the limp ends of the reins toward the mountains, "to El Rancho de Dos Fuentes, the land o' my fadher and his fadher and his before him for seex generations."

She tried to curb her impatience. "A rancho?" she said. "You mean a ranch, like with livestock and corrals."

He nodded. "A cool, green place een de mountains, wit' two—how do you say?—*agua*. Water come up from de groun'."

"Ah, springs," she supplied. "Well, that's lovely, I'm sure, but about the car...? Couldn't you at least take a look under the hood?"

He clucked his tongue and rattled something in Spanish that made his companions chortle.

"*Señorita,*" he began with a sigh, "my men an' I, we ride, we no drive. We could look at your car from now to de Secon' Coming an' we could no' make eet go. You come wit us or you stay. But I mus' tell you—eef you stay, you pro'ly goin' to die."

Rebecca stiffened. Die? She had to admit it was a possibility, but she didn't want to think about it. "You're trying to frighten me," she said. "Why, I'd be insane to get on a horse and ride off with three Mexican cowboys I've never even seen before. If you won't help me, I'll just wait here until someone else comes along."

He inclined his head. "As you wish, *señorita*. You can pro'ly hol' out. Jus' watch for snakes an' spiders, take eet easy on de water and stay out o' de sun."

"A-all right. I can do that."

"De Indian," he went on, "dey wander dis way. Now no Indian ees going to make your car go, but dey will give you water an' food. You got food to las' five or seex days?"

Five or six days! She gulped. "It wouldn't be that long— would it?"

He shrugged. "Eet ees har' to say how long or what kind o' man will come nex'. We will say a prayer for you. God be wit you." He moved toward his horse, but Rebecca suddenly couldn't let him go.

"Wait!" she said. "Let me think a minute, would you?" He nodded and reached up a hand to pat the jaw of his horse. It was really quite cool out, and she shivered again, the skin prickling along her arms. Five days stranded on the edge of a desert! Could she bear that? Could she even survive it? And what of that face? Had it belonged to an Indian? Was he out there still? Maybe that person would come again after these men had left. And what if all this man said was true? Did she dare take the chance? Being with this English-speaking man seemed far preferable to waiting here alone for even another hour, but what might she be getting into? She swallowed a tremor in her throat and took a deep breath.

"Could . . . would it be possible for you to take me to my brother in San Benito?"

He glanced at his confederates. "*Sí*. No' righ' away. My people, dey need dese supplies. Eet's a busy time o' year."

"Might there be a telephone where you're going then? Maybe I could call San Benito and . . ."

But he was shaking his head. "No *teléfono*. No *teléfono* for fifty mile."

She put both hands to her head, struggling desperately for some answer to this dilemma.

"Perhaps if I spoke to your boss . . ."

He folded his arms. "You are speaking to de boss a'ready."

"Oh. I see." That was that, then. His terms or nothing, and, of course, he knew that.

He shrugged impatiently. "My men and I, we come back dis way een maybe two mon's. We can check for you den. Perha's we jus' find your bones, but we can look, eh?"

Rebecca took a deep breath. "If it's really as you say . . ." She hesitated, not just because she was uncertain, but also because she hated having her mind made up for her, even by a tall, good-looking man. Still, what option did she have? Anyway, if he really wanted to do harm to her, he could have done it already, and he did speak English. She licked her lips. "I'll go with you. But I have to get to San Benito at first opportunity."

"On my word o' honor, *señorita,* we'll get you dhere. As I say, eet ees a busy time, but we do de bes' we can."

She sighed. "I guess I can't ask for more than that."

Something very like relief softened his features and he gave her his first genuine smile. "You make a wise deceesion, *señorita*. You will no' regret eet, I swear."

Nodding reluctantly, she extended her hand. "I suppose introductions are in order. I'm Rebecca Jane Harper from Los Angeles."

"Ah." He seized her fingertips, his thumb running over her knuckles. His manner had become most deferential, and he seemed to know something of Los Angeles—or was it only the Spanish name of the city that he recognized? He gave her no opportunity to ask. Instead, he made a truncated bow, as deep as the proximity allowed. "Rodrigo Felipe Marcos Junípeo Avilés o' de Ranch o' Two Springs, as you say, a' your service." He finished with a flourish.

She could only smile. "And what should I call you?"

He gave a shrug, still holding fast to her fingertips. "I am Don Rigo to mos'."

She nodded. "Don Rigo, then, and you may call me Rebecca."

"Rebecca," he said, rolling the *R*. "A pleasure to know you." He released her hand, finally, to gesture toward his men. "De small one ees Paco an' de odher, Luca."

She nodded toward each, wondering if they would prove equally galant in manner. Somehow she didn't think so. She shivered again, feeling exhausted. "You wouldn't have something warm I could wear, would you?"

Don Rigo said something in Spanish, and the little one, Paco, stripped off his outer garment and tossed it to Luca, who tossed it to Don Rigo. "Allow me," he said around a display of fine teeth as he held out what appeared to be a piece of hemp-colored blanket with a bound hole in the center. He lifted it and slipped it over her head. It was heavy and a bit smelly and scratched the sides and back of her neck, but once she'd fished her collar out and turned it up, the garment was comfortable enough and thankfully warm.

"Thank...uh, *gracias*," she said to all, but Don Rigo was already giving orders. In response, Paco dismounted and

moved with an odd clinking sound toward the car. Pushing
and elbowing his way past the big white horse and Don
Rigo, he swept off his hat, an overlarge cowboy-style one
with a flattened brim, and grinned at Rebecca. He was a
fully grown man, no child this, as evidenced by a reddish
beard and gapped, broken teeth stained by the tobacco
tucked between his gum and lower lip. He was a dirty little
man, but not threatening.

She intuitively pushed the door wide, and he scrambled
inside, booted feet and clinking spurs disappearing last. She
moved away and found herself in Don Rigo's hands, being
guided smoothly toward his mount. First, he lifted her knee,
bringing her foot high, and pushed her foot into the stirrup
cup, then his hand moved to her waist, and he lifted her
easily into the saddle. She swung her right leg over, feeling
her foot plucked from the stirrup at the same time, and
landed hard against leather. The whole thing then shifted as
his hand grasped the pommel and he heaved his own weight
aboard. Close behind her, he wrapped his arm around her
middle and lifted her against him, settling her comfortably
between his legs. It seemed a strangely intimate position but
was not unpleasant.

Don Rigo gathered the reins in his left hand, said something in reply to Paco, who was retreating from the car with
her suitcase and water jugs, and frowned. Without so much
as looking up, Paco swiftly opened the case and began to go
through her things, tossing away some and stuffing others
inside his opened shirt. She let out a yelp.

"My clothes!"

"De burros are a'ready heavily loaded," Don Rigo's
smooth voice said into her ear. "We take only what ees
necessary. De odhers we lock eento de car."

Rebecca's face burned as she saw Paco stuff a handful of
lacy panties into his shirt front, but she said nothing,
knowing it was out of her hands. Apparently satisfied with
the products of his rummaging, Paco tossed an additional
pair of jeans over his shoulder and shoved the empty suit-

case into the car. At a command from Don Rigo, he twisted inside and plucked out the keys before hitting the lock and slamming the door. Finally, he scooped up Rebecca's supply of water jugs and carried two of them to the man called Luca, who began tying them on either side of his saddle. Then Paco mounted, turned his comically small burro and rolled his spurs over its shaggy sides. With a shrill bray, it trotted away, trailing a string of six or eight others behind it, each piled high with its own clumsy burden. Luca went racing ahead, while Don Rigo turned his fine white mount to follow. Rebecca held on to the arm that circled her middle and tried to quell the doubts that were even then rushing to fill her thoughts. To the east, above the ragged tops of rocky mountains outlined thinly in a dark, bloody red, the sky had turned from black to gray with the slowly coming dawn.

Rebecca felt the sensuous rock of Don Rigo Something Something Something Avilés's hard thighs aside her own, and it came to her that she could have been found by some ugly, offensive brute with body odor and dirty hands instead of this attractive, interesting man. The chill air ruffled her hair, but she was warm now beneath the layers of her clothing, and it didn't have nearly as much to do with this blanket as it did with the man who held her. She thought this thing was called a serape, and she suddenly realized that it had come right off Paco's own shoulders. What sort of man, she wondered, ordered another to sacrifice his comfort and was rewarded with instant obedience? And what sort of man, all things considered, picked up a strange woman in the middle of nowhere and carried her by horseback to his home? The same sort of man, she was sure, who could warm a woman's body with even the most impersonal touch. She was either very lucky, she decided, or riding toward the rawest sort of danger.

Oh, Matthew, she thought, what have I gotten myself into?

Chapter Two

He sat with his head slightly cocked, his forearms resting on drawn-up knees, listening to her every word. When she had finished describing what she had seen in the car window, he plucked a clod from the ground and crumbled it between long, nimble fingers before replying.

"Aw, eet was some crazee," he said. "Indian pro'ly. De deser', eet ees hard, and de Indians are de poorest o' de poor here. Dey wander from place to place, dhose who keep to de ol' ways."

Rebecca bit her lip. "You don't suppose he—or she—needs our help, do you? I mean, maybe he's lost."

Don Rigo shrugged. "Who ees to say?"

It seemed a lame answer for one she was coming to think of, in a way, as her savior. She stirred the dirt with her finger, putting space between words she half hoped would go away.

"Don't you care if someone's lost out there?"

"*Sí.*" He leaned back against the bank of dirt behind them, pushing his hat forward so that it rode low over his dark eyebrows. "But why worry abou' somet'ing you canno' change? I say a prayer for dis person and ligh' a candle in de chapel o' de rancho. De res' ees for God, no?"

She dropped her gaze, noticing that he wore a fine leather belt with a large oval buckle, and stirred the dirt some more, mollified by an answer both reasonable and romantic. What Rodrigo Avilés could not do must be left to God. He was Catholic, no doubt. A good man, it would seem. She had one more question for him.

"Listen, I've been wondering about my car. Do you think it's going to be okay back there?"

He seemed uncertain for a moment, but then he leveled his gaze, his light, oak-colored eyes frank. "Eet ees jus' a car," he said. "Ees no' your life more *importante* dan a car?"

She sighed. "In other words, I should just forget about it." His eyes did not falter. His expression did not change. An honest man. She looked away, thinking that she could have done worse, much worse. Besides, it was an old car. She put it out of her mind. "How long," she asked, "before we reach your home?" She was wanting a bath and a clean bed to snuggle into, though neither seemed required by her escorts. Both Luca and Paco had earlier thrown themselves down in a patch of shade provided by a rocky overhang and were already snoring. Don Rigo seemed to relax of an instant and was even now stretching out for a snooze, his hands laced over his flat middle and his hat shading his face. His reply came through the crown.

"Eef we make good time tonigh'," he said, "we be a' de rancho tomorrow before siesta."

"Tomorrow!" Another night in the desert! She groaned.

Don Rigo pushed up his hat with an extended index finger. "You mus' sleep before eet ees too hot or you no' sleep a' all," he warned. The hat went back down, and the fingers relaced themselves over the belt buckle. He had unbuttoned his jean jacket to expose the white shirt underneath, but had otherwise made no concession to the rising heat.

Rebecca glanced at her watch, noting helplessly that it was not yet 9:00 a.m. It seemed to her they had been traveling for days rather than hours, and also that they had gone backward in time, making the days now years. Soon, she would lose the twentieth century altogether.

She lay back upon the sand, surprised to find it cool against her body, and turned to her side, pillowing her head with her arm in an effort to keep her hair clean. She lay for a long while, too tired even to sleep, her worries creeping along her skin like spiders, until exhaustion and boredom numbed her mind so thoroughly that she at last found rest from her troubles.

Rodrigo stretched, using a minimum of movement, his arms straight in front of him, his toes turning upward, shoulders pressed to the ground. Slowly he sat up, pushing his hat into place and looked about him. Paco was sitting cross-legged on the ground some ten or eleven yards away, quietly gnawing on something wrapped in a tortilla, probably dried goat meat, maybe a fatty chunk of salt-cured pig. Rodrigo felt his own belly asking for some of the same, but first he must address the need of another part of his body. His belly wanted filling, his bladder wanted emptying: that was always the way with life, conflict of one sort or another.

He looked down at the woman. She had a nice curve to her, a fact her position emphasized. She lay upon her side, finally sleeping, it seemed. He'd felt sorry for her earlier, sensing her discomfort; yet he knew that this was nothing compared to what she would feel after another five or six hours on horseback. He checked the sun hanging low on the western horizon, and judged the hour. He thought in terms of the daylight left to them: an hour at most. It was time to be moving. They would stop again before midnight to rest the animals, and the woman would truly suffer then. He would have to make her walk before he could let her rest again or she would not be able to walk at all later.

His gaze went to the fall of light-colored hair that spilled over the ground. It was blond but not as light as if she had used chemicals to bleed the color. It was instead a soft, pale brown streaked unevenly with the yellow-white that came from spending time in the sun. He thought of the women he had seen in America, nearly naked in their little bathing garments, lolling beside their cement pools, and in his mind he saw Rebecca, the pale gold of her skin exposed for the eyes of any man, and felt both interest and disgust. *Americanos,* what a strange lot they were.

He would feel better about this one if she weren't so pretty. *Madre de Dios,* what eyes! It wasn't just that they were blue, but that they were *such* a blue. He had nothing with which to compare them. They were darker than the sky, less green than the Sea of Cortés, not so gray as the mountains on the horizon, and only a bit more purple than the shadows that grew at dusk. He had spent some pleasant minutes this morning contemplating those eyes; yet he knew that it would be easier for him—and for her—if she were less lovely. Too bad she wasn't ugly. Then his people would look and shake their heads, their disgust tempered by pity, and they would befriend her, even Tía Elena, his aunt, the self-appointed conscience of his people. As she was, this Rebecca was going to be trouble, but he was partly to blame. He wished fervently that he had not told his men so many stories about the *Americanas* he had known. But the words had been said, many times, and he could not undo them. Besides, most of them were true. Only the most lurid details had he made up, to make the stories seem more exciting.

In truth, his experiences with *Americanas* had been empty and tawdry. He did not understand women who gave themselves so freely and with so few expectations. He had been hurt in the beginning when his conquests had failed to fall madly in love with him, but then he had realized that passion, like all else in American society, was fashioned for convenience. They treasured nothing above their convenience, these *Americanos,* not even love.

At least Glorieta, his most recent mistress, fancied herself in love with him, as was proper for a Mexican woman, even one with Glorieta's reputation. Of course, it was Glorieta's reputation that made her the proper choice for his *amante,* but it also made her a poor replacement for the mother of his sons. This caused him sorrow in one way and relief in another. He understood Glorieta's need for a man. Having been widowed himself these many, many months, he knew how hard it was to do without that pleasure that a beloved mate brings. Also, he felt sorry for her because she had no children of her own. Yet he was glad that he could not marry her, because he could never feel for her, outside of bed, what he had felt for his Sofía. But it would not do to dwell on Sofía. All the thought and wishing in the world would not bring her back, and they were losing time while he sat and brooded on these things. Besides, his bladder was threatening to pain him if he did not pay it heed.

He got up, snatching his spurs from the ground, and walked toward the large rock around which Luca had just appeared, hitching up his pants. He saw the man's eyes go at once to the woman and set his jaw. Yes, she would be trouble, this Rebecca. He could not, on his honor as a gentleman, have left her unprotected in the desert alone. Yet he had no time to deal with her. So much depended on what happened during these next few weeks, and there was the matter of the dwindling water supply on the lower range. That was not something he could ignore. Indeed, there were more immediate concerns than the woman, many of them.

Rebecca felt the hand close upon her shoulder and flinched, but the slumber was too heavy to throw off all at once. She fought her way to the surface like a swimmer in deep water, bemused by the incongruent feeling of lungs expanding with fresh air in the process, and came awake.

Don Rigo had hunkered down beside her, his weight balanced on the balls of his feet, his eyes calm and steady. "We make ready to go," he said softly, handing her her small canvas purse. "Eat, drink and relieve yourse'f quickly."

Relieve yourself? Of course. She sat up, switching her gaze before he could see the embarrassment in them. But where? He rose to his feet and, as if reading her mind, looked deliberately toward a large rock some fifteen or twenty yards away, then strode off with a jingling of spurs. She dusted off her forearms and shoulder before getting stiffly to her feet, her handbag clutched to her side. She supposed Paco had taken it from the car seat, and she was grateful, for there were tissues inside and a comb and a few cosmetics. She was sore and cramped, especially in the seat, but felt surprisingly rested, all things considered. It was hot still, but not unbearably so, and the sun did not beat down as it had before. She conducted her business speedily and got back to the others.

Don Rigo was tightening the girth on his saddle, with Luca by his side speaking forcefully. She did not understand, despite the years of Spanish classes, but the bold look the man gave her let her know that she was the topic of conversation. Don Rigo said something stern, and Luca closed his mouth and stepped away, but the worried look on his face told Rebecca that the matter had not been settled. Rebecca set her chin and walked forward as Luca slipped away, her heart thumping noticeably. Rodrigo gave her a perfectly composed smile, which helped to soothe her concern somewhat.

"A problem?" she asked.

"Life ees full o' problems," he said. "No' to worry. Paco has somet'ing for you to eat. Bring eet along, eh? I wan' to get started."

She nodded and went quickly to Paco, who hunched over the ground. He was wrapping something in a piece of white fabric about the size of a bandanna and tying the ends together to make a sling. She stooped and timidly smiled at him. He beamed back a gapped grin. Perhaps she had two friends. He held up the bundle, his shaggy eyebrows arching in invitation, and indicated her canvas bag. She understood. He would carry her purse for her so she could carry the food. She handed it over.

"It's not as if you're going to charge up my credit cards," she muttered. He nodded and chattered, stuffing the bag into his shirt front, where once her clothing had ridden. She wondered where her things were now.

Paco looped the ends of the bundle over her wrist and began to roll up the supple hide he had used for a work surface. *"Vaya,"* he said with a jerk of his head. *"Vaya pronto."*

She understood that all right. It was time to ride. She stood and moved swiftly toward Don Rigo and his horse. He was waiting for her, one elbow hitched up onto the saddle. His denim jacket had disappeared, and he had rolled back the cuffs of his sleeves. His hat sat far back on his head, but he pulled it forward as she approached. She stepped close, and once more he boosted her easily into the saddle. She made a softer landing this time and purposefully moved as far forward as possible, the saddle horn pressing into her crotch. He swung up and settled, the reins in his hand.

"Back," he said. "Come on. Come on." She slid a fraction of an inch toward him. He made a disgusted sound through his nose and wrapped his arm about her, giving her a yank upward and back. "Eet ees easier for you dis way," he told her, his voice loud in her ear. "You will no' be so—" he snapped his fingers a couple of times before finding the word "—sore."

She nodded, color staining her cheeks, and they moved off, Luca in the lead again and Paco following with the pack train. Don Rigo kept his horse behind and a little to the left, avoiding the dust that followed the string of burros. Rebecca was keenly aware of him, of his long legs flanking hers and the strong arm encircling her waist.

They rode swiftly as long as there was light, but darkness restricted movement to a careful walk. After a bit, Paco began to sing in a surprisingly clear, lilting voice. Rebecca's stomach rumbled, and, remembering the food, she spread her little bundle in her lap. Inside were three white tortillas, each wrapped about a strange, grayish meat. She chose one, sniffed delicately and, detecting no offensive odor, bit into it. It tasted strongly of pepper, with a strange, musty aftertaste. She chewed swiftly and swallowed, trying not to think about what it was she had just sent down to her stomach.

"No' ezac'ly a Beeg Moc, eh?"

She swiveled her head and looked at him over her shoulder. "No, it isn't a Big Mac. You know about hamburgers?"

"*Sí.* Gimme a burger and French fries and Coca-Cola anytime. Dat ees good eating. I like peetsa, too."

"Peetsa?"

"*Sí.* You know. Big roun' t'ing wit cheese an' meat an' all dat goop."

"Cheese and meat and goop? Oh! A pizza! Where did you eat pizza?"

There came a little pause for effect. "Los Angeles."

She twisted about. "You were in Los Angeles?"

"*Sí.*" And he told her how he had come to be in that city so faraway, how his old tutor, the village priest, had died and no other had come to take his place, leaving him with no one to complete his education, how his father had sent him, barely fifteen, to La Paz, the capital, for schooling. "He t'ought o' himse'f as *patrón*," he explained, "an' de *patrón*'s son was to be…educated. Eet was, umm, okay for de odher chi'dren to be ignoran', but no' for de *patrón*'s son. He was a hard man, my fadher, but a good man."

He went on, explaining frankly how that taste of life beyond the *sierras* combined with his father's sternness to produce rebelliousness in him, how at seventeen, thinking himself worldly, he had talked his way onto a pleasure boat owned by rich Americans and traded work for his passage to the United States. He had spent the next three years dodging immigration officials, learning English and working at odd jobs, everything from dishwashing to gardening.

"But you didn't learn to drive?" she asked innocently.

"Hell, no," he declared, waving his arm around. "American highways scare me to death. You *Americanos* are crazy! You kill each odher all over de place. I jus' wan' a good horse like my El Pescado under me." He leaned forward and patted the long, lithe white neck of their mount.

"El Pescado," Rebecca said absently, less aware of what she was saying than the arms that surrounded her. "Guess that means horse."

"No." He chuckled. "*Pescado* mean fish."

"You named your horse Fish?"

"*Sí.* In La Paz, de guides—umm, for de tourists to go out in de sea—de guides, dey alway' say, 'I gonna find you a fish big as a horse!' An', hey, I seen some, too, and dis 'ere, dis ees a big horse, so..."

"So, El Pescado," Rebecca said, patting the horse. "I like that. It's clever."

"I yam a clever hombre," he came back. "You know hombre?"

"*Sí.*" She sent a smile over her shoulder. "It means man."

"Ah. So you have some *español,* eh? Perha's you will get some more before you see your *hermano.*"

"*Hermano,*" she said, "brother."

His smile was white against the dark shadow of his face. She settled against him, Paco's song floating to her on the night. Who would have thought such a man could be found here in this Mexican desert? This could turn into quite a little adventure, as she no longer doubted that Don Rigo could be trusted. She felt certain that he would eventually get her to Matthew; it was just a matter of time. Yes, indeed, it could have been a lot worse. A lot worse.

The night grew chilly. Don Rigo retrieved his jacket and her borrowed serape from a roll tied immediately behind the saddle. She put away the food and slipped into the serape, then held the reins nervously while Rodrigo brushed down his sleeves, shrugged into his coat and buttoned it. They had lost time doing this, and once they were both appropriately garbed, Don Rigo took hold of the reins, wrapped his arm about Rebecca again and kicked El Pescado into an easy canter. They quickly regained their position behind the others, but Don Rigo kept his arm about her.

Paco ended his song and the silence combined with the steady rock of the horse beneath her, the snug safety of Don Rigo's arms and the cool blanket of the night to suggest sleep. Though she struggled to remain alert, she continually felt herself slouching, her eyelids slipping over her eyes. By the time the little band drew up to the chosen resting place at the foot of the rocky *sierra,* Rebecca felt as if she hadn't slept in days and days. She wanted nothing more than to lie down, but the pain that shot through her when she dismounted was very nearly incapacitating. Don Rigo was at her elbow.

"You mus' walk," he insisted. "Come, I will help you."

She held on to his arm and moved like an arthritic old woman. While she gradually worked out the stiffness, Paco and Luca made camp. Yet somehow, wherever Rebecca and Don Rigo walked, whatever they were doing, both Paco and Luca kept an almost constant watch on them. They muttered together, chuckling at times, then sobering too quickly when Don Rigo looked their way. Rebecca sensed that he was growing angry, and the safety she had felt earlier was replaced by a stiff wariness.

The atmosphere grew so tense that when the meal was prepared, Rebecca took her tin plate to a rock some distance from the fire, where she picked at her food, the only readily identifiable portion of which was the gray meat of uncertain origin. In her absence, the men seemed to relax, making conversation in low, even tones. Then sudenly Don Rigo came to his feet, shouting out sharp, quick words that made his men wince and Rebecca start. Don Rigo stomped past her, his face set in angry lines. She watched him stride into the dark, and she shivered, confused and frightened. Should she follow or wait, call out or keep silent? She looked to the men huddled about the fire, but they were studiously ignoring her. She set aside her food, her gaze going back to the place where she had last seen Don Rigo.

In a while, Paco crept forward and took her plate with a pained grin and a quick nod, slinking away again with a minimum of eye contact. Rebecca held herself and waited, eyes and ears poised for evidence of Don Rigo's return, while Luca and Paco cleaned the supper things with sand and ash. Just as the men were settling down for the night, their blankets spread upon the sand, Don Rigo walked into camp. It was all Rebecca could do not to go to him and slip beneath his arm, seeking the protection and reassurance she had felt earlier.

He walked to the pile of gear on the far side of the fire and, stooping, snatched up two blankets. He shook them out and came to stand beside her, then spread both blankets on the ground. With a jerk of his head, he indicated the one nearest the rock for her. She knelt upon it, so much relieved at his presence that she didn't even care at the moment what the blowup had been about, but he seemed intent upon telling her. He sat on the rock and removed his spurs, then gripped his knees and waited until she got into a more comfortable position, her movements still stiff and slow. She stretched her legs out in front of her and leaned back upon the heels of her palms, her expression open and inviting. He looked away and back again, clearly uncertain how to begin.

"What is it?" she prompted. "It's about me, isn't it?"

He scratched an ear and leaned forward, forearms braced against knees. "Eet ees jus' de men, dey worry. My people hold to de ol' ways, but dey hear de *Americanos* do no', an' now I bring dem a *Americana* woman who de men find—" He took a deep breath and blew it out again. "Eet ees your color. Dey have no' seen a blon' woman before or a woman wit eyes so blue. You are beautiful to look at, an' so, being men, dey t'ink o' perha's taking you to dheir beds.''

Whatever she'd expected, *that* wasn't it. She stiffened, her hands going to her throat. "You're frightening me."

"Dey woul' no' hurt you," he assured her. "But you mus' comprehend. Eet ees a diffrent world we go to. Dhere are no roads, no shops, no electricity, an' you are no' like our own women. You are *Americana,* an' so dey t'ink perha's you no' ezpec' a man to—" he paused, searching for words and finding them "—behave wit honor."

Her mouth fell open. "Are you telling me those men might try to force me to have sex with them?"

"No' force," he said quickly, "but dey t'ink perha's you might be willing."

"Willing?" She closed her mouth with a snap and struggled up to stand despite the pain. "Oo! Ah!" She bent and snatched up the blanket practically from under her own feet. "Willing!" She gathered it into a sandy heap and stomped away a few steps. "I'll have you know, Rodrigo Whoever-you-are, I am *not* willing. How dare you ask if I'm willing!"

"I did no' ask!"

"Well, you implied! And that's as bad!" She shook out her blanket, spitting at the sand that pelted her face, and spread it in a separate place. "You tell your men, *señor,* that if they so much as come near me—"

"I tol' dem a'ready!" he declared, coming to his feet. "I defen' your honor likē de men o' ol'. I tell dem dis gringa ees diff'rent. I say dat eef dey even suggest such a t'ing, I rip ou' dheir lungs an' feed dem to de vultures!" This dramatic statement was accompanied with suitable gesticulations, demonstrating how the hand would descend, grasp and tear away. Then warm brown eyes twinkled and the mustache twitched.

Rebecca felt her anger melting. "You did not!"

He relaxed at once and chuckled. "I did no' have to. Dey are good men. No one harm you, *señorita,* I swear eet. But you mus' comprehend wha' kind o' place you go to. Eet ees no' like Los Angeles, believe dis.''

"I believe you," she said quietly, but he seemed to feel the need to drive the point home more surely.

"Eet will no' be jus' de men, Rebecca, and dis ees wha' worry dem. De women will no' wan' you dhere." He spread his hands helplessly. "Wha' woman wan's a beautiful blon' wit sof' blue eyes hanging aroun' her man, eh?"

That was the second time he'd called her beautiful, and a thrill shimmered through her, a secretive kind of personal pleasure that she immediately struggled to suppress. She turned on her heel, putting her back to those brown eyes. "Your women have no need to worry," she said.

"Eet ees o' no concern to me," he told her lightly. "I do no' have a woman."

No woman? A man like Don Rigo without a woman? It didn't seem likely. Yet, her heart was suddenly whamming like a pile driver as she remembered his arms about her. But this was foolishness, lunacy, especially after what he'd just told her. She busied herself straightening the blanket, then sat down upon it. "You'll forgive me if I say that your people sound a bit small-minded."

He shrugged. "You may say wha' you wish, but eet ees dat you do no' comprehend, really. How can you? Los Angeles ees so very faraway from dis place an' dese people."

She crossed her arms over her knees and hung her chin on them. It was true, of course, perhaps more so than she had even realized, which brought up another question. "Why did you come back here?"

He walked over and went down on his haunches beside her. "I came home," he told her simply. "I came to know dat my place ees here on dis mountain, wit my people an' my fadher's people—"

"And his father's before him," she supplied.

"For seex generations." He grinned and swirled a finger in the dust. "I did no' fit een Los Angeles. I no' comprehend how so many peoples can live so close an' be so far apar'. Dhere wa' such wealth, but no..." He reached for the right word but closed his hand on emptiness. "I had to come back. Een de end, I walked. An' when I saw my home again, I wept like a *niño*."

She pictured this strong man weeping and found the scene poignant, yet some part of her, some deep, empty part, could not quite understand the emotion that had so moved him. She thought of Matthew and how glad she would be to see him again and decided the feeling must have been something like that.

"I'm a great inconvenience to you, aren't I?" she asked.

"You may come to t'ink de inconvenience ees yours," he warned her.

"But you're going to have trouble because of me, aren't you? I'm beginning to realize how much. It makes what you did, bringing me with you, seem pretty courageous."

He shrugged. "A man mus' do wha' ees right. Perha's you will no' be so gra'eful after a while. Now go to sleep, an' do no' fear." He tossed the ends of the blanket over her and rose.

"Rodrigo," she said, "I'm sorry..." She meant to say more, but couldn't find the words.

He smiled down at her. "Beautiful women shoul' never be sorry," he said, and he left her, her whispered parting seeming to waft behind him on the weightless silence of the night.

He was near, she reminded herself, and he would not let anyone hurt her, not that these were bad men. They just had some unfortunate ideas about American women. This truly was a different world, but she'd be all right as long as she watched her step—and that meant with Don Rigo, too.

Chapter Three

Rebecca was so stiff she couldn't move, and when she tried to, tears came instantly to her eyes, but Don Rigo was unsympathetic. He took her by the hands, stood over her with one foot on either side and pulled her up, walking backward as she rose. It did no good to protest, to threaten or even to cry, but once she was on her feet, he brushed the tears from the hollows of her eyes with the pads of his thumbs and chucked her beneath the chin.

"Eet will pass in a shor' while, an' *mañana* when you wake, eet will no' be so bad as today. Soon you will be tough and proud, you see."

But she felt only fragile and sore with a great, desperate yearning for her own bed in her old room in the big house in California, Grange Albertson's house now. Moreover, she was dirty and bedraggled, with sand in her socks and athletic shoes and her hair. She was hungry, but the meat smelled positively rancid that morning, if one could call such a black hour morning, so she settled for the leathery tortillas and, surprisingly, two small, dark, very sweet oranges that Don Rigo proudly presented her, saying they were from his own orchards.

The idea of citrus orchards in this hot, vast emptiness seemed ludicrous, but she couldn't deny the reality of those two dark-yellow orbs. She wolfed them down, tearing the peel from the membrane with her fingers and breaking the whole into sections that squirted with dark, rich juice. Afterward, she licked the sticky juice from her fingers until the last trace of sweetness was gone. Don Rigo laughed at her, calling her a child, and she found herself smiling despite the chill and the grit and the overriding fatigue.

They mounted—Rodrigo literally handing Rebecca up into the saddle because she was too sore to help herself—and began the slow circling of the mountain. The ground was especially rocky, and their little train wound carefully in and out among the boulders, until they came to a wide cleft in the wall of rock. A sharp right turn led them up a narrow gully of loose shale that cracked and popped beneath the hooves of the horses and burros. Presently, the trail bore right, and the little train of travelers strung out in a long, single-file line that curved gently left and upward. Occasionally, Rebecca's foot or knee brushed a rocky outcropping that crumbled beneath El Pescado's hooves, disappearing silently into the darkness beyond the narrow rim of the pathway. As they climbed steadily higher, her discomfort increased and she grew tense, reacting to innocent sounds, small collisions and the pressing darkness with jerks, gasps and trembling.

"Relax," Don Rigo said quietly into her ear, so close that she felt the edges of his teeth against its upper curve, but even that made her jump, her tension adding to the strain on her battered muscles.

Gradually, the sky about them brightened, going from black through progressive shades of gray to a dusky blue washed with morning gold. It was an incredible experience, moving there on that narrow thread of trail suspended between the black striated rock of the mountain and the cloudless sky. The sky, like a sheet of glass on her right, the mountain, a wall of stone on her left, Rebecca curled her fingers tightly into the arm about her waist and gazed with wide, frightened eyes. She forgot her pain, the dusty feel of skin chafed by cold, even her tension as the horse carried her higher and higher in the fold of Don Rigo's arm.

The air grew warmer as the sun rose, crowning both dirt and sky with a light so bright and brittle and white that it wounded. Don Rigo made her keep her sleeves rolled down and button her shirt to the very top, warning her that her pale skin would burn as if held over a flame. Warm air became hot air as the morning wore on, yet it lacked the stifling weight of that which blanketed the desert below. They passed a real tree, a spindly thing that clung to a basketful of dirt gathered in the crevice of a rock, its malnourished limbs and pale foliage offering no shade to the small cactus that grew by its side. Ahead, the path, if indeed it was a path, narrowed alarmingly and seemed to come to a dead end against a cracked wall of sheer rock, only to veer sharply to the left into a crevice barely wide enough to admit them.

Suddenly the sky was blotted out by a thick overhang of greenish-black rock that made Rebecca duck her head, though the clearance was easily half-a-dozen feet. Just as suddenly, a new vista greeted her, a true mountain oasis nestled, green and fragrant in a narrow valley cradled on all sides by the naturally terraced slopes of the mountain.

"We stop below," Don Rigo told her, pointing to nothing in particular, as far as she could see, "to prepare ourse'ves for homecoming."

The nothing in particular turned out to be a steep, narrow trace that led down into the green valley. They followed the pack train, which seemed simply to fall, animal by animal, over the edge of the precipice. Rebecca closed her eyes as Rodrigo urged El Pescado after them. Even blind, the descent was harrowing, the angle so steep that Rebecca felt herself thrown backward against Don Rigo's chest, her hips thrust forward as the horse's shoulders seemed to drop from beneath her. Her eyes popped open, widened at the sight of palm trees rising up to meet her, and snapped shut again as her fingers twisted in the fabric of Don Rigo's shirtsleeve. Then suddenly it was over, the horse righting beneath her as Don Rigo whooped triumphantly.

She couldn't believe they had survived the ride. Even when Don Rigo slid off the horse and reached up to lift her down, she felt only shock at being unscathed. Numbly, she allowed him to aid her dismount, and then, with solid earth beneath her feet, looked up into sparkling brown eyes shaded by the brim of his hat and felt her knees buckle. Instantly, he pulled her up and against him, both arms closing about her.

"Rebecca!"

She gasped, her head reeling sickeningly, and laid her cheek against his shoulder. Oddly, she was not as sore as before, but that didn't seem to help.

"I'm sorry," she muttered. "I can't seem to get my breath."

"*¡Dios mío!* What a stupid I am! Come, I hold you to de water." And so saying, he scooped her up, bearing her quickly away. She felt herself smile, the sickness already receding.

"Carry," she muttered against his shoulder.

"Eh?"

"Carry," she repeated, her tongue thick. "Not hold. You should have said, 'I'll carry you to the water,' not 'I'll hold you to the water.'"

She caught the flash of his smile as he bent to deposit her gently upon the ground. He knelt on one knee and reached across her, bending to the little stream. "Rebecca," he said teasingly, "I have carry you to de water." He straightened and began to stroke her face with wet fingers, forehead first and then cheeks. The water felt surprisingly cool and refreshing against her skin. She managed a smile.

"Thank you. *Gracias*. Again."

"De air," he said, "eet ees too t'in for you, but you feel better after—ah, how you say, *el baño,* ah, to wash?"

A bath? She struggled up onto her elbows. "Do you mean I can bathe, wash myself?"

"*Sí.*"

She looked around her. The ground was littered with browning palm fronds, speckled dark and light with a soft mixture of shade and sun. At her elbow trickled a rivulet of water, certainly not enough in which to bathe. He pointed behind her. She pushed herself up into a sitting position and twisted around. Luca and Paco were drawing water from a shallow pool against a jut of rock curving out into the narrow valley. It could not have been a more welcome sight. She clutched at the dirty blouse in which she had slept and sweat and ridden, thinking how good it would feel to have something clean against her skin once more.

"Might I have a change of clothes, too?" she asked tremulously.

"We will all change," he answered gently. "Eet ees better to go home clean, eh?"

Home. The word sounded hollow and foreign to her. Where was her home? With Matthew, of course, wherever that might be.

Gradually, as her head cleared, she began to recognize a certain order around her, an order beyond the random consequence of nature. There were two types of trees, the skinny palms with their full crowns of fronds, and a sturdier, shorter specimen with real branches and dark green, waxy-looking leaves. These other trees, the small ones with limbs, seemed to grow in orderly clusters of ten or fifteen.

Rodrigo noticed her interest. "Dis arroyo," he said, "dis ees one o' my fadher's orchar's. We grow de frui' here. Wha' you say, de or'ges?"

Orange trees! "It's beautiful," she said.

"De water was here. Eet come from a spring high een de mountain. But de, ah, eart' was no' deep enou' for de frui' to grow. On de mountain was de eart' but no water. So, my fadher an' his people carry—ees correc', no?—eet down een baskets.''

"The earth? You mean the soil? Your father and his people carried soil down here from the mountaintop to plant their orange trees?''

"*Sí.* Dey carry down de soil an' make, umm, pipe from, uh, *la palmera* to carry de water from de pool to de frui'.''

"They made pipes from the palm trees—the trunks, I guess—to carry the water from the stream to the fruit trees. How incredible!''

He smiled proudly. "Now we have no' on'y de pool for de horses to drink an' de travelers to 'fresh demselves, but de or'ges, also. Since dat time when the orchar' began, we have lay much more pipe for water to make more range, an' eet has been a custom since den to stop a' dis place.''

"And a welcome custom at that,'' she told him sincerely.

He stood. "I will make ready. You res', eh?''

She nodded, and he left her, returning some time later to help her to her feet. Luca and Paco had unsaddled the horses, then strung a pair of blankets in front of the pool, using a plaited leather riata secured to a stake driven into a crack in the rock wall of the mountain and the thin bole of the closest palm tree. Before this crude privacy screen lay the bundle of clothing Paco had taken from her suitcase and a smooth white oval she took first to be a bar of soap but which turned out to be nothing more than a small, porous stone smoothed for use in scrubbing the dirt from one's skin.

Grateful but nervous, Rebecca slipped behind the curtain of blankets and slowly, nervously removed her clothes to sit in the cool water and scrub herself clean. She lay on her back to wet her hair, regretting that it was not possible to shampoo it in the little pool, and reveled in the sensuous feel of the water, so precious in this arid place. Knowing the others were waiting their turns, she tried to hurry, yet her efforts produced only a languorous kind of movement. Finally, as clean as she was going to get in a stone-lined pond high in a mountain oasis, she left the water to pull on panties, bra, jeans and a pink cotton T-shirt, the tail of which she tied in a jaunty knot just above the curve of her left hip bone. With her soiled blouse, she dried her hair and emerged from behind the curtain with it tousled and damp.

Luca and Paco quickly abandoned their half-eaten lunches to take their turn, bathing together. They kept their eyes averted as they picked their way, barefoot, toward the pool, clothing slung over their shoulders, but she was not thinking of them. Her attention centered on Don Rigo. He stood before a shard of mirror tacked to the trunk of a palm tree, intently shaving the stubble from the flat of his jaw with a straight razor. He had removed his hat and shirt, and the muscles glided smoothly beneath his nut-brown skin as he stroked the razor over his face and straightened to review his work. Apparently satisfied, he turned to catch her staring. Rebecca flushed and instantly dropped her gaze, only to find it lifting again. He cleaned the razor against his jean-clad thigh, slipped it into his hip pocket and rubbed both hands over his face. Only the neat mustache remained, its droop no match for the sensual upward tilt of the corners of his mouth.

"Eet ees good to be clean again, eh?"

She nodded, aware of the pulse beating in the hollow of her throat. Here was a truly stunning man. The clean, proud lines of an aristocratic face were no longer blurred by the scruff of beard. Light brown eyes sparkled beneath the slash and curve of inky eyebrows. His upper torso was smooth, the muscles taut and clearly defined by a lifetime of hard physical labor. His flat middle tapered to a narrow waist, below which rode the waistband of his jeans, his navel peeking over the stitched rim. Muscles bunched in his upper arms and corded from elbow to wrist. This was the man who had become her lifeline, her protector, her only link with what lay behind and what lay ahead. The very thought made her shiver.

Abruptly, she abandoned the trail along which her thoughts had skipped, color first suffusing and then draining from her face. She turned away, hoping he had not noticed, but she was still learning how sensitive a man Rodrigo Avilés was. He came swiftly to her side, hands reaching for shoulder and chin, gently but firmly urging her to face him.

"Rebecca?" he whispered, "somet'ing troubles you?"

She shook her head. "No," she lied, searching for a reasonable explanation for her behavior. "It's just that, well, you're going home, but I . . ."

"You will go home someday soon, Rebecca," he assured her, strong hands cupping her face. "I swear dis."

It all served to undo her, everything she'd been through, her fears, and now his virility, his kindness and generosity, his good intentions, his nearness. She felt her lower lip begin to tremble, tears springing to her eyes as a wave of self-pity engulfed her.

"Rebecca!" He whispered something in Spanish, then his arms came about her, folding her against him. She turned her face into the hollow of his shoulder, wallowing shamelessly in her private misery and his intimate comfort. He smelled faintly of leather and horse and hot flesh, a purely masculine scent, heady and rich. Her tears wet his skin, her breath coming in quick, ragged gasps, but she was no longer certain why she cried. "Eet has been a bad time, eh? But de village ees jus' above us. Eet may be *dificil,* but no one will dare harm you. Believe dis."

"I—I believe you," she murmured. "I'm not frightened, because I know you wouldn't let anyone harm me. It's only that I lost my own home recently, and if I don't f-find my brother I don't know what I'll d-do or where I'll g-go."

He sucked in his breath. "*¡Caramba!* I no' know dis! Why you no' tell me dis, eh?"

"W-would it have made any difference, really?" She sniffed and lifted her head, encountering the grim line of his mouth with its carefully trimmed embellishment. Her breath caught in her throat. She pushed it out with considerable effort, unable either to lift or lower her gaze.

"Perha's no'," he conceded softly, and his sigh fanned her eyelashes. "Be patien' an' remember you are wit friends."

"One friend, anyway," she countered thoughtlessly.

His fingers curled beneath her chin. *"Sí,"* he whispered, tilting her head back.

She froze, her heart stopping, her lungs paralyzed. Somehow her hands had found the sensitive flesh covering his ribs, and it rippled now beneath her fingertips, sending shock waves of sensation up her arms. His mouth hovered over hers for an agonizing moment, then descended swiftly, seizing hers with stunning fierceness.

Her first impulse, when shock gave way, was simply to enjoy this deeply sensual experience. She was safe with him, after all. Or was she? Had he not said that the men thought of taking her to their beds? Was he not a man? Had he not hinted that if she was willing, no man among them would hesitate to do as he wished? She pushed away from him, suddenly uncertain.

Don Rigo blinked, then stiffened, his arms going down to his sides, hands tightening into fists. "Forgive me," he said. "I did no' mean . . ." He lifted his chin and began again. "When a beautiful woman ees een tears, a man, simply because he ees a man, will . . ." He paused, as if rethinking, then gave it up, finishing with, "Forgive me, *señorita,* I will no' again forget myse'f."

"I—it's all right," she said. "You've been so kind to me, and anyway it wasn't all . . . Let's just forget it, please." She knew it was as much her fault as his, more, because she'd been warned, and that wasn't the only reason. The truth was that their worlds were as different as black and white, and in her own world, she knew she wouldn't have looked twice at him. He would have been out of place there, as out of place as she was here. She was appalled at herself. Perhaps he was, also.

"Eet ees forgotten, *señorita*." He bowed stiffly and backed away.

She pushed her hands into her damp hair. Whatever she'd said, that kiss would hardly be forgotten, nor should it be. This was not just a different place, it was a different time with different standards. She had to walk a line here. Her behavior must be proper. Proper. That was a word seldom heard in L.A.

Paco emerged from behind the curtain, his hair slicked back, clean trousers replacing his dirty jeans. Rebecca went to him and pantomimed her need of a comb and how she might extract one from her purse until he got the idea to retrieve her handbag from one of the packs.

She had started to comb out her rapidly drying hair when Luca gave up the luxury of his own bath and returned to them, loudly proclaiming in Spanish his evident pleasure. Don Rigo pushed past him without comment, his personal gear slung over his shoulder, and disappeared behind the blanket barrier. Luca's gaze went instantly to Rebecca, as if she alone could account for his companion's mood, and she felt a guilty blush come to her cheeks. She turned away, pulling and tearing at her hair with the comb. By the time Don Rigo returned, she had managed to tame her hair, but only just. It dried so quickly in this arid environment that she was hard put to get all the snags and snarls combed out.

Don Rigo had not lingered with his bath as had the others, which made his transformation all the more stunning. The rough peasant was gone, and in his place stood a proud, meticulous aristocrat. Black pants and shirt, embroidered heavily with silver, fit like second skin, except where the pants flared below the knee to the ankle to accommodate the tall black boots. His belt was an intricate work of silver inlaid against black leather and closed with a buckle as large as a man's hand and embellished with gold. The slide that held his narrow black bolo tie between the twin points of his collar was silver, as were the shirt buttons. His hair was combed back sleekly, giving his clean-shaven face a narrow, sculpted look heightened by the pencil-thin line of his mustache.

Paco appeared at Don Rigo's side with a plain black jacket, which he brushed hastily with his hand before holding it out. As Don Rigo plunged first one arm and then the other into the slender black sleeves, he twisted about just enough for Rebecca to see that the upper layers of his hair had been pulled into a taut tail just above his nape. The rest was left to curl gently about his shirt collar. The jacket was collarless and had been cropped short so that its hem just covered his belt. The effect was striking.

Don Rigo extended his hand, and Luca hurried to place in it a neat black hat that he had taken from one of the burro packs. It was a curious thing: not a conventional sombrero, it was too wide of brim and shallow of crown for a cowboy hat. Don Rigo turned it over in his hands. He pulled the string down, loosening the black bead of the slide, then lifted the hat and settled it carefully on his head. His hands dropped to the string hanging down the back of his head. With a single movement he brought the string beneath the bound tail of hair and pushed the slide tight against his head.

He was magnificent. A living, breathing specimen of nineteenth-century *California* vanity, a peacock in black and silver with a touch of gold. He was lord here, dressed as befitted his station. Here, on this mountain, Rodrigo Avilés was boss, top honcho, a master of men and land and who knew what else? Rebecca could only stare, painfully aware of her own bedraggled state.

Don Rigo strode forward, calm and controlled. Within minutes, he had dressed his horse in the appropriate finery, a medallion here, a medallion there, all fixed with drapings of plaited black leather, then seized the reins and vaulted into the saddle, the great animal rearing beneath him. His teeth flashed white against the brown of his face, and suddenly the pair of them was bearing down on Rebecca. Startled, she backed off a step, her blue eyes going wide as she realized what was about to happen. Don Rigo leaned to one side, his long arm sweeping down to lift her off her feet. His arm slid about her waist, and the next instant, she was hauled up and onto his lap.

"Hold tight!" he said, and touched his silver spurs to El Pescado's flanks. They surged forward, man, horse and woman, pounding through the orchard and then, with a lurch, up the steep incline of the valley wall. Rebecca held on for dear life, hiding her face against Don Rigo's chest. Sooner than she could believe, they crested the ridge and were traveling over level ground again, the horse prancing and pawing.

Don Rigo turned his mount back toward the precipice. El Pescado halted on the very rim of the valley oasis, snorting and blowing from his exertion. Below, Luca and Paco scurried amongst the pack animals. They had thrown on leather chaps and vests and were trying to reload all they had taken from the packs earlier. Don Rigo laughed, the sound reverberating from the base of his throat, then he turned El Pescado toward the trail.

"Now," he said, "I take you to my village above. We call eet La Fuente Uno, meaning Spring Number One. Dhere ees anodher, for dis ees de Rancho o' Two Springs, but La Fuente Dos ees no' so large. Perha's eet will be strange to you, but eet ees all I have to offer, an' a man canno' give more dan all he has, eh?"

"Not even the most generous of men," she replied softly, realizing for the first time that her arms were about his neck. She moved them and fixed her eyes on the square of silver at his throat.

"These are interesting clothes you wear," she said. "I'm wondering why you chose them."

"Ah. Eet ees dis way—I return to my people—how do I say? Victorious? Successful? I have made wha' you could call 'a big deal' for cattle, an' eet will mean much to my people. I took a chance, dividing de range for de goats an' de cattle. Mostly we have had goats. Dey survive drought better dan cattle, but de market ees more for cattle. For some years now, I build de herd, an' a' las', we sell. De clothing ees a way o' saying all ees well. Eet ees de costume o' *el hidalgo,* de nobleman from de ol' days. You comprehend?''

She nodded. "It's like a message to the people, so they'll know right away that the deal has been made, *sí?*"

He nodded. "No' dat I ezpec' anyone to notice."

"No? Why not?"

He settled his disturbing brown eyes on her. "Rebecca," he said, "mos' o' dese people have never seen a gringa. To dem, you will be no' on'y strange but a worry. To one mos' o' all. But do no' fear. We have a saying, *'El grajo grazna, pero pica solamente al impotente.'* It means, de crow caws, but it bites on'y de helpless. Remember dis when you meet my aunt, eh? An' trust een me—eef you can."

"Oh, I can," she replied unthinkingly, then looked away, remembering with shame that only minutes before, she had suffered great doubt. Don Rigo clucked his tongue and touched rowels to the flanks of the horse. El Pescado shivered and bolted forward with an eagerness Rebecca could not begin to match. And why shouldn't he? He was going home, after all. He hadn't lost his place in the world. She wondered if she would ever go home again, and if she did, where it would be—and when.

Chapter Four

It was pandemonium from the first bark of the first scrawny dog to the last gasp of Don Rigo's five sisters. It was everything he had warned her to expect and more; yet, Rebecca was unprepared for the shock caused by her presence in the ancient pueblo. No sooner had they entered the dusty, winding lane that led to the village than they met a pack of barking dogs. This was to be their escort through the small community of palm-thatched cabanas. A throng of children gathered, accompanied by their parents, groggy from having risen early from their afternoon siestas. On every side, from every mouth came the wondrous words, *"¡La gringa!"* Many openly gawked, and one woman, brought up short in her doorway as they passed, put her hands to her head and shrieked.

"My eldes' sister, Teresa," Don Rigo explained. He did the same for sisters Ana and María and Beatriz and finally for Isabel, who as the youngest of the sisters was only a year older than her brother. The others were shocked, but Isabel simply stood and smiled until her husband, his arms waving, sent her off at a run. "She will be going for Tía Elena," Don Rigo said with a sigh, but Rebecca was too caught up in the scenery to pay much attention.

All in all, there weren't as many as a dozen houses in the village, each tucked into its own narrow cranny, and they managed to ride by eight or nine of them. What surprised Rebecca was the abundance of flowers, red mostly, with a few yellow ones, and the tiny gardens sown on every available patch of soil. Around the barren square were arranged a saddlery, a blacksmith's shop, a small church, and *el hospital,* which was truly little more than a shed enclosing a single dusty examining table and a trio of cots. In the center of the square was a palm tree standing beside a well with a low, circular cistern bordered by colorful tiles. A small fountain in the shape of a girl with an urn burbled into the cistern, and beyond that was an old-fashioned hand pump below which sat a water trough flanked on each side by a post with rings for tethering horses.

Don Rigo rode to the nearest post and tossed down the reins to a small, excited boy, who knotted them expertly through the rings, then gave El Pescado's probing muzzle a pat before skipping aside to call, *"¡Papá! ¡Papá!"* and to speak excitedly to Don Rigo in rapid Spanish. Don Rigo bent to make a reply, but suddenly they were engulfed by the villagers, everyone jostling and shouting. Don Rigo shouted for calm and handed Rebecca down, sliding her off his lap and setting her feet to the ground, his hands beneath her arms. Instantly, the crowd fell back, silence descending like a weight. Rebecca absently reached for support, her fingers grasping the flared portion of Don Rigo's pants just above his ankle. The boy who had tethered the horse stepped forward, looking over Rebecca with interest.

"¿Padre," he said, *"quién es la gringa?"*

It was the question on everyone's mind. Who is the gringa? Don Rigo made the introduction. "Rodolfo, *esta es* Señorita Harper. Rebecca, this is my son Rodolfo."

His son! How did a man without a woman manage to have a son? She stared at Don Rigo, but he was intent for the moment on the boy, so it was the boy to whom she looked next. He paid rapt attention to his father's explanation, while Rebecca paid rapt attention to him. He favored Don Rigo. Or was his mother tall and lean and sinewy, too?

The crowd parted suddenly, and Don Rigo ceased his explanations, turning his light brown eyes in that direction. Rebecca followed his gaze. An elderly woman hobbled toward them. Tiny but unbowed and clothed entirely in black from her long, gathered skirt to the rebozo draped over her coiled white hair, she clutched a string of rosary beads. Her eyes were small and black and sharp, her face a canopy of dried wrinkles beneath the arch and sweep of whimsical eyebrows, still sooty dark despite the white of her head. So this was the crow. The description was apt.

Don Rigo stepped down from the saddle. As the old woman drew near, he made a slight bow, then widened his stance, feet planted in the powdery dirt.

"Tía Elena," he said.

Rebecca remembered that *tía* meant aunt. She tried to smile. It was an abysmal effort, but no one was looking at her anyway. All eyes were directed at Don Rigo and his elderly aunt. The latter stopped at the side of the well, some two yards separating her from her nephew. For a long moment neither moved or spoke. Then suddenly the old woman threw her hands in the air, beads slinging and rattling. Both she and Don Rigo erupted in torrents of loud Spanish that seemed to roll on and on. Rebecca had no doubt that she was the main topic of conversation.

In the middle of it, Paco and Luca arrived with the pack animals, but not a single soul tore away from the fracas to bid them welcome. Gradually, Don Rigo's sisters were drawn into the fray. Teresa came out squarely in support of Tía Elena, Isabel seemed to align with her brother, and the remaining three wavered. Finally, Don Rigo put a stop to the argument, the command given not as a shout but as a deadly hiss that drew startled responses from the crowd. Elena merely straightened and looked down her narrow nose at him, her thin mouth clamped into a wizened wrinkle. Rodrigo turned to Rebecca.

"Do no' be co'cern," he said in a low, rough voice. "I ezpected dis. De pro'lem ees to fin' you a place to stay. Dhere are but two of us wit room for you. Me." He paused for effect. "Or Tía Elena."

Rebecca gulped. "I'll stay with you."

He sent her an understanding look but shook his head. "Eet ees no' so simple as dat. Dis ees no' Los Angeles, Rebecca. Unmarry men an' unmarry women do no' jus' stay togedher een de same house alone."

Rebecca sighed. "All right, but if that old crow carves me up during the night, it's on your head, Rodrigo Avilés."

There came a gasp from the crowd. Don Rigo sent Rebecca a sheepish, apologetic look. "Here, Rebecca," he began in a very low voice, "I yam afrai' eet mus' be *Don* Rigo. Eet ees a title o' respect, an' *importante* to dese people who t'ink o' me no' on'y as *el dueño*, or landlord, but also as *el hidalgo*. Een private, you may call me wha' you wish."

Rebecca nodded, eyes downcast. Like so much else in this place, the casual intimacy of given names was not to be taken for granted. "Certainly, Don Rigo."

"*Gracias,* Rebecca. Now I yam afrai' I mus' ask my aunt to be de—how you say?—wa'ch dog for us. But do no' worry," he told her, eyes twinkling. "I do no' t'ink she will agree."

He turned back to his glowering aunt and began to speak in a mild, conciliatory tone. He went on at length, the model of patience and reason. This time, Rebecca caught many of the words, but stringing them together into a cohesive pattern was something else again. When he had finished, Elena sniffed, huffed and rattled a negative sounding reply. Don Rigo spoke again and received the same reaction. He turned to Rebecca.

"She will not be the *acompañante*," he said, "nor will she invite you to her home, and my, umm, houseworker is no' acceptable because she ees old an' fond o' me."

"What now?" Rebecca asked.

Don Rigo went back to his people with arms outstretched. At once a woman stepped forward. With her, she brought a teenage girl whose dark eyes seemed to smoulder when she fixed them on Don Rigo. The girl thrust her shoulders back, emphasizing her voluptuous curves, and her glossy brown hair hung thick and loose down her back. She had a look of raw sexuality about her. Here was a girl looking for a man to make her a woman, and the man upon whom she had set her sight was Rodrigo Avilés. He was not unaware. Rebecca saw it in the set of his jaw, the careful movement of his eyes.

There was a good deal of discussion. At last, the girl was given a pointed shove forward. "Rebecca," Don Rigo said, "meet your wa'ch dog."

"More like a watch puppy, if you ask me," she muttered.

He chuckled. "She ees young, *sí*. Her name is Clara. Her modher, Ochéa, ees my cook." He made the necessary introductions in Spanish. Both the girl and her mother nodded politely, but their eyes were cold with dislike. Rebecca sighed. So she would spend a few days watching the girl moon over *el hidalgo*. That was preferrable to Tía Elena's stern, sanctimonious presence. She watched the old woman's haughty departure and felt great relief. Nevertheless, when Clara too happily attached herself to Don Rigo's arm, her smile one of calculated invitation, Rebecca felt an intense and immediate regret.

The crowd began to break up. Don Rigo detached himself from the girl and gave orders to some of the men, who moved toward the pack animals supervised by Luca and Paco. As they left, the women sent sidelong glances at Rebecca. One in particular seemed bolder than the others, her look more hostile. Intimidated, Rebecca turned away to

watch Don Rigo speak to his son. He slipped a stick of cin-
namon candy into the boy's hands, and a moment later,
Rodolfo skipped off happily. It was then that Isabel came
forward and handed the don a younger boy. Don Rigo
dangled him overhead, laughing, and the child growled
good-naturedly, drool spilling from his lips. "Enrique ees a
big, big boy!" Don Rigo exclaimed proudly.

"Another son?" Rebecca asked with raised eyebrows.
"Tell me, how does a man without a woman come by such
fine sons?"

His smile grew tattered. "A large rock fell from a place
no' far from here," he said. "My wife was beneat' eet. She
live jus' long enough to give birt' to de boy. Eet was early,
an' he was small. But look a' him now!" He dangled the
baby again. "Enrique ees a big boy."

Rebecca looked at the boy. He was definitely younger
than two years, which meant that Don Rigo had lost his wife
less than two years earlier. She felt compelled to offer the
grinning child a finger, which he promptly grasped and
pulled into his mouth, fist and all. Warm drool ran down the
back of her hand. She disengaged nervously, wiping her
hand on her jeans. Don Rigo handed the fat toddler to his
sister, who carried him away, and went to the hitching post
for the horse. They were three now, too many to ride, and
so they would walk. The girl put herself on Don Rigo's
right, but he ignored her and looked to Rebecca.

"Don't your sons live at home?" she asked.

He shook his head. "My sisters care for dhem. Dheir
abuela—grandmodher—ees ol' an' has much to do."

They were traveling a smooth-walled lane broad enough
for four to walk abreast with ease. Every five or six feet,
there were niches carved in the rock at about shoulder
height, a fat, greasy candle in each. After perhaps a quar-
ter of a mile, the lane suddenly widened and ended at a
stockade fence with a tall gate in its center. Fence and gate
had been painted a vibrant turquoise and bordered top and
bottom with a simple pattern of flowers, vines and leaves.

They entered a private courtyard where cacti and small trees and flowering shrubs grew in large pots and baskets along tiled walkways.

The house surprised Rebecca. Long and low, with wide porticos and tall shuttered windows sheltered by the overhang of the thickly thatched roof, it was far larger than anything else she had seen in the village. The roof rested on heavy wooden beams protruding from the adobe walls and was broken in two places by tall, stuccoed chimneys.

"My gran'fadher's fadher build dis house," Don Rigo said, leading her onto the portico. He opened the door, and Rebecca stepped down into the living room, or *sala*. The floors were made of stone, and the walls were dazzlingly white. Low ledges protruded along two walls and were piled with large cushions, forming what amounted to long sofas. Tall carved candelabras stood on either end of the adobe mantel above the blackened fireplace. Candles sat inside lanterns hidden in niches between the glassless windows and woven wallhangings. There were no other furnishings.

Rodrigo ushered her down the narrow hallway opening off of the dining area that flanked the *sala*. The first door was that of a small bedroom. The narrow bed filled the room, leaving little space for anything else. A round wooden ball and a small, smooth stick lay upon the bed.

"I take it this is Rodolfo's room," she commented.

"*Sí*. Eet was once my fadher's study. We open a doorway into de nex' room, which ees mine alone now."

The end of the hallway opened onto a covered walk that led to the detached kitchen. It was here that they found Clara stoking the oddest stove Rebecca had ever seen. Rodrigo laughingly told Rebecca that it was made from the gasoline tank of an abandoned car. She shook her head ruefully, wondering if someone had already ripped the gasoline tank out of her car, but there was no point dwelling on it. Clara asked a question in Spanish, her manner saucy, and Don Rigo answered her in an impersonal monotone, explaining to Rebecca afterward that the girl's mother had ordered Clara to warm the stove so she could stew them a nice fat chicken for their dinner. Clara took down a small ax from the wall, and Don Rigo said that she was going to kill the chicken her mother would cook. The idea sickened Rebecca, but she supposed that without electricity there was no hope of finding a refrigerator on the place.

"Well, Toto," she muttered cryptically, "this sure as heck ain't Kansas."

"*¿Qué?*" Rodrigo asked, puzzled, but she shook her head.

"Forget it. Doesn't translate very well."

They left the kitchen to retrace their steps along the front hall and skirted the dining area, turning once more into a hallway. To the left, he explained, was the room Clara would use and to the right, behind the *sala,* was the room for Rebecca.

"De heat from de back o' de *hogar* will keep you warm on cold nights," he told her, opening the door.

The bed was built into the corner directly behind the fireplace wall. It was covered with a yellow blanket. The walls were the same brilliant white as those of the rest of the house, but someone had painted a red stripe perhaps four inches wide all the way around the room about three and a half feet above the floor. Likewise, the shutter from the one tall, deep window was painted red, as well as the interiors of the lantern niches.

"Is there a reason for this other than decoration?" she asked, laying a hand inside one of the niches.

"*Sí.* De candle give a sof', warm glow when de *nicho* is dis color. Eet ees de same een my own room. When I yam away a' nigh', I t'ink o' dis an' feel warm inside myself. I miss de *luz roja* when I was een your country. My *compañeros,* dey alway say, 'Look! Look a' dis electric ligh'!' But I alway' say, 'De ligh' een my room behin' de *hogar* glows wit a sof', red fire dat make a man feel a' peace wit his worl'.'"

"This was your room, then?"

"*Sí*, while my fadher live. Eet was dis room I long for dhose years I was away."

"I guess home is always special, isn't it?" she observed, melancholy sneaking into her voice despite her smile.

He curled a finger under her chin. "You have a home, Rebecca," he said gently, "even eef you have no' foun' eet yet. For a man, often his home ees where his fadher's home was, but for a woman, her home ees wit her husban', no?"

She lifted a shoulder in a halfhearted shrug. "I suppose that's the norm in this place, but where I'm from there are many women without husbands who somehow manage to have homes."

"Eet ees anodher diffrence between us," he said softly. "Here on'y a widow sometime live alone. Mos' marry young. Clara, a' *diecisiete*—dat's seventeen—ees consider somet'ing o' a *soltera*. I no' know de *inglés*."

Rebecca was astounded. "Are you telling me that most girls Clara's age are already married?"

"*Sí*, an' modhers wit *niños* o' each hip. Clara herself has had offers. I know dis because eet ees custom for de bridegroom to inform *el dueño* before he approach de family."

"So someone's already asked for Clara's hand?"

"*Sí*, but she no' accep' dem."

"Maybe she wants more out of life."

A crooked smile curved his lips. "She wan's *el dueño*," he stated flatly. "Her modher pu's dis *noción* een her head, I t'ink. But I wan' a real woman, no' a girl."

They were standing very near each other, and the room seemed suddenly small. Rebecca thought of the kiss they had shared at the oasis and wondered if she rated as a "real woman." The pale brown eyes that held hers seemed to say so, but she didn't know what to trust in this place, and she was afraid to find out. Besides, she couldn't have him thinking she was "willing." She stepped away, dropping her gaze.

"I'm sure Clara will find someone else she wants to marry," Rebecca said lightly. "And I'm equally sure I'll be comfortable in this room. Thank you, Rodrigo, for your hospitality. Or should I have said, Don Rigo?''

"Rodrigo will do fine here," he answered quickly, "or even Rigo. De odher ees for pu'lic only.'' She nodded her understanding, only to have him amend his answer. "Perha's for Clara, also. Eet ees bes' no' to show too much *intimidad*.''

She didn't need a full translation to get the picture. "Of course. Now, if you'll excuse me, I'd like a little siesta.''

"I leave you, an' later I sen' Clara wit clothing and water to warm your bath, eef you like.''

"That reminds me," she said hesitantly, "where exactly is the bathroom?''

He smiled apologetically. "I t'ink you fin' what you wan' behind dat narrow door by de window. De priva'e house, however, can be reached by following de pathway beyon' de center door in de hall. I yam sorry to say dat here even *el dueño* canno' afford de luxury o' a flush toilet, but I t'ink you will fin' our *facilidades*—how you say?—adequate.''

"I'm sure I will.''

He turned to leave, pausing in the doorway for a final word. "I jus' wan' to say, welcome to my home, Rebecca Harper. I hope your stay here will be mem'rable.''

"Rodrigo," she told him sincerely, "this experience has already been the most memorable of my lifetime. I'm quite sure I won't forget a moment of it.''

"Eet may prove even more mem'rable," he advised, bright eyes gleaming. He went out, closing the door softly behind him.

Rebecca hugged herself and took another look around. Well, it wasn't the Ritz, but it was comfortable. In fact, it was rather nice. She sat down on the bed and smoothed the cover with her hand. It could be worse. Much worse.

She woke from a deep sleep to the dark and the sound of tapping. She climbed up groggily out of the soft mattress to sit on the edge of the bed in the blackness, her hand going to her head. Next time, she told herself, she would remember to light a candle before falling asleep. The tapping began again in earnest.

"Coming," she called, getting up to wander through the dark with her arms outstretched. "Coming." She found the door and opened it to Clara, who stood with a bucket of steaming water dangling from each hand and a sizable mound of clothing tossed over one shoulder. She had tapped at the door with the toe of her thick leather sandle.

Clara sauntered into the room, lighted by the opened doorway, set the buckets on the floor, and dumped the clothing on the bed. Then, taking a disposable lighter from her skirt pocket, she lit all eight of the room's candles and made a point of placing the lighter in Rebecca's hand. With a flip of her head she turned and left.

"Little witch!" Rebecca muttered, closing the heavy door. Now where was the tub? She opened the door Don Rigo had pointed out before, revealing a tiny room containing an old-fashioned hand pump and a quaint metal tub standing on one end over a drain hole in the floor. It reminded her of an oversize gravy boat. She pulled it out into the bedchamber and righted it, then dumped the contents of both buckets into it, adding a quantity of cool water from the free-standing pump in the water closet.

Quickly, she undressed and got into the tub. Settling back, she slid down until her head lay against the rim of the tub, her legs dangling over the sides. It was heaven. She put her arms over her head and luxuriated. She was learning a new appreciation for the amenities she had once taken for granted. She lounged in the tub until her stomach rumbled with hunger, then got out and toweled herself with rough linen squares left for the purpose.

Her lacy panties and bras and a pair of soft leather shoes were among the garments heaped upon her bed, as were several of her T-shirts and an extra pair of jeans. There was also a trio of full cotton skirts embroidered with zigzag designs and as many tops, each a soft color. These unfamiliar garments felt old, softened by years of wear and care, and smelled faintly of cedar. Perhaps they had belonged to Rodrigo's late wife. The idea disturbed her, but she chose her dinner costume from these unfamiliar goods, nonetheless—a blue top and a skirt of deep green. She combed her hair before a cloudy mirror set in the wall and went out to find her host. He was sitting at the head of the dining table, an additional place set to his right. She called his name and watched him rise and turn.

"Hermosa," he said, *"muy hermosa."* He made her a short bow, his arm folded across the waistband of his slim black pants. He wore a collarless white shirt that buttoned only to the breastbone and billowed softly against his firm chest, the full sleeves rolled back at the wrists. "My mod-her woul' be pleased to see her t'ings worn wit such . . ." He seemed to lose the words, but the ones that came to him were more than sufficient. "You are beautiful, Rebecca. Will you no' join me?"

He pulled out a heavy carved chair and held it until she was seated. At once, a woman appeared, her long hair white about her face and darkening to steely gray at the ends. She was small but round, her dark eyes beady but not unkind. Quietly, she delivered a pair of large bowls filled with chicken pieces and chunks of torn tortillas slopping in a fragrant broth.

"Dat ees Lupe," Don Rigo told Rebecca as Clara and Ochéa came in bearing platters heaped with corn and chick peas and sliced limes. "Lupe clean de house. She live be-hin' de *casa* een a mean hut I woul' tear down eef I coul' get her out o' eet. Wha' can a man do, eh, when de old ones are so settle een dheir ways?" He shrugged and sent Lupe a warm smile. She flipped a hand at him dismissively, but there was much affection in it.

Tall goblets of orange juice were set before them, and Rebecca sipped at hers, finding it deliciously sweet. The three serving women left them, and moments later, Rebecca saw Ochéa move past the window, rebozo about her head and shoulders. At about the same time, Clara returned to the *sala,* a bundle of mending and needle and thread in hand. She sat upon one of the cushioned shelves near a lantern niche and bent her head to her work, looking up occasionally with slitted eyes.

Don Rigo dropped peppers and lime slices into his soup. "Our wa'ch puppy takes her duties to hear', no?"

"Assuming she has a heart," Rebecca returned.

He steepled his hands over his bowl and laughed heartily, causing Clara's head to come up with a sharp movement of censure. He ignored her, his full attention turned upon Rebecca as she dipped her spoon into her bowl and lifted it to her mouth. The soup had a clear, simple flavor.

"Try the *lima,*" he instructed, reaching for a green wedge. He squeezed it over her bowl and dropped the remains, rind and all, into the broth. Rebecca tasted the soup. The lime added a piquant flavor.

They ate and talked, Rodrigo explaining that many of his men were in the hills with the goat herds and the cattle. "I will go ou' to join dem *mañana* and den I will know better when I migh' take you to your brodher."

"Do you think it will be long?" she asked.

He shrugged. "I hope your brodher will no' worry for you. When was he ezpecting you?"

"He isn't," she told him. "I didn't take time to write."

He stared at her, his expression one of incredulity. "*¡Madre de Dios!* A woman alone, you jus' begin a journey such a' dis witou' telling anyone?" He shook his head. "Eef I were your brodher, when I learn o' dis, I woul' be angry, very angry."

She sniffed. "Matthew knows I can take care of myself."

His dark eyebrows rose skeptically. "I mus' ask you to be patient while I take care o' t'ings here," he said. She frowned, but he ignored her and went on. "Dhere are books

een my room, several een English. You may take wha' you
like.''

"Fine."

They finished the meal and moved into the sitting area,
where a small but cheery fire blazed. Don Rigo stood with
one foot braced against the hearth, staring into the fire.
Rebecca was well aware of Clara's careful gaze but continued to ignore her. It was a relief, though, when the gate
creaked as someone entered the yard. Don Rigo went at once
to open the door and let in a tall middle-aged man. He and
Don Rigo spoke for several minutes, then the man left. Don
Rigo returned to inform Rebecca that he would be leaving
at first light.

"Is something wrong?" Rebecca asked.

He spread his hands. "Eet ees too soon to tell." Suddenly, Clara put aside her sewing, stretched and spoke to
Don Rigo. "De wa'ch puppy wan's to go to bed now. I can
tell her to wait eef you desire.''

Rebecca wasn't particularly sleepy, but shook her head,
afraid that to do otherwise would provoke an unpleasant
scene.

Don Rigo smiled. "Perha's you woul' like one of dhose
books now, eh?''

"Yes, thank you.''

He led her to his bedchamber to a bookshelf set into the
wall. While he pulled down the books, she took the opportunity to look around her. Only one or two of the lanterns
had been lit, but they gave off a warm, red glow. The big
four-poster had been turned down and a fire had been laid
upon the hearth, needing only a flame to ignite it. Rebecca
thought ironically of the disposable lighter in her own room.
It proved, along with the cookstove in the kitchen, that the
modern world did intrude in small ways.

Don Rigo presented her with several books. She turned
them over in her hands, scanning the back covers. When she
looked up, it was to find him standing near, his brown eyes
frank and bold. Her skin prickled, and the kiss they had

shared earlier came back to her in a rush of startling clarity. What if she hadn't jerked away? What would they be doing now? Her mind had a ready answer: she imagined herself going up on tiptoe, wrapping her arms about his neck and bringing her mouth against his. Almost as if she had actually made that move, his hands lifted to her shoulders, then slid away before they could settle. But his gaze held hers as if by some invisible string, and when he spoke, his voice was low and husky, so that each word came as a stroke, a tug, pulling her closer.

"Eet ees good, I t'ink, dat we have our little wa'ch puppy, eh? My good sense seem to leave me when I look into your eyes. Such eyes! I will alway' remember your eyes, Rebecca."

Her heart was pounding. Her throat was dry and thick, and though he did not touch her, she seemed to feel his skin against hers, his fingers skimming her arms, her cheek, everywhere. It was as if her nerve endings strained toward him, seeking sensation and, failing to find it, inventing it. She could lift a hand, and he would touch her, caress her. He wanted to. She wanted him to. But what of after? she asked herself. What would come after? Before Rebecca could think of an answer, Clara stepped into the doorway, shattering the illusion of isolation. Both Rebecca and Don Rigo stepped back, like children caught touching what they shouldn't. Clara's eyes flashed suspiciously. Don Rigo lifted his chin.

"Good night, Rebecca," he said. "Res' well."

She put her head down and escaped into the narrow hall, glad to leave him and at the same time sorry. He was far too compelling a man, and she was far too easily compelled.

He was gone when she woke in the morning. At loose ends, she read and lazed around and smiled at the women who came and went in Don Rigo's house. Once, after paying a visit to the facilities out back, she returned to find Lupe busy in her room with broom and dust rag. Employing many smiles and motions, she finally separated the old woman from her tools and took over the cleaning. It was something to do, and she didn't want special treatment. The broom wasn't much to speak of and did a poor job, but Rebecca returned it to the old woman with her thanks. Lupe stared at her for a moment, then shook her head and went away.

Rodrigo did not return for the evening meal, so Rebecca ate alone, then sat in the yard for a while, gazing at the broad, cloudless sky strewn with the diamond twinkle of stars. The night was silent and still, as was the house at her back. She felt very alone and frustrated because she could not ask for information about her host. Intuition told her something had gone wrong, and she spent a restless night, wondering when she would see Rodrigo Avilés again.

She found him the next morning at the breakfast table. His clothes were dirty and his face unshaven, the hat in his lap sweat-stained and creased. A cup of coffee steamed beside his plate, where a white, thick, cooked cereal cooled and congealed. The man had obviously gone without sleep.

"Sit wit me a momen'," he said.

She sat. He spooned some cereal into his mouth and swallowed. "Dhere ees trouble," he said. "I mus' eat and return. De odhers will be waiting." He sighed and looked at his plate. "Dhere ees no water een de lower range. De pipes mus' have collapse, or de spring eet has change eet's course. Some of de men search de lines, some dig, for we mus' restore de spring or sink a well—or lose de herds."

"What of the roundup of the cattle?" she asked.

He frowned. "A few of de vaqueros, de ones we coul' no' find, still ride. All de res' have come een to he'p. Wha' does eet matter? Witou' de *agua,* de cattle will die even before we reach de desert."

"And if that happens?"

The look he gave her was haunted, but even as she watched his face hardened, brown eyes glinting with steel. "We will no' starve," he said, "an' when we fin' de water again, we star' over. Dhere will be cattle from dis rancho for de *mercados* o' Sonora, I swear eet.''

She didn't know what to say. His concern was obvious, the problem severe, his determination strong. She pulled in a deep breath. ''Can I do anything to help?''

He gave her a smile. ''Your blue eyes, dey brigh'en my day. Eet ees enou'.''

Enough? No, it was not enough, but what would be? What did one say or do for a troubled man who had been so kind? ''When I find my brother,'' she told him, ''I know he'll want to reward you somehow.''

Don Rigo said nothing, but his smile was weak. He changed the subject. ''Fernando will remain een de village. Eef any o' de vaqueros come, sen' dem to him.''

''All right.''

He got up, his hand catching his hat as it slid from his lap, and went to the door. Rebecca followed him. He looked at her, then set his hat on his head and strode out onto the patio. A speckled horse was tied to the post beside the walk. She wondered where El Pescado was, but now was not the time to ask. He loosened the reins and climbed aboard.

''*Adiós, mi amiga.*''

''*Adiós,* Don Rigo.''

Clara came running around the corner of the house, a scarf wrapped tightly about her head and throat, a basket of foodstuffs in her arms. She shouted to Don Rigo, who frowned but sat waiting. Clara came to look up at him, her big brown eyes wide as she spoke. Don Rigo seemed to consider, then nodded. Clara practically whooped. She hoisted the basket up into his hands and scrambled up behind him, her arms locking about his waist, her striped skirt spreading over the horse's rump like an awning.

''I will take her wit me,'' he said. ''She can cook for de men. Her fadher ees dhere. He will see over her.''

Rebecca nodded and forced a smile. ''Good luck.''

''Eet takes more dan luck to survive een dis lan','' he told her. ''Eet takes all a man can do, an' to prosper even more.

Say a prayer for me, eh? Here on'y God can provide *agua*."
He turned the horse and rode through the open gate. Clara's striped skirt was the last to disappear behind the turquoise fence.

Rebecca stood for a moment, listening to the clop of hooves die away, the hand she had lifted in farewell drifting down to her side. She felt helpless and frightened for him and surprisingly resentful of Clara, but what could she do? She knew nothing about the kind of cooking that was necessary. She wouldn't be any good on the end of a shovel. Besides, even if she could have helped in some realistic way, prudence told her it would not be wise. Her task seemed merely to wait, and that she could do, at least, with patience. She went back into the house, time already weighing heavily upon her.

Chapter Five

An incredible amount of energy was required just to roll over, but Rodrigo Avilés had learned early that will was one of the stronger forces in life. He therefore willed himself not only over but up into a sitting position on the side of his bed, which sagged and bunched beneath him as he moved. Even with many recoverings and much care, the ticking had stretched over the years and the stuffing had flattened. It was, as Lupe said, time to retire this nest. Many of his people now slept on store-bought mattresses of foam rubber, and though he did not begrudge them any of the small conveniences not prohibited by their isolation, he couldn't quite bring himself to follow suit in this instance. In this bed, he had been conceived, taken a wife and conceived his own sons. It had been the same for his father, and his father's father. He had learned to value such tangible reminders of his heritage. His time in the California City of Angels had taught him to value much that he had disdained as a younger man. He kept those things close to his heart now, protecting them for his sons, as he must protect their inheritance.

The thought wearied him, and he allowed himself enough weakness to send his head into his hands for a few seconds, staving off the struggle that must resume soon enough. His mind went instantly to Rebecca, Rebecca of the blue eyes. They took his breath away, those eyes. He should not have brought her here. He hadn't seen her in four days, and it would be better if he did not see her again at all, for if—when—he saw her again, he would want to stay and care for her. The guilt he had been holding at bay would overwhelm him, guilt for leaving her alone these past days, guilt for hauling her across the desert with him, guilt for thinking the things he thought, for wanting her. He should not have brought her here.

But that was exhaustion thinking for him. He had had no choice but to bring her. He could not have left her there, uncertain when anyone else would come along. He truly didn't know how often the road was traveled, but in all the times he had crossed the road on supply trips, hers was only the third car he had seen in that place. He could not have left her there, an anglo woman alone in the desert, and he could not have stayed with her—but he should not have brought her here because he wanted her. From the moment he had seen those blue eyes staring up at him, he had wanted her.

Fool, he told himself. She was *la gringa* from the City of Angels, where all is new and fast and electric. What would she want with a man like him? Perhaps, as with so many others he had known from that place, a little sex would not be out of the question—for her. He sensed that it would not be enough for him, not this time.

He was ready to love again, the way he had loved Sofía. Sweet, soft Sofía, how she had filled his life! It had been so hard to let her go, but he wanted, needed, that kind of fulfillment again. Also, his children needed a mother. His sisters were generous with their attention, but his sons needed to be home again with a mother of their own to care for them. If only he could find a woman from his own people who would warm his blood and his heart as had Sofía, but perhaps that was the problem, a woman from his own people would be too much like his Sofía, and as dearly as he had loved her, he didn't want a ghost for his wife. That was the real problem with Glorieta. Though she fancied herself in love with him, he'd often found himself pretending that it was Sofía he held in his arms, and that was fair to neither of them. Now with Rebecca...

But he thought too much of Rebecca already. Perhaps if he coaxed her into his bed, he would find her not unlike Glorieta. But no, it was too much to chance. When she went from this place, she must not take his heart with her, for his children would have a mother again and he wanted to love her. If only she were not such a temptation, this Rebecca with the heavenly eyes. But there was always a man's will.

He willed himself up onto his feet and his feet into his pants. He pulled the soft brown jeans up over his thighs and buttocks. They moved into place and settled against him like a second skin. He worked the buttons through the holes with nimble fingers. It felt good to be clean again, to have slept in a bed.

Exhaustion had allowed him to make his mind blank, to forget his many problems and truly rest. But now the problems came back to him one by one: the lack of water on the range, the cattle drive, Clara, Rebecca... He went back to Clara.

He must do something about her before his annoyance with her became genuine anger, but he didn't know what to do. He had tried to speak with her calmly the day they had ridden out to the well site, telling her she must behave herself and find a nice boy to give her heart to. She had laughed throatily and declared that it would take a man to win her heart, and she had pressed her firm breasts against his back. He had gritted his teeth, angry words on the tip of his tongue, and afterward he kept his distance from her, but she had not been dissuaded. Countless times in the last days, she had approached him, always with those pouting lips and an invitation in her eyes. Her petulance because of his lack of interest irritated him most of all. He'd thought of speaking to her father but did not want to humiliate the man. Finally, the days wearing on, he had brought her back to the house and taken the time to bathe and sleep a night in his own bed. He must make her understand, or failing that, discourage her once and for all.

Sighing, he put the girl out of his mind and concentrated on more immediate problems. They had found two places where the palm-log piping had collapsed, but even when restored, the water traveling the pipes had been little more than a trickle. With so much evaporation, there would be too little to water the goats, let alone the cattle. He suspected a third break, even a fourth, but the low water volume bothered him nonetheless. The spring could be moving too far underground to tap into, or the aquifer that fed it could simply be running dry, so the men continued with the well, though that was a chancy business at best in this place.

They would hit water soon. They must, or it would be too late. They had already found the bloated bodies of an old bull and two fine brindle cows. There were surely others lying dead among the rocks and scrub. He prayed there was water in the sixth and seventh holes farther up the mountain. It would mean the spring had not died. Right now, though, he could not spare the men to ride out to check, and neither could they spare their *jefe*. He must dress, breakfast and ride out again. But first he would see those blue eyes, make certain that Rebecca was well. He was responsible for her, after all. It was his duty, one among many.

He pulled on socks and stamped his feet into his work boots, the spurs still buckled to them. He should wear *teguas* without socks like the others, but he was *el dueño,* and the hand-stitched leather shoes with the thick flat soles made him feel like a boy again. He was vain, he admitted, pulling on the plaid shirt and going to stand before the small, clouded mirror, his shirt still unsnapped. He grinned at his reflection, smoothing his mustache against his lip with his fingertips. Yes, he was vain, but he was handsome, too. Women had always liked him, nearly all of them.

He wondered if Rebecca liked him just a little, and thought of the stupid, impulsive kiss he had taken there in the oasis. Little enough, it seems, he thought wryly, remembering how she had wrenched free of him. And yet, he sensed in her a certain interest. Or was that his vanity again, his macho, Latino vanity? He had been given to understand by more than one *Americana* that his Latino blood made him especially susceptible to a certain kind of arrogance but also to an extreme depth of passion that each had found, for a time, quite compelling. Which was his curse, he wondered, the vanity or the passion? Little matter, for in this instance, he must struggle to suppress both.

Even with that in mind, he took the time to shave and to trim his mustache to that neat, spare line he favored simply because so few other men could wear it without looking sinister. He fancied it a bit of dashing flare on himself, and in this he did not think he was mistaken. He combed his hair, leaving it unbound to wave against his neck, cleaned his teeth and snapped his shirt front closed. Store-bought clothing was a convenience he approved. His most formal attire, of course, had been made by hand, and he felt a marked preference for the fine shirts his mother had stitched for him over the years, but store-bought was good enough for work and often sturdier. He felt in need of sturdy things this day.

He opened his door to encounter Clara, who posed as if halted in passing, though he didn't believe it. He sent her a stony look and glanced down the hallway in both directions.

"Where is Miss Harper?" he asked in cool Spanish.

The question had its intended effect. The girl stiffened at once, then seemed to deflate, her attitude becoming sulky.

"The gringa is gone," she told him.

Gone? Gone from the rancho? But how? When?

"What do you mean?" he demanded. "Mother of God, if you let her go alone, if you—"

"I did nothing!" the girl protested. "She went with Lupe into the village. It is wash day. I imagine she dirties her clothes like the rest of us."

Rodrigo let go his breath, one hand spreading over his heart. Only to the village. Wash day. He was so relieved he was even willing to overlook Clara's sarcasm.

"Tell your mother I will eat," he ordered gruffly, dismissing her. He moved back into the room, snatching his battered straw cowboy hat from a peg on the wall. Wash day. It was probably far different from any other wash day his Rebecca had known. He remembered the convenience of coin-operated machines that washed and dried the clothing in minutes. He remembered, too, how he had shrunk his only pair of jeans, and as a result had worked for nearly a week in long-sleeved shirts, boots and shorts borrowed from a housemate. How the others had teased him! It had been some time before he could see the humor in that particular situation. He hoped Rebecca could be more sanguine in hers, because he was powerless at the moment to do anything about it.

He left the house through the back door and made a visit to the facilities before hurrying to the shelter carved into the side of the mountain that served as his personal stable. El Pescado, as well as the spotted horse, named Cierto for his sureness of foot, greeted him with an affectionate snort. There was a third horse, a proud little mare dubbed Jaqueca, meaning headache, because of her tendency to butt with her head any other horse around her. She remained aloof in her stall, munching the dry hay with which one of the older village boys had gifted her. Normally, Rodrigo would have taken a little time to give her a pat and an ear scratching, but not this day. Instead, he went directly to El Pescado's stall, took the bridle down from its peg and slipped it over the mottled nose.

"Your turn, my old friend," he muttered. "Your brother is tired." He spread the blankets over the horse's back, then led the animal to the saddle stand, took the comfortable rough-out working saddle, slick now with much use, from its sawhorse and placed it upon the broad back. Quickly, expertly, he looped the long cinch through the ring, tightening it after each pass and before securing the end. Patting the fine mount's graceful neck, he gathered the reins and swung aboard. Half a minute later, he swung down again and loosely knotted the reins in the ring of the post standing beside the walkway that led to his front door.

Inside, one of the women had laid the table with a platter of eggs cooked with cheese, peppers and bits of pork. A battered metal tankard of milk, a few tortillas and a mound of smelly but tasty goat cheese completed the meal. He made quick work of it, rolling a sizable hunk of the goat cheese and the leftover tortillas into a bandanna that he tied to a belt loop of his jeans, and called out his parting as he strode from the house.

As he stepped up into the stirrup, Clara came running from the kitchen, calling out in Spanish, "Take me with you!"

Calmly, he swung his leg wide and settled, his toe mechanically finding the other stirrup. He straightened the reins, looking placidly at the girl on the ground.

"Not this time, Clara. Stay here with your mother and Miss Harper."

"I want to go! You need me!"

"Stay here, Clara!"

She stomped a sandaled foot, spitting with anger. "I will go!"

"You will do as you're told, little sister, or suffer for your disobedience! So help me, I will lift my own hand to you if your father does not!"

She glared at him, clearly unsubdued, then suddenly melted, reaching out her pretty hand to touch the skirt of his saddle, her features softening, lids lowering to hood sparkling eyes.

"I will be very good, my chief, and obey your every wish if only you will take me with you."

"You would not like what I would wish on you, Clara. Stop behaving like a strumpet and obey your chief!" He jerked the reins, wheeling the horse toward the gate. Behind him, the girl huffily folded her arms beneath her breasts and watched, her eyes narrowing. He sent her a last glare as he turned his mount into the lane and caught the toss of her head as she whirled toward the house. Let her sulk, he decided. Later he would speak to her again, and this time he would make her understand that he was not meant for her. But then, he wondered, for whom was he meant? Certainly not a blue-eyed, light-haired anglo.

Now that he was on the move, El Pescado proved a bit frisky. He was well-rested from the arduous trip to and from the salt merchant near Guerrero Negro and had been exercised by the boy Rodrigo hired as a stable hand. The horse was ready for a good run. Rodrigo let him go, standing in his stirrups and hoping they would encounter no one moving toward them down the walled lane. Too soon for the animal's satisfaction, they were bursting upon the village square, Rodrigo hauling back on the reins as the energized horse fought him. It was a battle fought and lost many times, and this incident was no exception. Recognizing the touch of his master, El Pescado dug his hooves into the dirt and subsided. Rodrigo laughed, as exhilarated by the contest of wills as the horse had been by the race.

Before him, the washtubs of the women ringed the tree by the fountain. A familiar figure in blue jeans bent over a scrub board, her neatly rounded posterior presenting a fetching view. The elation he felt deepened, moving through his chest and down into the region of his groin. Instinctively, he kicked the horse forward and rode up to the tree, where he halted and leaned a forearm against the saddle horn, a fingertip pushing his hat brim back. He grinned down at her, taking advantage of her preoccupation. She was struggling, her slender arms pushing and pulling the wadded, sodden fabric over the ribbed board, her hair falling forward, slipping free of the scarf with which she had tied it back. One of the other women moved over to give her a shot with an elbow, jerking a chin in Rodrigo's direction when she finally looked up.

"Oh." Rebecca straightened, her wet hand going to her lower back. "Ow." She smiled limply. "I'll tell you something. I've learned a new appreciation for the electric washing machine—among other things." She looked around her. "Like clean clothes."

"Eh, you learn to conserve all t'ings here," he told her in what he felt was very good English. "Even clean clodhing."

She cocked her head to one side. "You know, I think that's good. Being here, working like this, well, it's sort of given me a whole new perspective on life. But enough about me. How's it going out there?"

He lifted a shoulder. "We will find water because we mus'. Eef no', dis may be de las' wash day for a long while."

"Yeah, Lupe said something like that," she acknowledged to his surprise.

"Has my ol' servan' sudde'ly learned English dat she may talk wit you?"

She laughed, the sound seeming to lift his spirits. He felt unaccountably lighter and childishly pleased with himself.

"I have a little Spanish, you know," she said, pushing sun-streaked hair from her face. "We've sort of built on that. She's been very patient with me, and she's very fond of you."

He actually felt himself blushing. The things this woman did to him! He pulled his hat forward, striving for nonchalance. "De ol' woman ees jus' gra'eful I do no' beat her," he returned flippantly, but instead of the laughter he expected, Rebecca presented him with an oddly solemn visage. "Wha's wrong? Eet was jus' a joke."

"Oh, I know you don't go around beating these people," she told him dismissively. Then those blue eyes settled on him, heavy with frankness. "Why didn't you tell me that Lupe was your mother-in-law?"

His dark eyebrows lifted. "Your *español* mus' have improved very much."

"It wasn't hard to figure out. There's a picture of your wife on the little altar in your room and another in Lupe's hut. She was very beautiful."

He felt his heartbeat in the base of his throat, a dozen different thoughts occurring to him at once. When had she seen that picture? Had she been in his bedroom again? For what reason? Had she stopped and stared at his bed, wondering what it would be like to—

Abruptly, he derailed the train of his thoughts, feeling the impact in his groin. He shifted uncomfortably, afraid of giving himself away, of being found out displaying the grossest sort of disloyalty. Rebecca had been speaking of his wife, his poor, dead Sofía, and all he could think of was getting Rebecca into his bed. For months he had struggled to banish his wife from his thoughts, and now suddenly, because of this anglo woman, he struggled to bring her to mind.

"I loved her!" he blurted almost defensively, the outburst startling the animal beneath him.

El Pescado skittered backward, and a dozen female faces were turned in his direction. Embarrassed, overcompensating, he yanked hard on the reins. El Pescado almost went down on his haunches, his back legs buckling as he drew up sharply. Rodrigo growled at him, cursing himself for a fool in low, guttural Spanish. In sharp contrast, Rebecca stood very still, seemingly frozen in the moment, and he had never been so aware of her as he was just then. He noticed, ironically, that the fronts of her thighs were wet where she'd sloshed the wash water onto herself and, conversely, that the unbound nipples of her high breasts stood firmly against the soft cotton fabric of her blouse. He noticed, too, the sharp intake of breath, the stiffening of limbs, the widening of eyes an impossible blue, as if she suddenly found herself perched precariously on the brink of a great chasm.

"I've upset you," she was saying. "I'm sorry. I didn't mean to pry."

He looked around at the curious faces, saw Ana whisper to María, and Teresa scowl, her wet hands making dark spots on her broad hips. His aunt would undoubtedly hear of this. He could only wonder what significance would be attached to it. Roughly, he urged El Pescado forward again, angry with himself and the staring women.

"I have no time for dis," he told Rebecca briskly. The blondish head bowed, bringing him a sharp pain in his chest. "Rebecca..." But then she faced him again, a brilliant smile contradicting the moist sparkle of her eyes.

"I haven't seen you in days," she said, "and right away I put my foot in it."

Another time, he would have grinned at the metaphor, but this debacle was his. If she'd stepped in anything, it was of his creation, not hers.

"You have no' offen'ed me," he said quietly, intensely aware of their audience. "De fault ees mine. I yam too much o' edge. My problems wit de rancho an'—" He couldn't stop himself from glancing at his oldest sister. She was staring daggers at him, trying to discern his words despite the fact that he spoke in a language foreign to her. "Odher t'ings," he finished lamely, his gaze flitting guiltily back to Rebecca. Her smile had faded, but so had the glitter of her eyes.

"You have enough to do without worrying about me," she said, lifting a hand to scratch El Pescado's ear. "And I have to help Lupe finish your laundry." Abruptly, she dropped her hand and backed away. "Go on. Go find that water."

You're a most remarkable woman, Rebecca Harper, he told her silently, but he didn't dare say it aloud. Instead, he offered a gentle smile and allowed his eyes to hold hers for a moment. He could almost feel their color, so cool, so vibrant.

"I will return soon," he said confidently. "An' dhere will be water."

"Yes."

It seemed a simple affirmation of everything in which he needed to believe: his luck and ability, the strength of his will, the continued prosperity of his people, the futures of his sons. He felt the familiar swell of pride, the stony determination to succeed against all odds and the glad surprise because she seemed to care that all went well with him and his people. He backed the horse into the dusty street and headed him north.

"*Adiós,* Rebecca."

She waved as she bent over her scrub board, her gaze following him as the horse started into a trot, and in that moment, he made himself a promise. Soon. He would return soon.

Rodrigo turned his face toward the north, enjoying the feel of the horse beneath him. El Pescado was a sturdy animal. Hadn't he carried two people for as many days over burning desert and rocky mountain trail without the slightest falter? Confident in his mount, Rodrigo pushed for a swifter speed than was probably prudent, but already he was wishing to be back at the *casa* again. He remembered the one meal he and Rebecca had shared at his table and wished he had been able to join her every evening. Perhaps he should make the long ride back to the *casa* more often. Perhaps he should even make that long ride tonight. His legs moved as if of their own volition, knees bending, heels rising. El Pescado felt the touch of metal against his sensitive flanks and lengthened his strides accordingly.

The sun was high in the eastern sky when Rodrigo reached the well site, but the day was yet young. He greeted his men tersely, not wishing to delay the work a moment longer than necessary, then listened to those who had been riding the pipeline in search of a break. Another collapse had been found, and it would be necessary to lug up repair goods by hand, but where the palm-wood pipe had broken, a sizable puddle had accumulated, and there perhaps a dozen of the big-boned brindle cows had been milling about. A pair of vaqueros had gone up to drive the cattle toward the holding pens, one on foot and the other on horseback by way of a different route. Meanwhile, work was progressing on the well. They had at last broken through a shelf of rock that had defied their shovels and were now hauling up the debris left behind by their picks. Soon they would be digging again.

"It is but a matter of time, Don Rigo," his *capataz* assured him, returning to his supervision of the work. But time, Rodrigo reflected silently, was ever the enemy, and he took up a shovel himself, following his *capataz* down into the well.

He drove the men by simple example that day, bending his own back to the work with such fiendish determination that the dirt flew far faster than it could be removed by barrels and pulleys. The men above were hauling at twice their usual pace just trying to keep up, but if a quick end to the day was Rodrigo's goal, his efforts were moot. In the early afternoon, the slender beam supporting the trio of pulleys gave way against the weight of three fully loaded barrels moving upward at once, and only a shouted warning prevented Rodrigo and the men below from being seriously hurt. As it was, one of the men remained trapped but uninjured beneath some of the shoring that had been erected. By the time the workman could be freed, the shoring replaced, a new beam mounted, the pulleys rehung, lines restrung, barrels filled once more and hauled upward two at a time and the day's digging cleared away at last, the sun had set and the last rays of light were slipping away.

The men who crawled up out of that hole were exhausted, grimy and slick with their own sweat. Their bellies were rumbling in chorus for the caldron of stew bubbling over the camp fire, but they paused, every one, to stare openmouthed as their *jefe,* their leader, *el dueño,* saddled his big gray, mounted, and wished them a good night's sleep before riding off into the gathering darkness.

Rodrigo himself marveled at his behavior. He ached, and he reeked, and dinner would be over and cleared away before he even reached the village, but he urged El Pescado over the narrow, rocky trail. And for what? he wondered. A night of passion? A conversation in which he might not embarrass himself? Another opportunity to look into those eyes? He couldn't name the thing for which he hoped or identify his own motives, but he rode on beneath a black sky bright with billions of stars. In Los Angeles, he reminded himself, even on a clear night, not one tenth of the sky's bounty could be seen. Men there did not even know how liberal the Creator had been. They thought their neon was bright! He wondered if Rebecca had turned her eyes on God's roof at any time these past nights. Perhaps he should direct them for her.

The village was sleeping when he slipped into it. A barking dog soon roused one household, setting the baby to howling and a tired mother to scolding, but by the time Rodrigo turned El Pescado into the walled lane leading to his home, all had settled into silence again. He recognized his folly in the stillness that pervaded the night as he walked from the stable toward the house after caring for his horse. Not a light showed from any window, either in Lupe's poor hut or the big *casa.* Everyone had gone to bed.

He let himself in through the back door, pausing on the narrow step to sweep his hat from his head and allow his eyes to adjust to the deeper darkness of the interior of his house. On his right, Clara would be abed in the room of his sisters. On his left, not four steps away, stood the door to his old room, where Rebecca would lie sleeping. He moved even before the conscious thought to do so had formed, his feet easing soundlessly over the flagstones. The door yielded easily to his fingertips, swinging inward with a faint sigh.

A single candle cast a gentle light from a niche across the room. She lay upon her side in shadow, her back to the light, her slender arms flung across the bed that had once been his. He knew instantly that she was sleeping and moved no farther, merely gazing at her from the doorway. He tensed as she rolled onto her back, his heart suddenly hammering, but the next moment he knew she slept on. Her chest rose and fell gently, one arm bent across her body at the waist. She wore a T-shirt without sleeves or neck binding, and the soft white fabric molded the mounds of her breasts and the slender taper of her torso before disappearing beneath the covers. But it was her face that held him. The sandy lashes lay against her smooth skin, and her light hair fanned across her pillow. Her lips were slightly parted, contributing a note of sensuality to her peacefully composed features and evoking a response in him so intense that it was painful, his swelling manhood betraying the true nature of his intent in coming here this night.

With a strangled groan, he stepped backward into the hallway, pulling the door closed in the same extended movement. Sighing deeply, he laid his forehead against the door, feeling the throb of desire in his groin and the hollowness of disappointment in his chest. He should thank God that she was asleep. Only that had kept him from making a great mistake. She was not the right sort of woman for him, this Rebecca, and now was decidedly the wrong time for a lusty dalliance.

He had experienced genuine love and lost it, and though the many months had taken the edge off his grief, he was lonely. He wanted a wife, but not one that reminded him of his Sofía. He was ripe for love—but not with Rebecca Harper. Too soon, she would be gone. She probably hated this place and could not wait to be gone. He understood. It was not her home. She wanted her brother. She would go, but he would stay, for he was a part of the rancho, and the rancho a part of him. Yet the look of her there upon his bed would not easily be forgotten. She was one of the exotic women about whom he had fantasized as a beardless boy. Let her be that then, he told himself, and nothing more.

The exhaustion that had permeated these last days settled over him like a heavy cloak. Sluggishly, he straightened and turned from the door. He thought fleetingly of seeking out Glorieta, but his appetite for the lovely widow had waned since he'd met Rebecca Harper, so much so that he preferred the solitary comfort of his own bed to the sultry charms of the widow's. What an incredible development. He'd have laughed at himself, had he not been so miserable.

Chapter Six

Rodrigo listened to the faint sounds of his own footsteps in the dark, narrow hall. He was tired and frustrated, wanting only his bed now and a respite from his thoughts. Instinctively, he turned into the doorway of his room, his hand finding the lever unerringly, pushing down, feeling the weight against his palm as the bar on the other side lifted. He pushed the door wide, surprised to find that someone had lit the wall-mounted oil lantern he had purchased for his mother in a gift shop in Tijuana. More decorative than serviceable in its place beside his mirror, its hammered-tin holder reflected the merrily dancing flame despite the ugly black smudge in its center. Irritated, he strode toward it, his boots clumping over the rug-strewn floor, all attempts at silence now abandoned.

A sudden movement, a small gasp, the instantaneous realization that he was not alone brought him up short and sent him whirling. He gaped at the young woman sitting bolt upright in his bed, her long dark hair disheveled, her pale cotton nightdress twisted and rumpled.

"Don Rigo!"

Her! "Mother of God, Clara, what are you doing?" he demanded in Spanish, but he didn't really expect her to answer.

She did not, her features settling into stubborn petulance. He considered that she had been waiting for him, perhaps hoping to seduce him, or was this merely a bit of girlish pretending? Her initial reaction had seemed one of shock. Indeed, it had seemed that he was as much a surprise to her as she to him. And that gown, that nightdress...

Of a sudden it struck him. He strode forward and grabbed a handful of it, sensing rather than seeing that she shrank from him. Sofía's, from the chest beside his bed, sewn by Lupé's hand as a gift after the birth of Rudolfo. She had sewn another, he remembered, after Enrique, this one a burial garment for his wife. Furious, he switched his gaze to Clara's face even as he released his hold on the gown, Sofía's gown. She would play that role then, would she? But in reality, it would never be hers and it was time she understood. Let her pretend. Two could play at that game, and he was betting she wouldn't like his version. In fact, he was counting on it, for though she at times attempted to entice him, she was as yet innocent, unaware of what consequences her actions could have.

Purposefully, he planted his feet and dropped his hands to the fly of his pants. One button, two. Her dark eyes widened in shock, but she stuck out her chin, keeping her place, daring him. Three buttons, four. She expected him to stop, to play the gentleman. She believed that if she could make him want her, he would marry her, and marriage was the means of satisfying her ambitions. He pushed the fifth button through the hole. Let her understand that he was a flesh-and-blood man who could be pushed too far, that a man could want in more ways than one. Let her see what way he would have her and decide if she wanted him on those terms. He freed the sixth and final button, watching the bravado begin to wane in her eyes. Fine. Let her decide how far it would go. He ripped the snaps open on his shirt, then crawled up onto the bed, boots and all. She lifted a hand as if to ward him off, recoiling despite the thrust of her chin.

"Come now, little one," he crooned. "You want me. You have made it known. What better time than now, eh?"

She attempted a sultry look, but fear sent her eyes skittering furtively, and her voice trembled when she answered. "Yes. But not like this. It is no..." The word she finally chose was *apropiado.* Rodrigo sent his eyebrows upward.

"Appropriate?" he questioned, reaching out a hand to bring that haughty chin down. "Was it appropriate for you to tease me? To tempt me? To wait here for me in my own bed?"

"No. Yes! That is, I did not think you would return tonight. I only wanted..." She licked her lips, her gaze fleeing his. "After we marry, Don Rigo, then—"

"Marry?" He laughed and twisted his hand in the front of her gown, raking the softness of her heavy breasts. "It is not marriage I am thinking of."

"But, Don Rigo—"

"No more talk!" he ordered, tugging her gown as if to bring her to him.

Her mouth fell open, arms flying out, hands clawing at the bedcovers. Instinctively, she resisted him and he tugged again, grinning at the sound of ripping fabric. She gasped and bolted, rolling away to hit the floor, naked as the day she was born. He stifled his laughter, collapsing against the bed as if taken off guard, the shredded gown still clenched in his hand.

He gave her ample time to get to her room, chuckling into the mattress until the thought of the torn gown sobered him. Sighing with exhaustion, he turned over onto his back and brought the ruined gown to his chest, Sofía's gown. He fingered the delicate fabric, remembering how she had looked to him that night after the long, healing separation that followed childbirth. How she had stirred his blood! But he should not have kept the gown. Sofía was gone, and he never wanted to see another woman in Sofía's things, certainly not Clara, and not even Rebecca—especially not Rebecca. Yet, if it had been she in his bed . . .

He let himself imagine seeing Rebecca there, her firm breasts molded by the soft T-shirt, and thoughts of Sofía receded. Clara did not even exist. Somewhere in the distance he heard what sounded like a door closing, but the fantasy of Rebecca shimmered before his mind's eye, and exhaustion was even then pushing consciousness away. He saw her there in his bed, a smile curving her lips, and he imagined sliding under the blankets beside her, lifting his hand to cup her breast, feeling it swell as she arched her back, her arms lifting about his neck, her mouth settling against his. He imagined pressing her down onto the bed, moving between her parted thighs, pushing his throbbing shaft into her warm body. She moved beneath him, bringing pleasure, taking it. She loved him. He saw it in her eyes, and seeing it, he spilled his love into her, shuddering as it gushed from him in a torrent. He felt her sigh into his ear, felt her lips forming words he could not hear, but it didn't matter, for he knew what she said. She was his woman. She loved him, and that was all that mattered—in his dreams.

Rebecca woke early, put on her jeans, athletic shoes and a shirt one of the women had given her the day before, and trotted outside to visit the facilities. The sun was not yet up, but the sky had lightened to a gray blue, and the clean air smelled and tasted of crisp yellow sunshine. It was really very pleasant here. Because of the altitude and the pueblo's position between the two oases, one above and one below, the temperature remained far cooler than on the desert floor. It still got hot, of course, but she no longer found the heat oppressive, even without the central air-conditioning to which she was accustomed.

They built smart here, used every scrap of shade and every waft of breeze, and the thick adobe walls provided excellent insulation against both heat and cold. In truth, it was the cold that bothered her most. Some nights she shivered beneath her blankets, but only for a little while. She wondered how Rodrigo and his men stood it, sleeping out-of-doors almost every night.

By the look of him, at least the few times she'd seen him since this crisis had begun, he hadn't managed all that well. She supposed exhaustion was a pretty good insulator, too, but she couldn't help wondering how long he and the other men could keep up with the pace they'd apparently set themselves. Still, she mustn't forget that Don Rodrigo Felipe Marcos Junípeo Avilés was a man in his element. He was used to the rigors of life in this remarkable land, and a remarkable land required a remarkable man.

Such a man deserved five distinguished names. Lupe seemed to think so, anyway—as far as Rebecca could ascertain. Being here on her own without a translator had done quite a lot for her understanding of the language, but her Spanish was still far from proficient. Perhaps with time . . . But time was an uncertainty, one she no longer wished to ponder for some reason.

She relieved herself and returned to the *casa,* feeling light and— Was she actually happy? She stopped inside the back hall, feeling the peacefulness of the house, and pondered her feelings. Well, perhaps she wasn't actually happy, but neither was she unhappy, and that said something, didn't it? This whole experience was turning out to be very good for her. Life was really worthwhile when one stopped to think about it, despite the difficulties. She was beginning to understand that happiness did not depend upon physical luxuries.

She hated to admit how much in the beginning she had grieved the loss of the easy life she'd led in Los Angeles. It all seemed rather pointless and cowardly now, the do-nothing job with the family company, the lack of responsibilities or challenge. She had never even used her degree, and here there was not even a primary school. She had been shocked when she'd realized that the village had no school. Realizing this, she felt rather selfish and small. She wondered if Matthew had experienced a similar revelation in San Benito. She hoped he had. They would both be the better for it.

She shook off her musings then and stepped down from the flagstone of the hallway to that of the *sala*. It really was exceptionally quiet this morning. Clara was usually up and around by now. In fact, Clara seemed to take pleasure in waking Rebecca most mornings. It seemed to be her little way of letting everyone know that she was a lazy layabout. Perhaps Clara was the layabout this morning, or perhaps Lupé had put the precocious child to work in order to keep her out of mischief. Lupe was a wise, wise woman. Rebecca was beginning to understand what her daughter must have been like, why Rodrigo had not yet gotten over her loss.

Rebecca stepped up into the front hall and turned right toward the kitchen. She was ready for her coffee and a little something to fill her stomach, perhaps a scrambled egg with chopped peppers and wrapped in a soft, warm tortilla. She walked past Don Rigo's bedroom door, surprised to find the door standing open, when something caught her eye, halting her, dragging her back for a second look. Something poked up from the foot of his bed, something very like . . . She stepped inside the room, craning her neck to get a better idea of just what she was seeing. She stared for a long moment, not quite believing what her eyes told her was there. It was the toe of a boot that poked up above the turned rail of the footboard. Quietly, she moved closer.

Don Rigo lay upon the bed fully clothed, a piece of fabric clutched in his hand. He looked dirty and bedraggled and had evidently been too tired even to undress, though he had begun, for his shirt and pants were open, revealing his firmly muscled torso, flat middle and . . . She turned away, both

thrilled and appalled by the feelings the sight of him produced in her, but she wouldn't be caught spying like some
curious schoolgirl who'd just discovered the difference between the sexes. She turned and slipped away, carefully
pulling the door closed behind her.

She was trembling, and there was a tightness in her chest
that made her breath come in gasps and her nipples peak
beneath the thin fabric of her shirt. Don Rigo Avilés made
a woman think about just what it meant to be a woman. He
was an exciting man, as male as a man could be. She could
not help thinking of that great depth of passion for which
the Latin lover was famous. She was right to fear him a little, for he made her aware of him as no other man had done.
But he was a gentleman, the true *hidalgo,* and she had come
to believe that he would take advantage of no one.

It was not him she feared but herself. It would be so easy
to fall in love with him, with this place, even, to let herself
believe she could belong. But she knew that was foolishness. She belonged here even less than he belonged in Los
Angeles. Besides, Don Rigo was obviously not over the
death of his wife. Anything that developed between them
would be purely physical, and Rebecca knew she would
certainly regret that. She couldn't keep from worrying about
him, though.

He looked so tired, so stressed. He needed someone to
take care of him, someone like Clara or Glorieta, that
woman who so obviously disliked her. Glorieta seemed to
keep to herself, and the other women seemed to expect Rebecca to do so, as well. There was something strange there,
but that Glorieta was beautiful, her every movement graceful and fluid, could not be denied. Rebecca had tried to
question Lupe about her, but the language barrier was too
great. The only thing she'd been able to learn was that the
woman's husband was dead. That would seem to give her
and Rodrigo something in common, but it didn't explain
why the women had ostracized her.

There were one or two others in whom Rodrigo might eventually take an interest, but they were awfully young, just girls, really, younger even than Clara. Rebecca wondered again where Clara was, but it really wasn't any of her business, and she wanted to be sure that Ochéa knew her *jefe* would be wanting his breakfast eventually.

She moved on down the hall and out onto the path and into the kitchen, but Ochéa was not there. In fact, it did not appear that Ochéa had been in at all. The stove had not been lit, the work table was clear, the coffeepot empty. This was strange, but before she could really think about it, Lupe came in, her skirt full of fresh eggs.

"Ah. *¡Buenos días, mi amiga!*" She rattled on in Spanish as if Rebecca were sure to understand every word.

"*Despacio, por favor,*" Rebecca interrupted, laughing. "*¡Despacio!*"

Lupe flashed her a look of mock irritation and spoke with exaggerated slowness. "*¿Dónde está Ochéa?*"

Rebecca frowned. "I don't know where Ochéa is." She shrugged by way of translation, and Lupe really stopped now and studied her face for a moment before taking a long look around. "Clara hasn't shown up either," Rebecca went on. "*¿Dónde Clara?*"

Lupe shook her head, muttering in Spanish, and her watery eyes narrowed. Rebecca bit her lip.

"I'm going to wake up Clara. Uh, *buenos días,* Clara. Uh... Oh, to heck with it." She turned and started toward the door. Lupe followed close behind her, complaining in Spanish. They crossed to the house and went in, Rebecca remembering to inform Lupe of Don Rigo's presence. The old woman seemed not only surprised but perplexed. "Yeah, me, too," Rebecca mumbled.

They stepped down into the *sala,* skirted the dining table and were just about to step up again into the back hallway when the front door opened and Tía Elena entered, her tiny figure dressed exactly as it had been the day Rebecca had first seen her, right down to the prayer beads, rebozo and frown. Lupe stiffened, obviously offended by the other woman's presumptuous behavior, but it was Rebecca at whom the woman in black pointed her bony finger.

"*¡Ramera!*" she proclaimed.

Lupe gasped, drawing herself up rigidly, but Rebecca could only blink, confused. The word meant nothing to her, but the disdain was painfully obvious. Suddenly, a number of other women pressed into the room, Ochéa among them. The cook glared at Rebecca and folded her shawl protectively about her shoulders. To Rebecca's astonishment, Lupe lifted a knobby fist, shook it at the intruders and rushed forward, shrieking in angry Spanish. The room erupted with shrill voices, everyone shouting at once, and Rebecca begging them all to hush, mindful of the sleeping don, desperate to understand what was going on, all to no avail.

"*¡Silencio!*"

Don Rigo strode into the room, eyes wild, hair disheveled. His shirt hung open, his cuffs loose, but he'd managed to do up his pants. He held a hand to his head as if nursing an ache there and again called for silence, though only final syllables were falling from mouths at that point. He glared at the assembly, ignoring Rebecca who stood apart at the far end of the *sala*. Straightening, he pulled his shirt closed and snapped it together in two or three places before speaking again, clearly demanding an explanation. For a moment it was pandemonium once more. It was Lupe who finally won the ear of the *jefe,* however, drawing close and gesticulating wildly. Whatever she said clearly enraged Rodrigo. His dark head came up sharply, and he shot Rebecca a look of such venom that for one insane instant she thought his anger directed at her! But then he rounded on the faction crowding his door, shouting with such vigor that they recoiled as one, all except little Elena.

Rebecca had to hand it to her. That little old woman faced her raving nephew with pure relish, screeching back at him, shaking her beads, stamping her feet against the floor, giving not an inch. Don Rigo finally abandoned her, shaking his finger in Ochéa's blanched face instead. Ochéa said nothing, but there was a flurry of movement behind her, and she drew aside as someone pushed Clara through the crowd and into the room. Instantly, Don Rigo seized her wrist, shaking her like a doll, spewing angry words that Rebecca didn't even attempt to follow, her confusion so complete that she couldn't have deciphered English just then!

Clara began to weep, but Don Rigo was merciless. Time and again he forced her to speak, and it was clear as the story unfolded that sentiment was running against the girl. At one point, Lupe threw up her hands and turned her back on all of them, her whitened head bowed. At the end, Ochéa stepped forward and slapped her daughter's face, even as the tears poured down her own cheeks. But when it was done, poor Clara's humiliation seemingly complete, Tía Elena again had her say, folding her hands over her heart, her face utterly implacable. Don Rigo stood fuming, growling replies and comments Rebecca neither wanted nor hoped to understand. Finally, his back straight as a board, he turned and strode toward her, his agitation painfully evident. Rebecca literally held her breath. He stopped short and pushed a hand through his hair, only then lifting his gaze to her face.

"She—Clara has tol' dem—" He stepped closer, swallowing his anger, and began again. "I return las' nigh' to find Clara een my bed, playing a' *dueña*. You comprehend dis?"

Rebecca let out a long breath and nodded. "It means owner or mistress." It meant that Clara had been pretending to be the wife of Don Rigo. His jaw clamped, a muscle working in its center.

"I make a mistake, Rebecca," he told her in a harsh whisper. "I pretended to welcome her, but no' een de manner she imagine." He twisted about and lifted a hand to his head, thumb and forefinger pressing against his temples. "Rebecca, I t'ink on'y to discourage her, an' she run like a mouse wit *el gato* on her tail! But she no' go to her bed. She run home to her modher, an' dis morning she tol' ev'ryone dat I ha' t'row her ou' because I was—wit you.''

Rebecca closed her eyes, her heart sinking, and popped them open again, seeing behind her lids the picture of Don Rigo as she'd seen him earlier in his sleep. He'd said he'd "made a mistake" with Clara, but somehow she couldn't quite bring herself to ponder this. She did not want to think how his clothing had become so disarrayed or what she might have done if she'd been in Clara's place, if it had been as Clara had claimed. A guilty red flush burned her face, and she had to remind herself that it wasn't true. She had not been with Rodrigo. Of course, Clara would say that Rebecca had been, under the circumstances, just to save face. Clara hated her. That had been obvious from the beginning. And perhaps she even hated Don Rigo, if only because she couldn't have him, couldn't be the *doña*. But surely he'd made them see that the girl had lied.

"You told them, didn't you," Rebecca choked out, "that it wasn't true?"

"I tol' dem!" he declared angrily, dropping his hand. "Clara tol' dem! But Elena..." He stopped to draw breath, tamping down his anger. "To Elena—an' perha's eet ees so—you are for me..." He seemed to search for words and found them resignedly. "For me, Rebecca, you are a temptation. Dis much ees o'vious, but I woul' no' have dem t'ink dat we...dat you..." He licked his lips. "Rebecca, you canno' stay here anymore. We no longer have *la acompañante*." He broke off, finishing lamely with, "I yam sorry. I mus' make for you odher—how you say?—*preparativos*."

She must leave! Plainly it could be no other way, but suddenly this place had never seemed more welcoming, safer, familiar. Hot tears welled behind her eyes, but she managed to keep them at bay, her chin up, shoulders squared.

"Our watch puppy," she said, struggling with a light tone, "seems to have been more trouble than she was worth."

Don Rigo had bowed his head, but he raised it now, smiling wryly. "You shoul' be angry wit me, Rebecca. Las' nigh', I did no' t'ink why she was here, an' now you mus' suffer no' on'y dese lies but also, I fear, discomfort."

She took a deep breath, wanting to make it easier for him, for both of them. "I don't imagine it will be so bad. After all, I rode horseback across a desert, double, slept on the ground, froze at night, broiled during the day. And you insulted me. Remember that? Oh, I've been meaning to ask you a question." She was thinking that she might not get another chance. "Just where did Paco and Luca get those ideas about American women, anyway?"

He actually chuckled, but his gaze flitted away guiltily. "Forgive me, Rebecca. I yam twice a fool, eet seems."

Twice a fool? This man? She wouldn't have him think that, even if she couldn't help wondering what experiences had prompted him to malign American women to his men. Once again, she found that she didn't want to think about it.

"You're no fool," she told him. "You're just a man with problems of his own and an unexpected guest to complicate matters. It'll be okay. Besides, it won't be long now until we'll be off to San Benito and Matthew."

"To San Benito," he repeated softly, "and Matthew." She nodded encouragingly, forcing a smile. He took both of her hands in his, stormy eyes meeting hers and holding them. "Rebecca, I fear I canno' leave dis place a' soon a' you may hope. De water pro'lem mus' be solve, an' a'ready we are behind wit de cattle."

Rebecca was troubled by this news but would not have him feel guilty for things beyond his control. "So how long do you think it may be?" she asked evenly.

He cocked his head to one side, eyebrows drawing together. "I canno' say. De water ees mos' *importante,* but eef eet ees no' foun' soon, de sale o' de cattle will be—how do you say?—*comprometida*.''

She didn't know the word, but she had a handle on the problem. "Are you saying that there is a deadline, a date by which you must deliver the cattle?"

''*Sí*. A deadline an' also a number for de cattles. We mus' have time to gadher de number I have promise.''

"Have you thought of asking for a delay? I mean, this buyer, he's a businessman, isn't he? Won't he understand about the well?''

Don Rigo stroked his upper lip. ''Perha's. I will t'ink o' dis. But de problem now ees—''

"Me," she supplied flatly. He shook his head.

"No. De problem are dhose who make our business dheir own. Eef you stay here witou' de wa'chdog, dey will do an' say bad t'ings, an' I will no' be here so often to protec' you. We mus' find for you anodher place.''

She nodded. ''I understand.''

"I t'ink I will miss you," he said softly.

"Don't be silly," she chided, holding tight to the easy tone. "We've hardly seen one another for days. Besides, you're *el dueño, jefe*. Once you find water, drive those cattle to market and get me off your hands, some other crisis will crop up. Count on it.''

He shook his head stubbornly, and when he spoke, his voice was as soft as velvet. "I will miss you. I know eet as I know my name." He cleared his throat as if aware that he'd gone too far, said too much. "I mus' settle dis.''

He left her, his hands slipping from hers as he turned away. Sternly, he approached the women, some of whom were talking quietly amongst themselves. They hushed as he drew near, but Lupe positioned herself in front of him and spoke up. Rebecca understood every word.

''*Yo la recibiré*,'' she said. ''*Mándamela*.'' I'll accept her. Send her to me.

It was impossible, of course. Lupe's little shack was no bigger than a closet, with the memorabilia of a lifetime crammed inside, leaving only a path to the narrow bed in which she slept, and Tía Elena was quick to protest, on what grounds Rebecca could not guess, but perhaps it was that the poor cabaña stood so close to Don Rigo's house. Several others offered assistance, but Rebecca was beyond translating their words. Tears welled in her eyes at the thought of Lupe's kindness, and she longed to remain among friends, but she had been the source of enough trouble here, and the feelings she was developing for Don Rigo were dangerous. Did he really mean that she was a temptation for him? she wondered. But the very thought was dangerous, and she did her best to put it from her mind. After a few minutes of discussion, Don Rigo came back to her.

"I have accepted a place for you wit de Espinozas," he told her. "Dey are good people, and de *casa* ees o' some size, but dhere are many *niños.* Still, Señora Espinoza says you are welcome. Lupe will he'p you wit your belongings an' look in from time to time. Eef you have need, you mus' send me a message by her, an' I will come."

"I'll be fine," Rebecca said with much more bravado than she felt.

He nodded slowly. "My men wait for me."

"Well, then..." She felt a thickening in her throat and swallowed it down. "I'll see you."

"*Sí.* When de work permi's." He stood for a moment as if he would say more, and his hand came up to skim her cheek, but then he turned away abruptly and strode from the room, pausing only to speak to Lupe, his head jerking toward Rebecca, before he stepped up into the front hallway.

Already some of the women had returned to their respective duties, and Tía Elena was moving through the doorway, her hand on the forearm of Teresa, Rodrigo's eldest sister, whose head was bent so that her ear might catch the words the old woman was speaking. Elena slipped from view, taking the majority of the women with her, leaving only Lupe, a plump, short woman with a scarf tied over the thick, dark hair that hung down her back, and Teresa, whose eyes narrowed suspiciously. Clearly, Rodrigo's sister was left behind to make sure that the "temptation" was removed from his house.

Rebecca shook her head and went swiftly to her room, Rodrigo's old room. She began rolling her things into an awkward bundle. Suddenly, she felt a great need to get out of here, to find Matthew, to return to things and places familiar, to reclaim her life, and yet, as she looked around the neat, narrow room, she felt a sense of loss, too, but she had had enough of that. Angrily, she snatched her belongings from the nooks and crannies of the room, bundled them into her arms and swept clear of the place as quickly as possible.

It was one thing to mourn the loss of what had been legally and morally hers, but it was something else again when leaving a borrowed room brought the same feelings. She was becoming an emotional cripple, dependent upon the kindness of strangers. Well, it had to stop. She wouldn't let herself be some pathetic waif waiting for the world to suddenly become fair. She wouldn't let this place, these people defeat her. She was going to build a life of her own. She was going to be happy. She would find Matthew, however long it took, because she must. He was all she had in the world now. They were family. Together they would be happy, and she wouldn't miss Rodrigo or this place or even Los Angeles. She mustn't. Nevertheless, it was comforting to know she had made at least one friend here.

For Lupe, Rebecca lifted her head as she walked toward Señora Espinoza, aware of Teresa's watchful attention and the old housekeeper's affectionate one. As she drew near, Lupe reached out a hand to settle on her forearm and made a simple introduction in Spanish. Rebecca acknowledged her new hostess with a nod of her head and thanked her in halting Spanish for her generosity, then she turned to Lupe and opened an arm to receive her hug. No words were necessary. The knowledge that she had managed to endear herself to this old woman momentarily filled all the lonely, empty spaces inside. She kissed the old woman's papery cheek and gave her a smile before turning to follow Señora Espinoza from the house.

Chapter Seven

Rebecca sat up very carefully, acutely aware of the two little ones sleeping on either side of her. The baby, Eustacia, had slept only fitfully throughout the long night, waking almost hourly to gnaw her chubby fist and whimper before thrashing herself into exhaustion and sleep again. Rebecca suspected her of teething, but then she knew precious little about children. She didn't even know how old the child was, probably less than two years, not old enough to talk more than gibberish but old enough to toddle about and get into things.

Why, only a day after her arrival, Rebecca had caught the baby girl pulling the ear of an old goat that sometimes wandered into the village, and had snatched her away just as the thick teeth snapped together on the air her little fingers had displaced but an instant before. Baby Eustacia had squalled just as if she'd been bitten, and Rebecca had been hard-pressed to soothe and quiet her. But she had managed, and now, only a week later, Eustacia was somehow her responsibility, a notion that completely unnerved her. Despite being dirty, uncomfortable, tired and miserable, Rebecca's chief concern was that she'd unknowingly do something to harm the little innocent, and so she slipped carefully from the bed, grateful for the patch of lightening sky framed by the shutterless window that told her dawn was not far off.

In truth, her week with the Espinozas had been utterly miserable. For one thing, the three-room *casa* was packed tight with furniture and people from its dirt floor to its sooty ceiling. For another, in order to divert precious water to the herds, Don Rigo had almost immediately forbidden the use of water for anything other than strict necessities. As a consequence, neither Rebecca nor anyone else in the community had done more than wash face and hands in days. The baby had been running around without pants to minimize the chance of an accident as her potty training was not complete, and Rebecca herself had been wearing the same clothing going on three days now. All the children were grubby, and the crowded bed she shared with Eustacia and her older sister badly needed a change of linen. It was impossible to catch even a few hours sleep in that crowded, dirty bed, and lately she found herself longing for morning all night long. Most of all, she hated the dirt floors that caused grit to get into everything.

Silently, she stepped over the pallets of two more Espinoza daughters. The sons who had been born between them slept in the next room on a mattress that was pulled nightly from beneath the bed of their parents. The *sala* functioned not only as dining room but also as kitchen. There was no running water in the house, but light was provided by a quartet of modern kerosene lanterns hung from the ceiling, and Señora Espinoza was the proud owner of a pedal-operated sewing machine that made her the envy of every other woman on the rancho. It was to Lura's credit that she did much mending without charge.

She would be rising in a little while to make breakfast for her brood of children, three of whom were of school age. It worried Rebecca that they, as well as the other children of the rancho, received no formal instruction, and she determined to speak to Don Rigo about it before she left this place—if she ever did.

Sometimes it seemed to her that she had spent an eternity on this mountain and that she was doomed to spend another. It had not been so bad when she had enjoyed the hospitality of Don Rigo, but then he enjoyed a prosperity to which the villagers did not appear to even aspire. They were not an easy people to understand. If not for their provinciality, she would be sleeping peacefully in that good bed at the big house, and yet they were a happy people, readily sharing what little they had with her though she was a stranger, and a gringa, at that.

Shaking her head, she took the blanket that covered the room's inner door and wrapped it about her shoulders before slipping through one room and then another and out into the chill early morning. The sky had lightened just enough for her to make out the outline of the rocky cliffs in the distance. Soon, the sun would peek over them, warming all with its golden iridescence. Sunrise had become her favorite moment of the day, and she settled down upon the powdery earth to await it, her back to the planking of the door. She folded her legs, shivering inside the blanket, and hugged herself tighter.

Her mind, as always in these moments of stillness, went at once to Rodrigo. The don. His people truly respected him, and their welfare was undoubtedly his first priority. She wondered how he bore the responsibility alone, all the while fighting this fierce land, but before she could speculate an answer, her mind slipped into oblivion, finding the much-needed sleep that so far had eluded her. She was sitting there, her chin upon her chest when the sun lifted its light over the mountaintop, and she was sitting there still when, minutes later, a lazy cock crowed the advent of day and Don Rigo walked his mount through the village square.

It had been a long night for Don Rigo and his men, and he was beginning to wonder if this job would ever end. Many breaks in the pipeline had been repaired, and still the water only trickled. As far as the well was concerned, they were just chipping through solid rock now, working in shifts, hoping against hope and knowing that to give up would mean certain defeat and the prolonged suffering of their women and children. Life on this mountain without an adequate water supply would be difficult at best, and so they would find water. They must.

Don Rigo straightened, drawing himself tall in the saddle. He was dirty and tired and homesick, but he had not come to enjoy the luxury of his *casa*. He had made a difficult decision, and it was this he had come to implement. He wished the village again had a priest; it would be comforting just now to have someone pray for him.

He turned his horse toward the lane that led to his *casa*, and as if of its own will, his head turned to the right, his eyes following the short path to the Espinozas' front door. Instantly he drew up, hauling back on the reins, clutching with his knees. Rebecca sat with her back to the door, knees drawn up beneath the blanket tented about her, the curtain of her hair—very yellow now, he noticed, from exposure to the sun—hiding her face.

"She sleeps," said a voice in Spanish, and he twisted in the saddle to find Glorieta there, a metal pail on her hip. Glorieta was a comely woman, and he felt a sudden, sharp pity for her. Her gaze fell as if she sensed his emotion, but the next instant, she was walking forward, her shapely hips swaying rhythmically, her chin lifting in the direction of the Espinozas' little house. "She has not been there very long," she told him gently. "Still, it does not go well with the American woman."

"It does not go well for any of us just now," he replied, sighing.

"This is so," Glorieta acknowledged. "But the Americans live soft lives. You have said it yourself. We are used to the struggle, are we not?"

Did one get used to disaster? he wondered, pinching the bridge of his nose. To Glorieta he said, "I do not wish anyone to suffer."

She stepped close then and placed a hand upon the toe of his boot, her head falling back as she looked up at him. Her dark eyes were solemn, her pretty mouth soft and full. "You will not come to me again, will you, Rodrigo?"

He had not expected such directness, but he admired her for it. She deserved a direct answer. "No."

She looked away then, her head turning sharply in Rebecca's direction. "She should go back to where she belongs," Glorieta muttered, not unkindly.

Rodrigo sighed. "I expect that she will soon. A message is going to her brother."

She seemed surprised. "You can spare a man for this?"

He shook his head. "No, but the cattle shipment must be delayed, and it is as easy to send two messages as one."

"Ah."

He did not have to explain this decision to her. Even she knew that this was not good news. The delay might anger the buyer, who must make a special trip across the Sea of Cortés to receive the cattle. But this was better than having him arrive to inspect a few standing carcasses, which was all they would have left if they attempted to drive the cattle now. As for Rebecca, from the beginning it had been understood that she was on her way to another place. He hoped, for her sake, that it would be a place where she could belong. She couldn't stay here, living like this, sleeping against the front door. Like everyone everywhere, she deserved a place of her own, a real home. If it was in his power... But there wasn't much within his power just then, it seemed. His horse shifted beneath him, a sign of discomfort rather than impatience. He should be moving along, and yet he hated to leave her there like that.

"She may be stronger than we think," Glorieta said, following the line of his gaze.

He gathered his reins more firmly in his hands. "It is always hard in a strange place, even for the strong," he told her with the certainty of one who knew.

She narrowed her wide eyes, dropping her hand and backing away. She gave her long dark hair a toss, and he knew she was working her way up to something.

"If it makes you feel better," she began stiltedly, "I will try to keep watch over her."

He felt himself smile. "You're a good woman, Glorieta."

She laughed, her hand on her hip. "If I were a good woman, Don Rigo, you would never have come to me, and I would never have let you stay."

He gave her a dark look. "I know you, Glorieta, and I know that there is more than one way to be good just as there is more than one way to be bad."

"It is a pity everyone else does not share this knowledge of yours," she told him flatly, casting a derisive eye around the empty square.

He folded his hands over the pommel of his saddle. "There are others who share my view. If you would open your eyes, you might see them."

Her stance altered abruptly, the hand sliding away, the pail dropping to her side, shoulders sloping. "Truly?"

He grinned at her. "Did you never notice how some of the single men look at you? Paco, perhaps. Alonzo. Juan."

Her mouth shaped itself into a small O at the mention of the second name, and Rodrigo smiled inwardly with satisfaction, making a mental note to drop a word in Alonzo's ear at first opportunity. Glorieta quickly recovered, however, striking once more the pose of hauteur.

"Paco," she scoffed, "is an old man the size of a child!"

It was Rodrigo's turn to laugh. "So he is, and yet he is still a man."

Her stance softened. "He is that, yes."

"But not so much a man as Alonzo, perhaps."

It was not wise to tease her, but he couldn't resist. As he had expected, her face colored, and suddenly she was spitting words to singe his ears. Doors began to open in the houses tucked into the lanes leading from the square. Time to be off. His gaze went once more to where Rebecca stirred in the final moments of slumber. Then, frowning, he kicked the horse into a trot.

Lura Espinoza opened the door to her house and jolted Rebecca awake. She started and put a hand to her yellow hair, the blanket slipping from her shoulders. She looked around, her gaze colliding with that of the woman known as Glorieta. She smiled, letting her gaze settle for a moment, friendly, even needy. Glorieta returned the timid smile before slowly turning and walking to the fountain to fill her bucket.

Rebecca stretched as she got to her feet, working the kinks from her back and limbs. She had missed the sunrise, but at least she had gotten a little sleep. She took the bucket from Señora Espinoza's hand, smiling wanly, and shrugged in reply to whatever the woman said. She was too tired and stiff to attempt translation. The *señora* turned away, and Rebecca moved with the heavy wooden bucket toward the fountain in the square. As she turned from the lane, she saw Glorieta pumping water into her metal pail. It troubled Rebecca that the woman was ostracized by the others. She tended to treat them all with disdain, but Rebecca sensed that beneath that tough exterior, Glorieta was lonely, and that made two of them.

"*Buenos días,*" Rebecca called in greeting, walking forward.

The woman straightened, her hand on the pump handle, and to Rebecca's surprise, actually replied. "*Buenos días, Rebecca,*" she said softly. "*Me llamo Glorieta.*"

Of course, Rebecca already knew the woman's name, just as the woman knew Rebecca's, so this was not a mere introduction, which made it all the more surprising. Perhaps, Rebecca thought, it was a beginning, and she smiled again. Glorieta bowed her head, her own smile timid, and reached out her hand for Rebecca's bucket. With only the slightest hesitation, Rebecca relinquished it and bent to move the half-full pail beneath the faucet. Glorieta pumped the handle, sending a small stream of water into the wooden bucket. Rebecca's smile broadened. It seemed they'd made a connection, perhaps even a start on friendship.

Señora Espinoza offered a scrawny chicken wing hung with more loose skin than meat, and Rebecca's empty stomach roiled. In her opinion, one thirsty, skinny, demented old hen made neither an adequate nor appetizing meal for eight people, but it seemed she was alone in that judgment. The children around her were clamoring for the tidbit. The smallest, in fact, was smacking her mouth hopefully.

Rebecca had become extremely fond of Eustacia, more than was wise. She lifted her bowl toward Señora Espinoza and received the ghastly chicken part, then passed the unappetizing thing to the baby, switching her own little bowl with the child's. Eustacia plunged both hands into the thin broth and lifted the wing to her mouth, munching happily on the gristly joint.

Rebecca herself was hungry, but her stomach protested at the sight of the tough, stringy hen baked with a handful of dark pepper chunks and bright corn kernels. The meals had grown more unappetizing by the day now that the women, urged by Tía Elena, were conserving foodstuffs as well as water against the possibility of greater hardship. One did not live nor consume in this place without giving thought to tomorrow.

Rebecca pushed her bowl away and went to help the *señora* sift sand and ash with which to scour the dishes, but before long, she had reason to regret her finickiness: her stomach was rumbling. To her shame, the *señora* pressed an orange into her hands as soon as the children were in bed.

Tears stung her eyes. The *señora,* indeed, all of the village women, had been cool toward her for some days now. She knew they disapproved of her friendship with Glorieta. Don Rigo's eldest sister had even explained in slow, careful Spanish why Glorieta was to be shunned. Apparently, taking advantage of the fact that she was barren, Glorieta had enjoyed the company of men since the death of her husband. From the women's point of view, she seemed to constitute a threat to the sanctity of their own marriages. To Rebecca, it was a mean, outmoded, judgmental, unfair attitude, and without saying as much—in Spanish, anyway—she had resolved to stand by her new friend.

She did this by continuing to greet Glorieta whenever they met, by having a smile ready if the woman should catch her eye and by not looking away the instant eye contact was made. Glorieta seemed pitifully grateful for these crumbs of friendship, though she kept herself apart from Rebecca when the other women were present. Rebecca felt sorry for her, but more than that, she liked Glorieta. The woman employed a quick wit and a discerning eye, and Rebecca felt both protective of her and protected by her. She would not pretend disdain just because Tía Elena and her morality brigade of nieces and hangers-on dictated it. She had begun to think that Señora Espinoza despised her for her continued support of Glorieta, and it was a great relief to see that her hostess still possessed the good heart she had displayed in the beginning.

More, though, it was the entire circumstance that made Rebecca cry. She had begun to feel so alone. Except for the glances and signals and occasional quick chat she shared with Glorieta and the meaningless gurgles and blathering of the baby, no one even tried to talk to her anymore. Added to the already burdensome physical discomforts that she had endured since coming to the Espinozas, the situation had served to make her very unhappy, indeed. She no longer slept with the babies, for the urge to cry seemed constantly upon her, and she could not seem to get to sleep without doing so. Besides, the bed was so uncomfortable and crowded that a patch of sand was actually better, and looking at the stars calmed her, so she had claimed the whole of the out-of-doors for her bedroom. After all, it wasn't as if she had to worry about rain. The skies here remained perfectly cloudless day after day after day.

Clutching her orange, she sniffed and thanked Señora Espinoza, then quickly gathered her bedroll and slipped outside. The clean, cool night air washed over her skin, and she lifted her face to it, tears leaking from the corners of her eyes. The fragrance of the orange wafted to her nostrils. She walked out to the sandy spot she had found at the end of the lane and spread the rug she had appropriated close to the bushes that stood beside it. She wrapped the blanket about her, holding the orange beneath her chin, and sat down, letting the orange drop into her lap. She was so very tired, but the aroma of the orange was positively irresistible and she was hungry.

Carefully, she drove her thumbnail into the thick skin and began to peel it back, tossing away the pieces that fell into her palm until the heart of the fruit was bare. Meticulously, savoring the anticipation, she scraped away all of the white, stringy membrane, then gently broke the whole into plump segments. Slowly, with two measured bites to each section, she devoured every last morsel and licked the juice from her fingers, then let her head fall back upon her shoulders and enjoyed the feeling of a full stomach beneath the matchless canopy of the stars.

After a while, she felt agreeably sleepy and settled down upon her rug, but her fingers and chin were still sticky from the orange and clung lightly to all that she touched. She had come to hate the feeling of being even a little dirty, and try as she might, she couldn't put the matter from her mind. It was silly, of course, to worry about a little dirt while sleeping upon the ground on a rug, but she just couldn't help it.

The idea of waiting until the morning to wash made her want to weep again. She had this vision of herself waking to find her fingers and face covered in a sticky layer of dust which she could never hope to be rid of. Still, she worried about washing her hands and face. She had come to understand how precious every drop of water truly was. Not only the quality of life in this place depended on it; the very survival of this community was at stake. But, oh, what she wouldn't give for just a few drops of water to wash away this stickiness!

Finally, she couldn't stand it any longer. Promising herself that she would drink very little the next day, she made up her mind to go to the pump in the square. Guilt swamped her, but a sense of self-preservation rose to combat it. Just how much was a person supposed to do without, anyway? She lacked home, family, all the conveniences so much of the world took for granted, a bed, a roof over her head, even an adequate meal! Was it too much to ask that her face and hands be clean when she lay down to sleep? She had convinced herself that she was entitled to a few extra drops of water. Of course, no one else in this backward place would agree with her, but then, no one else had to know, did they?

Draping her blanket about her head and shoulders like a shawl, she got to her feet and slipped out into the square. The little church across the way gleamed white in the starlight, while the palm tree stood out in a thick, black, misshapen silhouette against the wheat-colored glow of the square itself. The now-dry fountain shimmered like dark silver. The place had a spooky feel about it. It put her in mind of the old westerns she used to watch back when television was something she had taken for granted, along with the water that ran freely from every faucet.

Holding the blanket tight about her, she swiftly crossed the open space to the pump beside the fountain and bent toward it. To her surprise, a big drop of water plopped onto her fingertip. That was strange. The pump usually only dripped just after it had been used, but she had seen no one there. Drawing back, she looked around her again, feeling deeply uncomfortable about the impenetrable shadow of the tree. Nothing. Besides, even if someone else had been here, it wouldn't hurt to use the water that dripped freely from the spigot. Shrugging, she bent toward the spout again, only to jerk away, startled by the snort of a horse somewhere nearby. The blanket slipped from her head, and she plucked at it desperately, the flesh prickling on the back of her neck. Someone was there, and suddenly she was frightened.

"Rebecca."

Her own name came to her out of the shadow of the tree, the voice unmistakably Don Rigo's. Relief swamped her, followed quickly by something very like joy, and suddenly tears were flowing down her face once again.

"Rebecca?" He stepped forward, the horse snuffling behind him. She swiped at her face, spreading stickiness with tears, then remembered why she'd come and quickly dashed her hands beneath the spout. The drip had stopped. She put her hands behind her, straightening.

"D-Don Rigo. You s-startled me."

"Forgive me. I did no' see you, you came so quietly."

She lifted the blanket about her head again and folded it about her shoulders, taking in what she could see of the rumpled jeans and jacket he wore. He had pushed his hat to the back of his head, but she couldn't really see his face, which meant that he couldn't see hers, either, and for that, she was grateful.

"What are you doing here?" she asked evenly.

"I stop to water de horse. Eet ees a long ride from de well, an' he has had little to drink een dese pas' days."

"Ah." That explained the drip.

"Why are you here?"

It wasn't a question she really wanted to answer, and she decided on an evasive reply. "I couldn't sleep."

"You t'ought a drink woul' help?"

"Ah, no..." What was the use? She'd been caught in the act, hadn't she? "I had an orange, and my face and fingers are a little sticky."

"Come den an' wash dem," he said, stepping up to the pump, but his generosity emphasized her selfishness.

"No, I really shouldn't."

"Come, come. Eet ees all righ', Rebecca. Soon we will have all de water we need once again."

"Really? The new well's a success?"

"*Sí.* De water comes even now. Eet ees jus' a matter of putting a pump wit eet. Till den, we mus' haul de water up een bucke's. De well, eet ees ver' deep, an' de water ees har' to haul, but soon I sen' a man to Santa Rosalía for a pump, an' eet will be much easier den. An' *mañana* de gadhering of de cattle starts again, dhough many o' de men will remain to haul de water till de pump works."

Rebecca clapped her hands together at this wonderful news, only to feel the cloying stickiness of her fingers. But if there was water... She thrust her hands under the spigot, laughing, and Don Rigo quickly pumped the handle. After a few seconds, water dribbled over her hands. Excitedly, she scrubbed them clean and splashed her face, drying off with the blanket.

"Oh, I can't wait to have a real bath again!"

"I have promise myse'f a bat' before I go to bed tonigh'," he told her, and instantly the narrow bed in her old room at his *casa* came to her mind.

"God, what I wouldn't give for a bath and a real bed!" she exclaimed.

"You do no' like your bed a' de Espinozas?" he queried quietly, and at once she regretted the impulsive outburst.

"Ah, well, it's not that I don't like the bed. I-it's just that... Actually, it's that I'm not used to sharing a bed, and... You know how children can be."

Don Rigo sighed and resettled the hat on his head. "Eet has been ver' har' for you, an' I yam sorry for eet, bu' eet will be easier now, wit de water."

Rebecca bit her lip and nodded. Had his own problems not been so grave, she might have told him just how hard it had been, but she knew that he had done his best from the moment he had come upon her beside the highway, and she would not repay his kindness with complaints. Neither would she display her weakness. She had some pride left, after all. Not much, but some.

"Eet will be easier," he went on, "an' eet will no' be much longer. De man who goes for de pump, he will also do somet'ing else. He will sen' messages for me, one to de buyer of de cattle an' one to your brodher in San Benito."

"Matthew!"

He nodded, going on. "Eef your brodher wish, an' I ezpec' he will, my man will bring him back here for you."

At last! She could hardly believe it. Matthew was coming! Don Rigo was sending for him, and soon he would be here!

"Eet will on'y be a few more days," Don Rigo was saying. "Soon you will once again—"

She threw her arms around him, cutting off the flow of his words, weeping with joy against his neck. "Thank you! Oh, thank you! Thank you! I thought I'd be dirty and hungry and sleeping on the ground for the rest of my life! But now that I know Matthew will be coming, it doesn't matter!"

"What ees dis?" he said, stepping back, his hand curling beneath her chin. "De lack o' a bath does no' make you hungry."

"No, of course, it doesn't, but with everyone on short rations around here..."

"I made no order to ration food."

"Perhaps not, but everyone understands that a shortage of water will eventually mean a shortage of food, and the *señora* has so many children to feed as it is."

"But de *señora* was given estra supplies so dat no one shoul' go hungry!" he insisted, and Rebecca began to understand that he was truly angry.

"She hasn't starved me, Rodrigo," she assured him. "Sometimes I just don't like the food, that's all."

"An' why you sleep on de groun'? De *señora* promise you woul' have a bed!"

"Not all to myself," she said. "And I'm just not used to sharing a bed. I prefer to sleep on the ground. Honestly. You mustn't blame Señora Espinoza. It's my choice. Besides, it's only for a few more days, until Matthew comes. You said so yourself."

He seemed to be considering. "Four days, Rebecca, perha's five. No. You have suffer enough. I canno' let you go on sleeping on de groun' when dhere are beds a' my house! Why di' no one tell me o' dis sooner?"

"No one is at fault here, Rodrigo," she said, but he was adamant.

"Where was Lupe? Where was..." He suddenly stopped, leaving it hanging.

"I would have had to tell Lupe for her to know," Rebecca pointed out. "But I didn't want to complain, and I'm not complaining now."

"Dhere ees no longer a' reason for complain," he told her flatly. "You are comin' to de *casa* wit me." And he turned away, striding into the darkness for the horse. Rebecca was flabbergasted. She ran after him.

"But, Rodrigo, nothing has changed. If I go back to the *casa* with you, this entire community's going to come down on your neck! I don't want that, especially now with the end in sight!"

"And I don' wan' you sleeping on de ground like a *vagabunda!*" he countered angrily, tightening the saddle cinch.

"But it's only for a few more days."

"No!" He whirled suddenly, grasping her shoulders, and just as suddenly, he released her. "You will come wit me," he said more calmly, adding, "Wha' woul' your brodher t'ink eef he come to fin' you sleeping on de groun'? He woul' be angry, an' I woul' no' blame him!"

She folded her arms. "You said the same thing before you sent me to the Espinozas, except then you were sure he'd be angry because I was sleeping in your house!"

"So eef he ees going to be angry an'way, you migh' a' leas' have comfort."

She rolled her eyes. "He's not going to be angry!"

"Den we have no problem," Don Rigo said, taking the reins in hand.

"Yes, we do! Your aunt isn't going to sit still for this! No one will! My God, they won't speak to me now just because I've befriended Glorieta!"

His head came around sharply. "*¿Qué?* Glorieta? You are a frien' wit Glorieta?"

Rebecca folded her arms, disappointed by the stressful quality of his voice. "Not you, too! What has that woman done to make you all hate her?"

"No, I do no' hate her. I do no' hate Glorieta."

"What then? What's wrong with me being friends with her?"

"Not'ing. I say not'ing."

"But you don't like it."

"How does dis matter to me, who your frien's are?"

"That's what I want to know!"

He pushed his hat back again, sighing, but after a moment, he began to chuckle. "Oh, Rebecca. I sen' you away because I do no' wan' my aunt an' dese people to t'ink bad o' you an' no' talk to you een de stree'. An' now you tell me eet ees so an'way. So wha' does eet matter eef you sleep een a bed een my *casa* till your brodher come, eh?" He shook his head, chuckling.

"Maybe I don't want anyone to think bad of *you* and not speak to *you* in the street," she said softly, and the silence that followed was broken only by horse sounds: chomping, blowing, the clop of a hoof. After a long moment, the shadow of Don Rigo's hand lifted toward her through the darkness, brushed her cheek, skimmed her shoulder and fell away again.

"Rebecca," he said, "you honor me wit dese t'oughts, bu' you forget dat I am *el dueño*. Dese are my people. No' even Elena will push me too har'. My co'cern alway' was for you. Do no' be too much co'cern for me now. You will come wit me, an' you will sleep tonigh' een a clean bed, alone. I have spoken dis. Eet will be. Come. *Mañana* I will get your t'ings. Tonigh', we will forget our worry an' rest."

She was inclined to agree, but it pained her to be the source of further discord for him, and she intended to say so. "But—"

Don Rigo clamped a hand over her mouth. "I am no' on'y *el dueño*," he told her firmly. "I am also *jefe,* an' I will hear no argument. You come wit me."

Quelled, convinced, she nodded, and he took his hand away, chuckling softly. He squeezed her shoulder, then turned and swung up into the saddle. Bending down, he reached out a hand for her. She put one foot into the stirrup and pushed upward as his arm came around her. She slid her leg between him and the saddle horn and settled into place against him. There would be hell to pay, no doubt, but it felt so good to be with him again, to know that she was welcome. And there would be a clean bed and real floors again and good food and water—and soon, Matthew. But just for tonight, she wouldn't think of that. Just for tonight, perhaps, she would pretend that she was home, where she belonged.

Chapter Eight

The basket of laundry was heavy. It was almost more than Rebecca could manage over the distance of the *paseo,* and she worried that Lupe's burden would be too much for her. After all, Lupe was an elderly woman, and her basket was as large as the one that Rebecca carried. Yet, the old woman had not faltered, and they were drawing near the square at last. Rebecca was relieved, even knowing what might well await her there.

An ugly scene had played itself out the morning after she had returned to Don Rigo's *casa.* Tía Elena and the sisters had shrieked and wailed and made solemn pronouncements. Don Rigo had roared and stormed and called them all names. Señora Espinoza, playing the part of peacemaker, had begged Rebecca to return with her, and when Rebecca would have agreed, Don Rigo had sent her to her room and had ordered the others to leave his house. Since then, he had pretended that all was well, and though at first he had said the roundup of the cattle would begin that very next day, two days had passed and another had begun and Don Rigo had yet to join his men in the field. At first, she was inclined to take advantage of the situation. He needed rest, after all, and she had been only too happy to spend time with him again. Also, she had found her chance to speak to him about the need of the village children for a real school and learned that Rodrigo was keenly aware of the problem, not that a solution presented itself.

Long ago, the village had had a real school. A building had been raised and a teacher had been hired, a sophisticated young man from Mexico City. After some time, that man had wed the old *dueño*'s daughter, Elena. It was apparently a happy match, but a few months later, the teacher had died and in her grief, Elena had persuaded her father that it would be disloyal to hire another teacher just as, she was convinced, it would be disloyal for her to marry again. The school had become the saddlery, and Tía Elena had become bitter and hard.

After that, the local priest had served as tutor to the *dueño*'s children but was forbidden by national law to operate a school, and the rancho had suffered a decline in revenue, making it impossible to hire a teacher. Now it was not even possible to have a tutor, for the village had been without a priest of its own for a long time. Evidently, the Church was having trouble filling its ranks. The itinerant priest who served them came only once every four months, and even though a layman in the village was training to conduct Sunday services and catechism classes in the future, he would not be available or qualified to teach academic subjects. Don Rigo's aim was to hire a real teacher, but such a project required money, and though the rancho was rich in many ways, it was poor in pesos. He sought to change this, to move the productivity of the rancho beyond the level of subsistence.

It was for this reason that he had carefully and selectively invested in cattle over the years, and now he had his first chance to sell for a profit. If all went well, he would be able to advertise for a teacher in the border towns of Tijuana and Mexicali and perhaps also in La Paz, and next year or the year after, the rancho would have a school. Rebecca could not help thinking that she had been educated to teach, but the idea, of course, was ridiculous, and she dared not allow herself to dwell on it, telling herself that it was only because she so enjoyed the time she spent with Rodrigo that the notion had come to her.

She was beginning to understand how dangerous it was to go on spending time with him. The more time she spent with him, the more difficult became the idea of leaving, but leave she would. Matthew was on his way, which was as it should be, so she had made up her mind to keep her distance from Don Rigo until Matthew came, perhaps tomorrow. Soon they would probably leave together, she and Matthew, in pursuit of that new life they would find. Somewhere. And she would never see Rodrigo again. The idea was daunting, painful even, but so was being with Don Rigo. She had begun to fantasize about making love with him. Everyone thought they were doing it anyway, but the reality was that he had not so much as touched her, and though one part of her was grateful, it had become painful even to be in the same room with him. So she had volunteered to help Lupe with the mountain of laundry that had accumulated during the forced drought.

She didn't mind the work. In fact, if she had learned one thing from this experience, it was that real work made one feel good about oneself. She regretted now all those years of doing nothing of real value, of adding nothing to another's life, of passing up chances to make a difference for someone beside herself. She had even wasted a college education. She had taken one look at that roomful of children with their snotty noses and their scabbed knees and had run back to the safety of Daddy's company, where nothing had been expected of her. Well, it would be different after Matthew came for her. Somehow.

Meanwhile, it was wash day, and everything she owned was filthy. Moreover, she owed Lupe her assistance with this burdensome task, even if her appearance in the square was bound to put some noses out of joint. Not that she expected real trouble. She was *el dueño*'s woman, after all, at least as far as they were concerned.

They entered the square, glad to see that the washtubs had been set up and a tendril of steam was curling from the big caldron that sat upon the fire. The water would be hot and the washing could begin right away, minimizing the possibility of conversation, not that such a possibility existed. Clearly, it did not, for as Rebecca and Lupe drew near, a dead silence fell over those already gathered. Rebecca forced a passive expression, ignoring the hard stares along with the averted faces, while Lupe glared a challenge from narrowed eyes at those bold enough to look her way. A few exhibited looks of silent pity, but only one person displayed a welcome: Glorieta.

As usual, the young widow had set up her own tubs, complete with a manual wringer, away from those used communally by the other women of the village, and she stood overlooking the scene, her hands on her hips, as the newcomers drew near the wash area beside the fountain. As Rebecca's eyes traveled over those present, she felt Glorieta's patient presence, and when at last she gave her friend her full attention, she was rewarded with a genuine smile and a silent invitation in the form of a jerk of the head and a wave of a hand.

Rebecca sent a questioning look to Lupe, who nodded her agreement. Heads high, they walked slowly by their self-appointed panel of judges, carrying their loaded baskets. As their intent became obvious, a series of gasps rippled through the small mob of washerwomen. Glorieta lifted her skirt, revealing several layers of thin, colored petticoats, and laughed with derision at their obvious disapproval.

"*¡Gallinas!*" she cried. "*¡Gallinas con faldas!*" Hens, she called them, hens in skirts, and turning, she thrust out a finger. *"¡Aquí viene la gallinera!"* Here comes the hen keeper!

Rebecca bent and dropped her basket heavily upon the ground, straightening to look in the direction in which Glorieta pointed. Tía Elena strode toward them, dressed as was her custom, and bearing in addition to her beads, an enormous black umbrella with which to shelter herself from the sun. Isabel was at her side, Elena's laundry bundled in her arms, a look of resignation upon her face. Elena's gaze was stony, bleak, and she employed it freely, heaping disdain upon everyone within her realm. Her coldest stare went to Rebecca, of course, and despite her best intentions, Rebecca found her hackles rising. She turned sharply, fighting the impulse to lash out at the old woman, and stooped to paw through her basket. But Glorieta was not so circumspect. She folded her arms and glared a challenge at the old *dama*. Within moments, they were shrieking at each other, the old woman pointing her finger as if she expected a thunderbolt to shoot from its end and incinerate the upstart. Glorieta stamped the dirt and shook her fists, spitting words like bullets from an automatic gone wild. Rebecca dumped a bedsheet into the washtub and threw her arms up, rushing at Glorieta.

"Stop! Just stop it! Both of you!" She knew they didn't understand the words, but they hushed, Glorieta first and Elena after Rebecca rounded on her, rage flashing in her blue eyes. She stared them all down, every last one, Glorieta included. "Now get to work," she muttered, marching toward the tub.

She set to it herself with a vengeance, scrubbing every inch of the sheet with the coarse bar soap provided by Lupe. Soon Glorieta joined her, arms plunged into the rapidly cooling water, and finally Lupe, moving slowly as if to give them time together. Presently, Rebecca glanced in Glorieta's direction, pausing to wipe her forehead with her upper arm, and caught a smile playing at the other's lips. Her own mouth quivered in response. The image of haughty Elena quelled by the shock of Rebecca's anger was too much and she could not hold the giggles inside. Lupe scolded them in low, hissing Spanish that halted the laughter but broadened the smiles, and they worked on in companionable silence thereafter, developing a natural sort of assembly line that had one washing, one rinsing and wringing, and another hanging the sodden articles on one of the many lines strung from the tree to the corners of the buildings fronting the square.

Periodically, by a kind of silent mutual assent, they switched positions, and in this manner, they worked their way through the mass of the laundry before taking a much-needed break. Lupe had packed a jar of corn relish and a roll of tortillas along with two cups in her basket, and to this Glorieta added a pair of the ever-present oranges and slices of marinated squash and a sizable chunk of caramel candy. The total was a veritable feast, which the three of them shared sitting on the tiled rim of the fountain cistern, separated by a little distance from the others. While they ate, some children came running into the square, chasing a dog to which someone had tied a colorful scrap of cloth. Rodolfo was among them, in the lead, in fact, and his little face, so like his father's, beamed with the delight of the chase, until suddenly the thick, stiff sole of one of his *teguas* slipped on a smooth stone. His foot flew out from under him and he fell, thumping his head upon the ground and crushing his arm beneath him as he tried to catch himself. He yelped and burst into tears.

Rebecca was up and moving toward him before she even thought. Lupe started after her, then stopped, the younger woman proving to be much faster than she was. Rodolfo had come to himself and stemmed his tears by the time Rebecca reached him, but he seemed grateful, nonetheless, for the attention of one who seemed better able than he to judge the extent of his injury. As if by rote, her recent experience with Eustacia and the other Espinoza children emboldening her, Rebecca crouched beside him and gently gathered the boy into her arms, speaking soothing words.

"Poor fellow," she said, hearing but ignoring Elena's strident voice. "Here now, let's have a look. What a bump you have there. How about that arm? Nothing broken? Just a scrape on your wrist. Burns, doesn't it? Well, a little water will help, and then we'll see what kind of salve we can find." But even as she said the last words, the boy was yanked from her arms. She went down on her knees, shocked to find herself surrounded by outraged aunts, all of them babbling at once. Clearly, they objected to her touching the boy. She wasn't fit, it seemed, to comfort the future heir, no doubt by Elena's specific edict.

Ana hustled the boy away. He cast perplexed looks over his shoulder, a hand to his injured head, while Teresa berated his would-be nurse, spitting names that needed no interpretation. The others nodded in agreement, María giving her little pushes every time she attempted to rise and Elena egging them on from her perch on the rim of the cistern, her black umbrella bobbing up and down in her excitement. As for the others, Lupe turned at once and toddled as quickly as her old legs would carry her for the walled lane, the *paseo* that led to *el hidalgo*'s house. Glorieta first gaped, then positioned herself directly in front of Elena, hands at her hips, elbows out in a defensive posture.

Rebecca knew at a glance that if she did not move quickly, Glorieta would. She launched a counterattack from her position on the ground, the first assault of which was aimed at María. Unable to rise, she decided the best course was to bring María down to her, and so Rebecca simply scooped the woman's ankles from beneath her, upending María neatly. A collective gasp followed, accompanied by shrieks of horror. Rebecca scrambled to her feet, prepared to strike blows if necessary, but it was evident by the looks on the faces surrounding her that no one had intended the incident to go this far. Nevertheless, Rebecca kept her guard up as she shoved her way through the circle of her tormentors, angry tears coursing down her face as she made her way toward Elena.

Onlookers and bystanders drew back, all but young Clara, whose dislike of Rebecca was well known. Elena had not even the grace to pretend indifference. She stood and lifted her chin haughtily, her mouth a grim sneer fixed among the furrows of her arid skin. This little despot needed to be put in her place, and Rebecca was just the one to do it.

"How dare you...?" she began, but Elena merely sniffed and turned her head away, her contempt touching off a rage in Rebecca even she found disturbing. "Oh!" She cast about in frustration, and her gaze fell immediately on the cistern before which Elena stood. Rebecca glanced at Glorieta, who seemed to read her thoughts. Her dark eyes were laughing, and her mouth threatened a hopeful smile. It was all the encouragement Rebecca needed. She gave Elena a little bow, then stepped forward, lifted both hands and shoved the old crone backward.

For a moment, nothing much happened. Elena seemed to teeter on some invisible precipice. Hands covered gaping mouths in silence, and Elena's umbrella trembled in the sun as she fought to retain her balance. Then suddenly, she toppled over, falling backward into the shallow pool of the fountain cistern, umbrella and all, the little heels of her old-fashioned button shoes sticking up over the tiled rim.

And that was how Don Rigo found them: Elena on her back in the fountain pool, Clara perched on its edge and staring down at her, and Rebecca standing before them both with arms adamantly folded. Glorieta, alone among the women, was doubled over with laughter, while the four remaining sisters were rushing forward as a body, questing hands seeking to restore their aunt's shattered dignity. It was Lupe, coming upon the scene last of all, who displayed the reaction most reasonable. Gasping with the effort of her recent run to fetch Rodrigo, she looked about her, realized what had just transpired and fell to her knees, lifting both shriveled hands heavenward. Rodrigo himself could only stare until his sisters had hauled Tía Elena out of the cistern and Clara had scurried back to her mother.

Soaked to the skin, her voluminous black skirt a circular waterfall, the sodden wool of her rebozo clinging to her head like seaweed, Elena drew herself erect, swished her heavy skirt in the mud and lifted her umbrella, water showering down on her from its upturned bowl. Droplets fell from the silver crown of her hair, dropped from her dark eyebrows, ran in rivulets within the creases of her face and trickled onto her heaving bodice. Her nieces covered their faces with their hands and keened. Glorieta howled, the crowd of onlookers chattered like magpies, and Lupe crossed herself hastily, mouthing her desperate prayer. Rebecca stubbornly stuck out her chin. Don Rigo exploded.

"¡Cállense, todos ustedes!"

Glorieta hushed, the nieces wailed and lapsed into muted grumblings, and Rebecca spun to face him, only then aware of his presence.

"Don Rigo!" The look on his face expressed something between dismay and fury, and for the first time, Rebecca felt doubt along with the beginnings of remorse.

He strode forward, looking her up and down, and at the end lifted his eyes to her face. They were troubled.

"What did dey do to you?"

Rebecca squared her shoulders. "It wasn't so much, really. The children were chasing a dog. Rodolfo fell and bumped his head. I went to help him, and Elena sent the others to separate us. They stole the boy away and pushed me to the ground." She shrugged. "I lost my temper."

Don Rigo seemed to let it all settle into place. "The boy?" he asked.

Rebecca lifted an open palm. "From what I could tell, it was minor, a bump and a scrape. A minute more and he would have been racing off after the other children."

"But dey—" he made a broad gesture inclusive of all his sisters, "—dey would no' let you tend him?"

"It was probably just a misunderstanding—" she began, but he turned away, glaring at the gathering.

Teresa, to her credit, ventured forward, offering her own explanation in Spanish. Don Rigo listened. After a moment, he slid a glance over his shoulder to Rebecca, his dark eyebrows aloft. She figured that was the part where she'd pushed Elena into the cistern, and she bit her lip. Teresa went on, her tone growing more vituperative with each passing moment. Finally Don Rigo had heard enough.

"¡Silencio!" he demanded, chopping the air with his arm, and he proceeded to upbraid the lot of them, wagging his finger in their faces, roaring out his criticisms and demands, grand gestures punctuating everything. He didn't leave out his aunt, speaking imperiously into her face and pressing the advantage when she winced.

Lupe got to her feet and wandered closer, her ears pricked to catch every word, while Glorieta grew increasingly subdued. Rebecca held her breath, waiting for her turn. At last, to her utter amazement, Don Rigo turned, pulled her into his arms and clamped his mouth over hers in a long, hard kiss that left her breathless and staggering. Everyone else gasped! *"¡Rebecca es mi mujer!"* he proclaimed. *"¡Lo que hacen a ella lo hacen a mí!"*

Shaken, Rebecca was uncertain what had been said, but she saw that the color had drained from Glorieta's face, her dark eyes staring at Rodrigo's chiseled profile, a hand covering her heart. In that instant, Rebecca knew the identity of at least one man whose company the comely widow had enjoyed. She felt a sharp stab of jealousy, and hot tears sprang instantly to her eyes. Rodrigo and Glorieta. Glorieta and Rodrigo. As if sensing what Rebecca was feeling, Glorieta abruptly switched her gaze to Rebecca's face, and their eyes held for a long, stark moment, then suddenly Glorieta recovered her poise. She tossed her long dark hair from her shoulders and with a wry introspective smile, began slowly to turn and address the crowd.

"*¡Ella es la mujer del patrón!*" she cried, flinging a hand in Rebecca's direction. "*¡Cuidado, hipócritas!*" And she turned with a flip of her skirt and strode back to her wash-tub, plunging her hands into the water. She glanced up at Don Rigo, the smile reforming itself on her lips, then put her energy and attention to scrubbing laundry. Rebecca dashed the tears from her eyes and felt Don Rigo's arm slip protectively about her shoulders.

Tersely, he issued what sounded like orders, jabbing at the washtubs and the women standing about. Finally, he dispatched his aunt and one of the sisters with her. Wordlessly, Elena moved away, her steps slow and burdened; Isabel, at her elbow, took the handle of the umbrella into her own hand. Rodrigo turned Rebecca and propelled her toward the lane.

"What happened just now?" she asked, her voice trembling.

"I have taken you fully under my protection," he explained quietly, keeping her moving. "Eet does no good, Rebecca, to deny what dey persis' een believing, so I turn dheir suspicion agains' dem. I have tol' dem dat you are my woman."

"You *want* them to think we're sleeping together?"

"No." He stopped now that they were beyond hearing distance and met her gaze. "I want some peace! Let dem t'ink wha' dey like, but let dem keep dheir complain's an' dheir prejudices een dheir own *casas!* My ears are too full of eet! An' I will no' allow dem to treat you badly, to send my son from one I choose as my frien'! Dey will no' harm you now. Dey will no' dare!"

"Well, they certainly aren't going to be fond of me!" she protested, folding her arms.

"*Sí*, eet ees so," he admitted. "But dey will leave you be till your brodher comes, an' when you are gone..." He frowned and shrugged. "Een a few days, de priest will come, an' I will make a co'fession to put an end to eet." He started along the path again, but Rebecca's hand went out to stop him, clasping his forearm.

"And Glorieta?"

He looked at her, his head cocking to one side. "What o' Glorieta? She ees your frien', I t'ink."

"She is your lover, I think!" Rebecca shot back hotly. "Does *she* understand this deception?"

He dropped his gaze and placed a hand over hers where it rested against his forearm. "Glorieta understan's much," he said softly. "Glorieta understan's a man's loneliness an' his pride. She understan's dat love has no part een some t'ings an' has de wisdom to preten' odherwise, but wha' Glorieta understan's best ees when a t'ing ees done." He looked up then, his gaze level and frank. "Dis she has understan' for some time. Now dey—" he jerked his head toward the square "—dey understan', also, an' eet will be easier for her. Eet ees de on'y protection I can offer eidher o' you, an' she knows eet well. Odherwise, woul' she have said to dem dat you are my woman?"

"She said that?"

"Because she knew eet was for de best."

Rebecca didn't know what to think. Perhaps it was best. What difference did it make anyway? They'd all believed the worst of her since she'd left the Espinozas'. Maybe this way they'd leave her alone, and it was only for a day or two, she reminded herself. Sighing, she turned and moved slowly down the *paseo* toward the house, tugging her hand from Don Rigo's grasp. He fell in beside her, and together they walked to the *casa,* each consumed with private thoughts. There, Rebecca remembered why she'd gone to the square in the first place.

"The laundry!" she cried, but Don Rigo pushed her firmly through the door.

"De odhers will he'p Lupe wash de clothes," he told her.

Lupe! Lupe knew Rebecca wasn't sleeping with Rodrigo and had defended her. It wasn't Lupe's fault the others hadn't believed her. Now she would think the worst, also.

Rebecca turned wide eyes upon him and he read her concern.

"I will explain to Lupe. Do no' be co'cern. She will no' t'ink bad o' you. On dis you have my word." Rebecca nodded, her fears receding into the great swamp of uncertainty that seemed to swirl about her. "Go to your room," he urged, "an' take a little siesta. Later, we will have dinner, an' perha's Fernando will come from de village an' play his guitar for us, eh?"

She hoped not. She didn't want Fernando or Lupe or anyone to see them together after what had happened. She would know what they were thinking, and Don Rigo would know, and they would sit there, pretending that no one thought of what everyone was thinking. She couldn't bear it. She turned quickly and left him, closing herself behind the door of the little room behind the fireplace with the *roja* light.

But she wouldn't care. She told herself as tears gathered in her eyes that she wouldn't care what Tía Elena and the sisters and the others thought of her. Why, if this were Los Angeles, no one would blink twice, even if it were true that she and Rodrigo were lovers. It was this nineteenth-century morality that was at fault, and she was a twentieth-century woman—and wasn't that really the reason she and Rodrigo were not, could not be lovers?

On the other hand, the very idea that Rodrigo and Glorieta had been lovers created a pain that twisted in the hollows of Rebecca's chest. Where was her twentieth-century morality where that relationship was concerned? After all, they were both adults. If they wanted to console each other in bed for their respective losses, it was really nobody's business but their own. But they didn't love each other. Rodrigo had as much as said so. And somehow, that put a whole other spin on it, made it rather unsavory. For Rebecca, love made all the difference. So there it was, the real problem: love. If Rodrigo truly loved her, if it were more than just kindness and a sense of responsibility on his part, then she wouldn't care what the others thought or at the least, she'd endure their disdain with a full heart. As it was, this deception only served to make her more keenly aware that she was the wrong person in the wrong place at the wrong time—again.

And that brought her back to the old same problem, where was her place? Where did she belong? As usual, the only answer that came to mind was Matthew. She belonged with her brother. They were family. Together, they could make a home, with or without Anita. That part was up to Matthew. She was honest enough to admit that she'd always pictured this happy home without Anita, but if Matthew loved the woman, that was reason enough to rethink the concept. Love, as she'd learned, made all the difference.

Rebecca dried her eyes, the thought of Matthew giving her strength. Reunion with him was the purpose for which she would endure. It wouldn't be much longer. Tomorrow or the next day or the day after that, he would come and soon they would leave this place behind. Once they started a life of their own somewhere out in the modern world, she would forget everything that had happened here—and everyone.

She went into the little water closet and pumped water to splash over her face. One day, she told herself, she would have a real sink with hot and cold running water. The notion didn't do much to cheer her, however. Running water just didn't seem as important as it once had. Nothing did. Except starting over with Matthew.

She lay upon the bed and found sleep eventually, despite playing all that had transpired over in her mind again and again. She imagined, too, that Matthew came and hugged her and rubbed her head with his knuckles, telling everyone how happy he was to see her and how grateful he was to find her unharmed. Eloquently, he told everyone how very much she had endured all her life and how, after losing everything, she had bravely started out to find him, her only remaining family. He listened with tears running down his cheeks as Rodrigo recounted all that she had gone through since leaving California: the car breaking down and having to be abandoned; the loneliness of that first long hot day and the terror of the evening; the rough ride across the desert; the conflict her arrival had caused in the village; the awful time with the Espinozas, being dirty and miserable and misunderstood, sleeping on the ground, eating revolting food and still being hungry; all the worry about Rodrigo and the lack of water and the delay in the roundup and the children growing up without an education, and finally, the defiant showdown with the old crow, Tía Elena.

Hearing it all in her mind, Rebecca was moved to fresh tears, but she knew that was self-pity. Self-pity was, in fact, an old friend. Having life reduced at times to a struggle for what seemed her very survival had made Rebecca recognize the self-pity in which she'd wallowed for so much of her life. She'd had enough of that and enough of regret. She focused willfully on Matthew and the life they would help each other to build, and this time she included Anita in the scenario she created, because she'd only just realized that Matt could have fallen in love with her. And it wasn't easy to stop loving someone once you'd started. It wasn't easy at all.

Chapter Nine

She woke long before dinner, feeling refreshed and calm. What was done was done, and there was no point in second guessing. Anyway, none of this was Don Rigo's fault, not even the way she felt about him, and she didn't want to cause him further trouble. Besides, it was only for another day or two, perhaps only for hours, and she wasn't going to spend it sulking in her room.

Rebecca bathed in cold water and washed her hair, wondering aloud how it was that she seemed to shiver as often as perspire in this arid land. She brushed her hair until it dried sleek and shiny. She noticed in the mirror that she was slim and firm and how the unrelenting sun had bronzed her skin and streaked her hair with pale gold. It was a healthy, fit look, and it suited her. She was pleased by that, finding it ironic that she should by accident stumble upon the style for which she had given up searching years before. Someone should tell all those struggling L.A. trendsetters that hard work, clean air and sunshine produced greater benefits than all the tanning beds, bleach and jazzy workouts in the world, not that anyone would believe it. She wouldn't have before coming here. But then, that was the irony of it.

Inspired by the image in her mirror, she dressed with infinite care. It was said that looking good made one feel good, and after the day she'd had, she wasn't above preening if it would help her to keep things in the proper perspective. She didn't have much choice in wardrobe, so she went with blue to match her eyes. She put on the blouse with the gathered neck, wearing it off the shoulders with the sleeves puffed, and a skirt in a darker shade. She brushed her hair again until it gleamed, and tucked one side behind her ear, liking the simplicity of the style. She washed the sandals Fernando had made for her and slipped them onto her feet, then searched out the pink gloss she'd brought from California and spread a light film over her lips. The mirror told her that she looked pretty good, all things considered. Don Rigo's gaze delivered the same message when she joined him in the dining area a few minutes later.

"Ah. I yam a man o' taste, am I no', to take such a beauty as my woman, eh?"

The teasing tone helped, but she could still feel the heat of the blush that spread through her cheeks. His woman! His burden was more like it. She wondered if he didn't regret stopping at her car. Later, as they dined by candlelight on small meat-and-vegetable pies soaked in a dark redbrown gravy, she found a way to ask him.

"Have you stopped to think what this is going to mean to you, Rodrigo?"

He shrugged. "No' so much as eet coul' mean to you, I fear."

"I understand that the double standard is alive and well," she said evenly. "A man might be forgiven that for which a woman is condemned, but I can't see Tía Elena forgiving you for a liaison, however short, with a gringa. I fear this lie may come back to haunt you after I'm gone."

But he would not concede the legitimacy of her concern. "My people may have wrong ideas abou' *Americanas,*" he told her, waving a rolled tortilla in the air, "an' dey may believe dat you are my woman, but dat has not'ing to do wit my aunt's opinion o' me. She has never forgive me for running away to America, no' even when I marry Sofía, o' whom she approve, an' she hates de changes I work for, any change, in fac'. I have live dis long wit her bad opinion o' me, I ezpec' to go on doing so, whedher you are here or no'. Do no' co'cern youse'f wit dis. Enjoy your dinner. Ees good, no?"

Rebecca smiled in spite of all that had happened that day, and why not? He could be so very charming, so comfortably strong, even if sometimes he seemed to work at it. The least she could do was to repay his efforts with a smile or two.

"Is good, yes," she said, and he laughed. She was pleased to have caused that, inordinately so.

They finished their meal and lingered at the table over glasses of bottled *cerveza* kept cool in a cellar beneath the house. A few decent wines were also kept down there, or so Rodrigo told her. He chatted on and on about them while she sipped her beer and his warmed in his hand. When the topic exhausted itself, they moved from the table to the *sala,* and they were sitting there in front of the fireplace, Don Rigo stoking a cozy blaze with real wood instead of dung or natural coal, when a knock sounded upon the door.

"Fernando," Don Rigo surmised with a twinkle in his eye, and he went to answer the summons. Both he and Rebecca were surprised when he opened the door and Luca stepped inside, his big hat in his beefy hands. Rebecca's heart did a flip-flop. If Luca had returned, then Matthew must be close by. She leapt to her feet expectantly, noting how the man's tilted eyes kept sliding over to where she stood. Matthew was here! She poised to fly to him the instant he stepped through the door. The blood pounded in her ears, while Don Rigo and his messenger talked in low, hushed tones. Then, unexpectedly, Luca turned and slipped outside. Don Rigo closed the door. She couldn't understand the reason for that.

"What is it?" she asked almost laughingly. "Where's my brother?"

Rodrigo came toward her, wiping his palms on the slim black pants encasing his thighs. His face was troubled, and his shoulders moved in a shrug beneath the padded yoke of his black shirt. "Luca contacted the *policía* in San Benito," he told her. "Dey claim no gringo live dhere. One did, de man say, but he has gone. He coul' no' say where."

"Gone?" Rebecca repeated. Matthew had gone? But how could this be? She had come so far, endured so much just to find him. How could he be gone? She laughed, disbelieving, but a look of compassion had set Don Rigo's mouth in a grim line draped by the arch of his mustache and made a furrow between his dark eyebrows. Rebecca sat down, numbed by this horrific reality.

"Eet ees o' no co'cern!" he proclaimed softly, going down on one knee beside her. "De man make a mistake. Or perha's he was protecting your brodher." He slipped an arm about her shoulders. "An' even eef your brodher has gone, we will find him. You will see."

Find him? When? she wondered. How? She realized she was trembling, but she felt powerless to stop it and her voice seemed to have disappeared. She shook her head. "T-too late," she managed. "We . . . we'll never . . ."

"Shhh. *Querida*, do no' say dese t'ings. Eet ees no' too late. I will take you dhere—I shoul' have done so a'ready—an' we will find dis Anita's family, an' dey will tell us where your brodher has gone. He coul' even be dhere, Rebecca, or he coul' come back. Dhere ees no way o' knowing dese t'ings, but some way we will find him. I swear eet. So do no' cry, my beauty. Remember, you are *el dueño*'s woman."

He stroked her hair while she trembled, unable to quite grasp the idea that Matthew was gone, out of reach, lost to her. It couldn't be, for where would she go? What would she do? Her teeth chattered. She was cold, so cold that she was frightened. Rodrigo drew her onto his knee and held her hard against his chest, her head tucked beneath his chin. He felt so solid, so warm. She felt fragile and small and terribly in need.

"I'm s-sorry. You've been s-so kind. You've tried s-so hard to help me, and all I do is cause you t-trouble."

He chuckled, the sound vibrating against her temple. "Eet ees no' true! I feel bad because I canno' go righ' away to take you to San Benito. I feel bad because my people have been unkin' to you. I have brough' you trouble!"

"It's not your fault!" she protested.

"It's no' yours," he countered softly, his arms hugging her tight. "Perha's eet ees no one's fault, *querida*. Perha's eet ees fate."

The thought did not comfort, for if it was fate, it was cruel fate, and yet, she was here with Rodrigo.

"What would I do without you?" she wondered softly, lifting her head. His hand cupped her cheek. The corners of his mouth lifted in a gentle smile.

"I have no' done so much," he said, "an' no' all I wish to do, a' dat."

"And then what is it you wish to do?" she asked innocently, and his gaze slid down to her mouth.

Her heart started a slow, pronounced thudding, her body seeming to blossom with sensation. She felt his hand most keenly against her cheek, his thumb sweeping across the corner of her mouth. But there was also the hard band of his arm about her shoulders, the rocklike solidity of his leg beneath her thighs, the muscled wall of his chest pressing against her upper arm, and the soft hair at the nape of his neck that curled about her fingers. How had that happened? She didn't remember putting her hand there, but neither was she aware of gently tilting her head back, bringing her mouth close to his.

Such a mouth! Lips sculpted in dark rose, not too full, not too thin, and she liked that mustache, trim, rakish, meticulously groomed. It seemed to celebrate the romantic in him, and she found that most compelling.

Deep within her, she felt the first brush of his lips on hers, and suddenly her heart was racing.

"*Querida,*" he whispered, and settled his mouth over hers. She was instantly, wildly aware, living totally in and for the moment. Nothing else mattered but the soft yet firm pressure of his lips, the light tickle of his mustache, his hand plunging into her hair, fingers splaying against the back of her head only to leave again, trailing down her neck and across her shoulder, along her arm, over her hip and beneath her thighs, lifting her easily against him. Bending from the waist, he laid her gently upon the floor and sank down beside her. His mouth wandered to the soft flesh beneath her chin and down the smooth column of her throat, breathing fire against her skin so that she dug her fingertips into the hard muscles of his shoulders, waves of heat radiating through her.

He came back to take her mouth again and again, his hands kneading her body, urging conformation with his, leaving her breathless and gasping, wanting so much to be a part of him that in desperation, she thrust her tongue between his teeth, exulting when he sucked it deeply into his mouth, his hand sliding between their bodies to knead the swell of her breast. Her nipple peaked against his palm. His tongue danced with hers. Desire liquified in her groin.

He found the bow in the string that gathered the neck of her blouse and untied it with a single tug, pushing the fabric away to lift naked flesh in his hand. Abruptly, he abandoned her mouth to capture the softness of her breast. She arched against him, feeling the pull at her nipple all the way to the pit of her stomach. She ground her teeth with the need to cry out, and just when she couldn't bear this brutal ecstasy a moment longer, he lifted his head and came back to her mouth, whispering urgently as he took it. She didn't understand a word, not that it mattered. She wanted only to make love with him, to really be his woman.

But she wasn't his woman, and she realized suddenly that sharing her body with him would not make her so. If it would, then Glorieta would be his woman. She jerked like a woman who had suddenly awakened from a dream. Don Rigo broke the kiss, levering his weight onto his elbow. Rebecca pushed herself into a sitting position, avoiding his gaze. She didn't have to say anything. He sucked in a sharp breath and launched himself onto his feet.

"I have done wha' I gave my word I woul' no'!" he said. "Wha's wrong wit me? Why can I no' t'ink?"

He put his hands to his head, obviously stricken with guilt. Rebecca was miserable. He didn't have to be quite so disappointed with himself. She was a woman, after all; he was a man. It was natural, given the circumstances, that they should be drawn to each other. Wasn't it?

"It's all right," she said dully, getting up off the floor to sit on the cushioned shelf. "I'm as much at fault as you are. This news about Matthew, I guess it just shook me up."

He spun to face her, his hands clasped behind him. "We will find him!" he said.

"And what do we do until then?" she demanded, her control suddenly snapping. He straightened, squared his shoulders, released his hands.

"Eet seems I have made us a problem," he said, a hand coming up to smooth the back of his neck. Rebecca closed her eyes, attempting to calm herself.

"It doesn't matter who has done what," she said tightly, opening her eyes. "But now I'm stuck here, and the whole damned village believes I'm sleeping with you! Do you think they're going to be even as kind to me as they were to Glorieta? Hell, no! Because I'm the slutty gringa. I'm the *Americana,* and that makes me trash, especially now that you've confirmed it for them!" She stopped and looked at him, took in the stricken face, the balled hands, the stiff posture. She saw that she had hurt him, and even though it was what she had intended to do, her regret was instantaneous. "Oh, God, I'm sorry. I didn't mean to blame you. I was upset. I didn't think."

He was shaking his head. "No—no. You are righ'. De fault ees mine. I have made matters worse, an' now I mus' find a way to make dem better."

Rebecca was truly miserable. "It's all right. Really. I just won't go into the village. I'll stay here. I don't have to see anybody. That way, I'll stay out of trouble and you can concentrate on getting those cattle to market. Problem solved."

He sighed. "How long can you hide, Rebecca? A week? Two weeks? Four?"

Four weeks! She put her head into her hands, moaning.

"Eet coul' even be longer, Rebecca," he said gently. "Perha's now you see how big our troubles are."

"L-longer?" She gulped and steeled herself. "I'll get through it," she insisted, pushing hair from her face.

"How?" he wanted to know. "By wa'ching television? Calling up your frien's on de telephone? Maybe you are going to have your hair done, eh?"

Rebecca swallowed, and her bottom lip began to tremble. Her bravado dissolved, and suddenly tears were spilling from her eyes. He sat beside her and leaned forward, his elbows on his knees. He didn't touch her, but his closeness was comforting, nonetheless.

"Do no' cry, *querida*," he told her. "I yam t'inking o' a way to fix dis, an' I t'ink—perha's—dat I know wha' we mus' do. De priest comes soon now. I tol' you o' de *padre*, did I no'?" She nodded and dried her eyes, hope rising in her. "*Bueno*. Den you know dat he comes an' den he goes again righ' away."

"Do you think I should go with him? Is that it?"

He shook his head. "No. Dat woul' be no good. De fadher travels nort' a' dis time, t'rough de mountains. He will no' retur' to San Benito for a' leas' two mon's. But I t'ink he will help us eef we tell him our problem. In fac', I t'ink dat he woul' sugges' eet himse'f."

"What?" she prodded hopefully. "What would he suggest?"

Rodrigo licked his lips, meeting her gaze, and said it. "Dat we marry."

It didn't register. It was just too preposterous even to think about. Marry? She and Don Rigo? Rebecca smiled. "What?"

He gripped her wrist, as if that would somehow make everything clear. "Consider, Rebecca," he urged. "Dey t'ink we live een sin togedher. How den can we make eet righ' wit dem, eh?" He paused, allowing her to come to the correct conclusion herself. Her mouth fell open. He squeezed her wrist. "Rebecca, dhere ees not'ing to do but marry."

He meant it! But at first she could only stare, dumbfounded. Then, suddenly, it came to her. Marriage was for people who loved each other. Did he love her, then? Could he possibly love her? She got up, aware only dimly that he still clasped her wrist.

"Is this . . . Are you serious?"

"Lis'en to me," he said, coming to his feet. "Lis'en an' den decide eef eet ees no' bes'. Padre Tomás ees a good man, an' a wise one. He knows me well, an' he will believe me when I tell him we have done not'ing wrong, but still, I believe he will t'ink eet bes' dat we marry, eef on'y because we live here togedher. But later, when you are gone—eef we have tell him eet ees our intention no' to live as man an' wife—he will believe me again when I tell him we have no slep' togedher, an' he will—how do you say?—make de marriage so dat eet do no' happen."

"An annulment," she said. "You're talking about an annulment?"

"*¡Sí!* So dat de marriage never was."

"Then we won't really be married?"

He let go of her wrist and scratched an ear. "Ah. De marriage, eet woul' be true, but later eet woul' no', unless o' course... But we will no'... Eet ees agreed dat we will no' *be* as man an' wife, an' so de marriage can be annul.''

So he didn't love her. Well, she hadn't really thought that he had, and it was better this way, after all. She couldn't stay here with him. She had to get to Matthew. She belonged with Matthew. But she had to find him first, and how long would it be before she could even begin? Perhaps, as it was proposed, this marriage was a good idea for her, but what of Rodrigo?

"I don't understand what you hope to accomplish with this," she told him honestly. "What do you get out of it?"

He smiled wanly. "Peace," he said. "An end to de co'frontations, a provision for you dat will no' cause screams o' anger. I wan' to find my cattle and drive dem to market, Rebecca, witou' worry dat you are een fear or pain. I wan' on'y to protec' you so dat I may no' worry. Eet ees no' so much to ask, ees eet?"

When he put it like that, she couldn't very well refuse. Still, just the idea of marriage to Don Rigo seemed—dangerous. She shook her head, then felt herself being shaken and looked up into eyes the color of creamed coffee.

"You mus' do dis," he said urgently. "Dhere ees no odher way. Believe me!"

She didn't know what to say, what to do, then she thought of the *padre*. If he was truly a wise man, a good man and a priest, would he not be able to think this thing through and come up with the best answer for everyone? It seemed safer, suddenly, to put herself in his hands than to try to make this decision on her own. She took a deep breath, lifting her chin.

"If the father actually agrees with this," she said, "if he says we should do it the way you say, well, then I will."

Don Rigo looked at her and let his hands slide down her arms, a smile growing on his face, then suddenly he released her and stepped back. "All will be well," he promised. "As de *doña,* you will be respected an' honored. No one woul' dare to speak agains' you."

"And afterward?" she queried.

"Eet will no' matter. You will be faraway wit your brodher, an' I will tell dem how dey misjudge you, dat de marriage was for dem on'y."

She doubted that they would believe him, but what difference did it make? As he said, she would be faraway. She nodded just to get it over with, for she was tired suddenly and she wanted the privacy of her room. For the first time, she just wanted to get away from him, to be free of him and what she felt for him.

"I think I'll go to bed," she said softly. "It's been a long, difficult day." She moved away, only to feel his hand at her wrist again.

"Dhere ees jus' one more t'ing, Rebecca," he told her apologetically. "I do no' wish to be made to look less dan a man before de odhers. Eet ees vain o' me, perha's, but my men woul' no' understan'. Eef you do' no' mind, we coul' let dem t'ink wha' dey woul', an' af'er I coul' make de es-planation."

She almost smiled. How ironic. He didn't want anyone to think they were sleeping together, but since they did, he proposed they marry, but once they married, he wanted everyone to think they were sleeping together. If she had not felt so close to tears, she might have laughed. Instead, she sighed and nodded again, then pulled free and walked away. When she looked back, she found him staring at the floor, his fingertips pressed to his temples.

My intended, she thought. God help us both. And it occurred to her that he was probably thinking the same thing. She left him with his thoughts and took hers to her room.

She wore a dress of Isabel's hastily made over. It had been white once, but with time had taken on a soft yellow patina. Snug and form-fitting from the high collarless neckline to the tops of the legs, it sported several fluffy tiers of skirts below, the bottom of which stopped at midshin in front and tapered to a long train that trailed on the floor in back. The long sleeves puffed at the tops and were so lean elsewhere that she could barely bend her elbows, and they as well as the bodice were embroidered in red and green. A long row of some four dozen pea-sized buttons closed the back and was marked top and bottom with bows, a tiny red one at the top, and at the bottom, an enormous, floppy green one that completely covered her bottom and stuck out on either side, its ends hanging down over the top tier of skirt.

On her feet, she wore Ana's red dress shoes with high, flared heels and a rhinestone nestled in leather flowers on each toe. They were thirty years old and looked like new, having been worn only on the most special of occasions, including Ana's own wedding. They were a little large, but this was compensated for by wearing heavy, red lace stockings belonging to Beatriz, both of which had been darned on the heels and along the seams in back. Luckily, the darnings didn't show beneath the long train of the skirt.

María had helped her put her hair up and dress it with a heavy white lace veil contributed by—of all people—Tía Elena. The veil was anchored with a crown of red silk flowers that had belonged to Sofía. Lupe had placed the crown, made by her own hands for her daughter's wedding, upon Rebecca's head, and then the old woman had kissed Rebecca by way of a blessing. Rebecca wept, knowing the old woman thought it joy and gratitude that moved her rather than the deep sadness of disappointment and misery. But then she dried her eyes and held her head high as befitted the bride of *el hidalgo,* even a sham bride in borrowed clothing.

The church was decked out with colorful paper flowers and flags. A hundred candles of all sizes were lighted upon the altar, save only the tall, fat, red one in the middle, which she and Rodrigo would light together during the ceremony. Upon her left wrist, Rebecca wore a corsage of red fabric roses set amongst green netting. Sewn to it with a single stitch was a worn gold band inlaid with a narrow strip of black onyx. It had belonged to Rodrigo's father. In his pocket, Rodrigo carried its mate, a small ring carved of a single black onyx, banded with a thread of gold. It had rested upon his mother's finger for fifty-seven years of marriage. It would reside upon Rebecca's for a mere month. She had begged him not to use it. He had insisted, saying that it would be expected of him since his parents were both deceased. She feared she would weep when he placed that ring upon her finger, but for now, the tears were held at bay.

Her arm linked with that of Juan, Teresa's husband, she paused at the back of the church, looking at those kneeling in rows upon the bare floor to witness her wedding. Everyone wore his or her best, and some articles of clothing were genuine antiques, handed down from generation to generation. The women wore their hair twisted up in tight braids or tied with ribbons and hanging down their backs. The men were all combed and shaved, many of them wearing the narrow pigtail wrapped in black ribbon at the nape, which Don Rigo himself had made popular and now wore, but none of them could match him for splendor.

His red lawn shirt was embroidered so heavily that it was difficult to tell fabric from stitching except by its thickness. Over this he wore a dark green velvet jacket cut short and lean with wide black satin lapels. At his throat, over the narrow, stand-up collar of the shirt, was a crisp black narrow tie fashioned into a small bow with dangling ends, a pronounced contrast to the red sash wrapped many times about his slender waist and tucked with the tail hanging down the side. His pants were black and tight fitting, flaring only enough at the ankle to cover the tops of short black boots, their soft, unembellished leather so highly polished, it fairly gleamed.

At his side, dressed in robes of creamy white overlaid with gold satin, stood Rodolfo and two other boys, still and dignified under the eye of *el dueño*. Clara stood across the aisle, dressed in buttery yellow embroidered with brown and gold, her hair separated into many looped braids tucked with waxy green leaves and a painted comb fastened to a short veil of brown netting. Rebecca had thought to suggest Glorieta as an attendant, but the woman's total lack of enthusiasm for the wedding had prevented Rebecca from doing so. Rodrigo had said that choosing Clara would be a signal to all the village that any rifts between Rebecca and the others had been mended. Rebecca had not argued, but the pout on Clara's face suggested that *she* had. And who could blame her? Certainly not the blushing bride—the unwanted, unloved, unhappy blushing bride.

Rebecca sighed, but then Padre Tomás—kind little Padre Tomás—looking like another boy in his flowing robes and vestments, made a sign to the crowd, and every head turned in her direction. She stiffened, chin high, and stared straight at the little priest, focusing upon his cherubic face with those protruding, oversized eyes. He had been a great encouragement, asssuring her in his broken English that all would be well for, as he stated it, "De 'oly God bless our attemp' a' good." This charade was more than a convenience as far as the sainted father was concerned; it was an attempt at goodness. The thought gave her comfort, but only a little.

Juan nudged her gently, urging her down the aisle, and it was then that she looked to Don Rigo. If this was an attempt at goodness, then it was Don Rigo's attempt and Don Rigo's alone. Like the padre, he seemed convinced that they were doing the right thing, and though she was not so certain, the genuineness of his smile gave her courage as she took that first, difficult step.

Right on cue, the boys began to sing a cappèlla in high, clean, surprisingly clear tones, the Latin words precisely enunciated as Padre Tomás nodded in time. Don Rigo beamed, his eyes never leaving her as she drew closer upon the arm of his eldest brother-in-law. Step by unalterable step, Rebecca advanced, pausing at the foot of the aisle as the boys finished the song. When the last note had died away, Don Rigo turned to face the priest, while Rodolfo did likewise, stepping close to his father with adoration in his young eyes. The other two boys put their hands in their sleeves and walked around the altar to flank the priest, one on either side.

Padre Tomás spoke, and in reply, Juan stepped forward, placed Rebecca's hand upon Don Rigo's arm and walked away. All else happened as if in a dream. Rebecca listened without hearing as Padre Tomás conducted the mass in Latin and Spanish. She knelt upon the dark blue satin pillow provided, rose again, spoke memorized words, lit the candle, received a ring and a promise, gave the same, and was blessed and pronounced a wife, all without meaning or emotion. Then Don Rigo kissed her gently, his fingers intertwined with hers, and it struck her suddenly that she was a legally married woman.

Her husband ushered her quickly through the silent church, then posed with her upon the steps as the wedding guests poured out to surround them. Spanish words of congratulations and blessing filled the air. Laughter bubbled up from dozens of throats, yet Rebecca could only tremble and wear a stiff smile, dependent upon Don Rigo's constant presence and protection. All through the afternoon and into the evening as the wedding fiesta proceeded, she kept close to his side, smiling as he played the grateful bridegroom. And, indeed, there was much for which to be thankful.

The village had been generous, laying out the best of their dwindling stores. A piglet and a kid had been killed and roasted on spits in the center of the square. Tables had been built of doors liberated from their hinges and covered with colorful cloths. Chairs were provided by every house, and several of the men brought instruments and provided music for dancing. Many of the vaqueros had been found and called in from the roundup, and despite her nervousness, Rebecca noticed Glorieta on the arm of one very tall young man. Identified by Don Rigo as Alonzo Rezítas, he seemed an independent sort, wearing a traditional sombrero rather than Western cowboy hats preferred by the others. Rebecca decided that she liked him on sight, a sentiment Glorieta seemed to share. For Rebecca it was an instance of genuine gladness in an otherwise torturous day.

But if it was a difficult day for Rebecca, it was a fiesta for everyone else. Barrels of home-brewed beer were tapped, and men and women alike indulged. The children played games, danced with the adults, stole sweets and soiled their clothing with abandon, all but Rodolfo. Having performed the part of attendant at his father's wedding seemed to have had a profound effect on him. He stayed close by the newlyweds, hastening to hold the chair for his new stepmother and refill his father's emptied cup. In short, he showed every little courtesy, as if eager to display his approval, and Rebecca couldn't help being touched. Even Tía Elena smiled and played at being gracious from her place beneath her umbrella. Though still quietly snubbing Rebecca at every opportunity, she was wise enough to know that open hostility toward the new bride would win her nothing but trouble from the groom. Dressed for a change in deep blue, she fanned herself and sipped her beer, even joined politely in a toast to the don and the new *doña*.

Rodrigo remarked, his hand covering Rebecca's, how this day of festival had been good for the people. He addressed her as *señora* and played the part of attentive husband, passing her tidbits from his own plate, drinking casually from her cup when his own was momentarily empty, draping his arm about her shoulders from time to time. When dusk came, he led her into the center of the square and guided her through a simple dance to the applause of onlookers, then delivered her safely into the care of Padre Tomás while he arranged for their departure. A horse and cart were brought, each decorated with paper flowers and tassels, and two chairs were loaded into it. Streamers were tied to the wheels and the reins, and bells were fixed to the corners.

When all was ready, Don Rigo came to collect his bride. Taking her hand and placing it upon his arm, he led her to the cart and assisted her as she stepped inside and sat upon a chair decorated with red tassels, taking his place next to her in a chair decorated with green. Padre Tomás came and made a final blessing over them, and to Rebecca's surprise, Don Rigo thanked him with an invitation to dinner.

"Will you join us, *Padre,* for de evening meal. I t'ink Rebecca woul' find your presence a comfor'."

"Oh, please do," she said, delighted that Rodrigo would think of this, and the little priest accepted gladly.

"Nine o'clock," the don advised him, and then they were off, Juan standing to drive the horse down the lane.

Children set off firecrackers in the square as the cart pulled away, and the adults called out blessings, some of them running alongside. Then as the noisy revelry of the square receded, their escorts grew quiet with dignity. Juan slowed the horse, and Fernando, walking close to hand, began to strum his guitar and sing in a deep, wavering voice something about two seas and two lovers who danced on a moonbeam.

The song had not ended by the time they reached the gate and stepped down from the cart, and the little procession followed them inside the fence, standing out in the yard while the newly married couple listened from the deep shadows beside the front door of the house. Don Rigo stood at Rebecca's back, his arms about her waist, his chin pressing against the top of her ear, and Rebecca forgot about the future and her brother awhile and remarked silently to herself that a woman really couldn't ask for much more than this. It was only as their escort left them, filing serenely through the gate, and they turned to enter the *casa* that she remembered none of this was really hers, not the house, not the feelings and good wishes and congratulations, not even the clothes on her back or the shoes on her feet, and certainly not the man who had made himself her husband as a matter of convenience.

Chapter Ten

"The padre has somet'ing for you," Don Rigo announced proudly, and Rebecca switched her gaze across the table to the little priest.

He cleared his throat and folded his hands almost in an attitude of prayer, his plate between his elbows. He had eaten a ridiculous amount of food for one so small, but his obvious enjoyment had added to Rebecca's own, and she laughed now, seeing him smile.

"Abou' your brodder," he said, his accent even thicker than Don Rigo's, "I have kep' dese words for—I do no' say de *inglés—ah, regalo, obsequio. ¿Comprende?*"

Rebecca could only shake her head. "I'm sorry."

He shrugged and tried again. "Fro' *amigo* to *amiga* for de marriage."

Friend to friend for the marriage. She got it. "A wedding gift," she said, and brightened as the full context struck her. "You've saved word of my brother for a wedding gift?"

"*¡Sí!* Ees good! I kep' word o' your brodher for wedding gif', an' de word ees dis—I mus' know dis man. I do for him wha' I do for you."

"You know Matthew!"

"*Posiblemente,*" he answered. "Een San Benito. Tall man."

Rebecca nodded eagerly. "A tall man, yes, with yellow hair."

"*Sí. Amarillo* hair an' your eyes."

"Blue eyes, yes!"

"But de skin ees, ah, *moteado.*" He pecked at the bridge of his nose with his forefinger.

"Freckled! Oh, yes! Matthew has freckles! You know him! Rodrigo, did you hear? Did you know?"

The don chuckled, obviously pleased with himself. "*Sí.* I hear, but I do no' t'ink you are lis'ening so good. Say eet again, Padre, how you know Rebecca's Matthew."

"I do for him wha' I do for you," the priest repeated eagerly, but Rebecca only blinked.

"You did for him what? The same you do for me?" She shook her head.

"De wedding!" he proclaimed. "I do for him and de *señorita* de wedding a' de *iglesia* San Benito."

Rebecca bolted up straight in her chair, her hands flat against the tabletop as the meaning sank in. "You performed a wedding for Matthew and Anita?"

"*¡Sí!* Anita!"

For the first time that day, Rebecca was truly thrilled. This same priest had married her brother and Anita! But even as she digested this joyous news, she saw that the priest was disturbed. She looked at Don Rigo for help in understanding this, but received only a piteous look that knotted her stomach.

"What? What about Matthew and Anita?"

Padre Tomás shrugged. "De *señorita,* Anita, *muy preñada. Muy preñada.*"

Muy. Very. Very *preñada.* It didn't click, until the priest began to move his hands from breast to hips in a wide arc and murmur, *"Bebé, niño."*

A baby! Anita had been pregnant! Rebecca reached across the table and seized the priest's wrist, signaling him that she understood.

"When?" she pleaded. "When was this? When did you marry them?"

"Ah. *Tres.*" He held up three fingers.

"Three." Rebecca nodded.

"Meses."

"Months," she translated. "Three months. You married them three months ago in San Benito, and Anita was pregnant, very pregnant, at the time."

She sat back in her chair, trying to think what all this meant. Matthew had married a very pregnant Anita three months ago in San Benito. The baby could be born by now. She could be an aunt! But better than that, this news meant that Matthew was bound to be in San Benito. He would not have taken a newborn child and a wife recovering from the birth from their home to a strange place. And where would he go? Not back to the States, surely, because as far as he knew, he was still a wanted man there. It just made sense to stay put. Rebecca felt certain that this news meant Matthew was still in San Benito with his little family, but when she put it to Don Rigo, he cautioned her not to jump to conclusions.

"But it would be too soon after the birth for them to travel," she insisted. "And where would they go? Anita's family is there, in San Benito. It was a mistake. I just know it! Matthew is there, and soon you'll take me to him!"

Don Rigo merely nodded, obviously not wishing to argue the point. "Perha's it is so," he said. "We will see, eh?"

But Rebecca was not content to leave it. She questioned the priest as best she could about his itinerary and made him promise, if he should get to Matthew first, to tell her brother where she was and that he should come for her. Padre

Tomás agreed at once, but she made Rodrigo put it to him in Spanish in case the priest had not understood her accurately. Don Rigo seemed to think it was an imposition, his tone was strained and words terse as he spoke, but he did as she asked, and she was happily grateful.

Padre Tomás left soon afterward, returning to his assigned quarters in Tía Elena's house. The arrangements that had been made on his behalf had been a matter of discussion and laughter at the table earlier. It seemed that Isabel had been drafted to sleep in the very same bed with her aunt so that there could be no question that the old *hidalga* had not tempted the padre to relinquish his vow of chastity. The father was gravely insulted but also amused to think that Elena could consider herself an object of lust. He left Rodrigo and Rebecca chuckling at the idea again, but as the door closed on his back, all the easiness evaporated between them.

A single candle remained burning upon the dining table, casting a soft light over the remains of their meal. Rebecca began to stack the dishes, her hands trembling slightly as she thought of allowing the evening to come to its natural end. But this was not the usual situation in which newlyweds found themselves, for she and Rodrigo would spend this, their wedding night—and every other—apart.

"Leave it," he said, coming to remove her hands from the work. "Sit wit me for a momen', eh?" He pulled out a chair for her.

She sank into it, feeling quite exhausted but unable to offend him after all that he'd done.

Rodrigo settled onto the edge of the table and folded his hands together against his thigh. After a bit, he broke the heavy silence. "Eet has been a good day."

Rebecca crossed her arms over her breasts, trying to banish the awkwardness that had come over her, and made no reply. He went on.

"I woul' no' have le' de people make so much fiesta, but dey have need o' eet. Dis ees a good t'ing we have done for dem, I t'ink, an' a good t'ing for ourse'ves."

"A good thing?" she retorted skeptically. "I wonder if a deception can be a good thing for anyone." She turned her face away from him, ashamed to have sunk at once into sarcasm. "I'm sorry. I don't know what's wrong with me."

"You are tired," he said softly. "A lie ees mos' hard when you need res'."

"I just want to change," she mumbled, and came to her feet, starting toward the back of the house and the little room behind the fireplace, but then she felt his hand upon her elbow, holding her back.

"Your t'ings are no' een de ol' room, Rebecca," he told her flatly. "I ha' Lupe move dem."

"Move them?" she echoed, resisting only enough to show her displeasure as he hauled her around to face him.

He glowered sternly, dark eyes hooded by dark eyebrows drawn low and together, but his voice went soft, soothing. "A wife's t'ings belong wit her husband's, do dey no'?"

"I am no wife!" she answered bitterly, tearing Elena's mantle and Sofía's circlet of flowers from her head. Rodrigo went rigid, his grip on her elbow tightening dangerously.

"You are a wife een all ways but one till you leave dis place!" he ordered flatly, but the next instant he was folding her into his arms and whispering comfort. "Eet mus' be so, *querida*. We have said dis. You are on'y tired, *querida*, an' dis make you forget wha' mus' be."

He was right, of course, hopelessly so, but she could only huddle against his chest and bite her lip to keep the anger—and the tears—at bay.

He hurried on, comforting her as he would a child. "We share de room but no' de bed. I will sleep een de li'l bed in de room o' de *niño*, dat I be near eef so'one come for me. Ees dis no' wise?"

Rebecca sniffled and nodded. "Yes. Yes, of course. I—I don't know what's wrong with me. I should be happy just knowing for certain that Matthew is in San Benito."

A troubled look passed over Don Rigo's face, but the next instant, he was smiling so indulgently that she thought she had imagined it.

"When you have rest you will feel *muy bien*." He turned her toward the front hall and urged her along, his arm about her shoulders.

"You're right," she sighed. "I think I could sleep for days."

He chuckled. "Eef you wish. Keeping my wife abed for so lon' woul' do much for my *reputación* as a lover—a' leas' till I tell dem de trut'!"

They laughed together, and though she still smarted deep inside, Rebecca was suddenly grateful to him for making it so easy to laugh at this predicament. He had done much to make her grateful, and it was more than simply foolish of her to feel hurt because he did not really want her for a wife. Don Rigo Avilés was a gentleman of the old school, one who would put himself out even so far as to marry a woman he did not want for her protection and ease.

As he escorted her across the dining area and up into the hall, she reminded herself that he, too, gained much from this arrangement, but she could not quell the feelings of gratitude, pride and admiration, or those of pain. And so, when she saw again the little room that was, in effect, the nursery, and the little bed upon which Rodrigo had pledged to sleep, she knew she couldn't allow it to be.

"Let me sleep here," she begged. "I will be more comfortable here than in your room. Besides, the bed is too short for you. Neither of us will be comfortable if you insist on sleeping in it."

"Eef you wish," he answered. Then with a dash of honesty that endeared him to her all the more, he declared, "I hope you woul' say dis, for I like my bed too much, I t'ink!"

They laughed together again, all the previous uneasiness gone now, and together they went into "their" room. Rodrigo showed her where her things were stored, those few items she had brought with her, as well as those she had been given upon her arrival and the new ones Lupe had quickly sewn. One of these was a nightdress of soft white cotton that was stitched in rows of tiny pleats over the bodice and fell full and loose to her knees. It was a modest garment with short, gathered sleeves, light enough to be comfortable but heavy enough for protection from cool nights and probing eyes. Rebecca took it into the little room that was now hers, undressed and slipped it on, then carefully folded her borrowed wedding clothes and, calling a good-night to Don Rigo through the door, went to bed.

As she lay upon the little bed, willing herself to sleep, she thought over and over again that all would be well now, until the phrase became a chant that sounded continually not only in her conscious mind but the subconscious, as well, so that it filled even her slumber and colored her mood when she awoke.

She was convinced that all would be well, and for a couple of weeks it actually was. She would rise early most mornings to find Rodrigo already gone, checking on the vaqueros and the progress of the roundup. He would come in and take a late breakfast with her, then ride out once more and not return until evening. Then he would bathe and change and join her for supper, and they would tell each other of the day's events.

Rebecca kept busy around the house, learning how things were done. She hadn't realized there was so much to maintaining a household, but Lupe was a patient teacher, and as her Spanish progressed, Rebecca was able to ask many questions. Aside from the predictable cleaning chores, she learned how to recycle the stubs of the many candles they burned and how to clean the candle niches of the smoke stains without damaging the paint. She learned, too, from a slightly less accommodating Ochéa, how to cook many of

Rodrigo's favorite dishes and how to store the foodstuffs properly without the aid of refrigeration. When it came to milking the goats and gathering the eggs from the chickens, she balked at first, but Lupe laughed and teased her until Rebecca gave in and let the old woman guide her hands under slick udders and feathered bottoms. It was not so difficult, after all, and she began to think of these small things as adventures to be remembered in a later time.

If these homey little things pleased her, however, there were others that bothered her. Twice during those early weeks, the villagers brought problems which they seemed to feel were hers to solve. The first came one afternoon in the form of two women, a boy and a dead chicken. It seemed that the son of one of the women had accidentally killed the chicken of the other, and they were squabbling over what should be done about it. The boy's mother contended that no real harm was done as the other woman would have eventually killed the chicken to cook it, anyway. The owner of the chicken wanted compensation for the eggs the hen would have laid until it was due to be eaten. Rebecca felt like a fraud sitting in judgment on this matter, but her attempts to put them off until Don Rigo could handle the dispute were futile. Was she not the woman of *el dueño?*

Finally, very ill at ease, Rebecca conferred with Lupe in her slow, painstaking Spanish and came to a solution. The boy's mother would replace the dead chicken with one of her own laying hens. The dead hen would then become hers, and she could cook it and serve it to her family. Once it was communicated, this solution seemed agreeable to both parties, and they all went away, if not completely happy, then at least satisfied.

When Rebecca told Don Rigo about the affair, he praised her judgment, and she was so pleased about this that she said nothing concerning her discomfort. Had she done so, he might well have spoken to the people about taking their problems to the new *doña,* using her poor Spanish as an excuse for her inability to deal with them. But she said nothing, only basked in his praise; so when the second incident came, she knew she was stuck, and this time the problem was not simply a dead chicken.

Only a few weeks earlier, a certain gentleman had bartered with another for a specific piece of furniture, a spacious chest, as a gift to his wife. The item bartered was a rug of uncommon workmanship, handwoven by the first gentleman's late mother. The chest had turned out to be too large for the couple's bedroom, so they had left it in the big room where the family gathered to eat and entertain one another and where the children slept. The wife had set the chest against a wall, made cushions for its top, and allowed her children to use it as a sofa. But it hadn't been long before one of its legs had broken, and now it just sat there askew, taking up space the family didn't have to spare, its heavy lid too difficult to raise to allow it to be used even for storage. To make matters worse, the man now deeply regretted parting with his mother's rug for this useless, space-eating monstrosity. The original owner of the chest had no use for it, either, in its present condition, and was fond of the rug. He was not amenable, therefore, to reversing the trade.

The conflict at first seemed without solution, and after much arguing and confusion, Rebecca had to send everyone home so she could think. Lupe proved of little help, and Rebecca resigned herself to failure, but then she began to think of how the chest might be repaired, and as she pondered, she began to wonder if it might not actually be improved. After a while, she struck upon an idea that seemed workable, and after an extensive search for something to draw on, she began to sketch her idea. That evening, she showed it to Rodrigo. He made a couple of suggestions to simplify things and left it at that.

Late the next afternoon, Rebecca nervously presented her idea to the two men and their wives. Discussion ensued, and before she knew it, the parties had reached a solution amongst themselves. The two men would repair the chest together, making the changes she suggested. This done, the chest would be much sturdier. That being the case, the original owner was glad to take it back and return the rug, which was something of a family heirloom, after all.

Now the two wives put their heads together and came up with a truly laudable idea. The notion of using the chest for a sofa appealed to its original and once-again mistress, and as it would be sturdier once repaired, she saw no reason not to do this. Moreover, she liked the cushions the other had made for this purpose, so she proposed trading a smaller chest in her possession for those cushions. Everyone was thrilled. The man got his rug back *and* the chest he had wanted for his wife. The other man received an improved piece of furniture, cushions and all, that would now serve two functions. And though Rebecca had done little more than suggest a way to repair the chest and make it sturdier, she garnered the credit!

With two successes under her belt, Rebecca was beginning to feel that she could handle anything the villagers might throw at her. Don Rigo flattered her by seeming unsurprised at the way these two incidents had turned out, and Rebecca sensed a new respect from the other women when she and Lupe went into town for wash day. She was Doña Rebecca, the wife of *el dueño,* and while the don was away or busy, she was expected to help out. She had proved herself capable of fulfilling her role, and no one would suspect that she was merely playing a part, especially with Padre Tomás gone on about his business elsewhere.

Both Don Rigo and Rebecca agreed that for the sake of peace, it would be wise to maintain the illusion of the *doña* until she was gone and the marriage annulled. They did this primarily by staying busy at separate duties during the days and keeping to themselves in the evenings so that they couldn't be observed together more than absolutely necessary. In public, they were constrained to display affection, but locked away behind closed doors, they could let Lupe and everyone else think they were enjoying this honeymoon period in the accepted manner without engaging in what, for Rebecca at least, had become dangerous physical contact. Meanwhile, they filled the time with talk and laughter, hitting upon the things that had happened during the day or in their respective pasts.

Rebecca loved to hear the stories about the rancho and those who had settled it. The stories were romantic and inspiring, and they helped her to understand more fully why Don Rigo had chosen to live here after all his travels, but she also liked, to her surprise, to tell him about her life before she had come to the Baja Peninsula. She realized that she had never talked so much of those things, and eventually it came to seem to her that no one in her family had really ever talked to anyone else and that perhaps that was why she had felt so lonely so much of her life.

All in all, married life seemed to be exactly what Don Rigo had said it would be, easy and calm and comfortable. The days had fallen into a pattern of domesticity that was both engrossing and enjoyable. Tía Elena still did not like Rebecca, but she veiled her disapproval with respect for Rebecca's position, and that was enough to keep the peace. Under the circumstances, Rebecca did not feel that she could ask for more, and Don Rigo did not seem of a mind to. He seemed so unmoved by their new marital status, in fact, that he was rather nonchalant about their contact in private. That made it easier for Rebecca to fool herself about controlling her romantic desires and to relax around him, so that it was inevitable that she should find herself lying across the foot of his bed one evening, deciding aloud that when she and Matthew were finally reunited, they would talk, really talk, from then on.

To her dismay, Rodrigo's face tightened, his mouth compressing grimly beneath the slender line of his mustache. It had happened before, once or twice, when she had spoken of Matthew, and she felt she knew why. "You don't believe he's in San Benito, do you?" she asked flat out.

His jaw clenched, but after only a slight pause, he relaxed it and gave her an indulgent smile, his dark head resting against the polished wood of the headboard.

"Wha' I t'ink do no' matter, *señora*. I wish on'y dat you no' hope too much an' your heart no' break because o' eet."

It pleased her to know that he cared in this way. In fact, it pleased her too much, but she pushed away the undue feelings and seized upon the friendship that had grown between them.

"All will be well, Rodrigo," she assured him, repeating the phrase that had sustained her throughout her wedding night and since. "If Matthew is not in San Benito, well, someone there must know where I can find him."

"We," he said, "where *we* can fin' him."

One side of her heart seemed to swell in gratitude, but the other shriveled a bit with the knowledge that he sought to be rid of her. This duality was not new to her. It had been so since the night he had proposed marriage as a solution to their problems, but as usual these days, she chose to focus on the positive, though that was not possible so long as she stayed there upon his bed. She got up, trying not to look at him and not to be too conspicuous about it at the same time. He looked so delicious sitting there with his dark hair curling about his ears and neck. His soft shirt was open to the waist, exposing the smoothly muscled expanse of his chest. His long fingers lay upon his snugly jeaned thighs, almost as if caressing them. She could not help thinking what it would feel like to place her own hands there and have his reach out for her. She shivered at the thought of it, and to her horror, Rodrigo shot up and came to her.

"You are cold?" He moved as if to put his arms around her, but she slipped away, drawing herself up tightly to stop the trembling.

"I'm just tired," she lied, "ready for bed."

"So early?" he asked, following her to the nursery door. There he caught her and made her face him with a hand gripping her upper arm. She jerked involuntarily as he laid that same hand across her forehead. "You are cool," he said, "but perha's you are sick, eh?"

"No, no. I'm fine."

"I frigh'en you wit my doubt abou' your brodher."

"Not at all!" She made herself laugh. "Why would I be frightened? If it turns out that Matthew is not in San Benito, I know I'll be safe with you until we find him."

That apparently satisfied him, for he stepped back suddenly, releasing her. "*Sí.* Safe wit me."

There was something about the tone of his voice that troubled her, and he seemed uncertain what to do with his hands just then, but she dared not dwell on it. It was a fine line upon which she walked in moments like this, and when he touched her, that line automatically blurred.

"I woul' no' harm you, Rebecca," he reiterated softly, and his hands skimmed over her hair.

He could be made to want me, she thought, then she tamped down the thrill that thought produced by reminding herself that desire and love were very often different things. They certainly were in this case. And yet, it would be so easy to let fiction become fact. She could truly become the *doña* by just letting herself do the things she wanted to do with him. A little encouragement would very probably make Rodrigo forget that there were reasons why they could not share a bed—for a while. Then he would remember and though he was too much a gentleman to say so, his regret would doubtlessly be very deep. They would both be unhappy, he because he had taken a wife he didn't love, she because he didn't love her. If she could just overcome the differences in their backgrounds, then perhaps she could make him love her, but that was a pipe dream and she knew it. Besides, there was Matthew to consider. Matthew was her family, and soon she would be with him again.

She smiled up at Rodrigo and carefully removed his hands from her shoulders, where they had settled. "I know you would never ever do anything to harm me," she told him lightly, "except maybe keep me from getting to sleep!"

He grinned self-consciously. "Ah. Forgive me. Eet ees jus' dat eet ees so early for bed dat I fear you were ill."

"Just tired," she assured him, and moved away. "Sleep well."

"*Sí*," he returned, "eef you are sure you are well."

She nodded and smiled. "Good night."

"*Buenas noches.*"

Quickly, she made her escape, letting herself into the little room that was her sanctuary in times such as this. She closed the door behind her, sighed with relief and changed her clothing before snuggling down under the warm covers of the bed. But sleep did not come automatically, and she could hear Don Rigo moving around next door, the sounds muffled by the thick walls. He seemed as restless as she felt, and yet she was tired, too, as he must be after a long day crawling over the mountain in search of cattle. She wanted to go to him, help him relax, make him happy and content as she had those of the village who had brought their problems to her.

But that could not be, so she settled down to sleep with Matthew on her mind, for Matthew was her refuge from the desire she felt but could not indulge. Matthew was everything, her hope, her future, her reality, and when the moment became too much, she went to Matthew in her mind, and all was well.

Rodrigo paced the floor in an agony of uncertainty. He could not say when his intentions had changed or even if they had, for it occurred to him now that he had wanted from the beginning to bind her to him. From the moment he had looked into her blue eyes and seen the fear there, he had wanted to protect her, to hold her close against his chest and whisper comforting words, but to comfort her was not enough. To hold her was not enough. To love her was not enough. He wanted those feelings returned. He wanted her to welcome his touch, not to recoil when his hand skimmed her cheek or settled upon her shoulder. He wanted her in his bed, and though they were married, he had found no way to accomplish that.

Indeed, it seemed that they were farther apart in that way than ever, because it was only when he pretended indifference that she seemed to relax with him. The moment he sought to deepen the intimacy they shared, to take it beyond the bounds of simple friendship, she backed away and fled into her room. He would like to have torn down the wall that separated them with his bare hands, but he knew that the wall between them was made of stronger stuff than adobe. It was made of electric lights and fast cars and movie theaters, all the stuff of the twentieth century, and perhaps even more, things he could not hope to define, let alone dispel. Yet he had to try. Not to try was certain failure, and Rodrigo Felipe Marcos Junípeo Avilés was not a man accustomed to failure. He was the don, and he had found his *doña*, if only he could make her see that she belonged with him. If only he could show her the passion he felt. He had to get her into his bed. He paced the floor, racking his brain for a way to make it happen, when suddenly, it came to him with a knock at the door.

He didn't connect the two at first, his problem and the persistent knocking that echoed down the hall from the *sala*. He was, in fact, rather perturbed to have his thoughts disturbed like this and at such an hour. But it was not late, he reminded himself. Another evening he and Rebecca might have talked on for hours yet, instead of retiring to their separate rooms. It was time, he supposed, to receive a caller. In fact, they were probably fortunate that no one had called on them this past week. The people had been generous in allowing them such time together. He wondered briefly if he ought to warn Rebecca, but decided that he would let her be. It would add a touch of authenticity to his pleas for one more night of peace if he could tell their caller truthfully that his wife was already abed.

He went out of the room and down the hallway, crossed the dining area and skirted the *sala* to reach the door. He lifted the latch and pulled it open just as a final knock sounded, to find the wrinkled knob of his aunt's fist raised at eye-level. He was surprised to find Elena on his doorstep, but surprised more to find her in the company of his sisters Teresa and María and his own two sons. He laughed softly, for it was somehow comical, the five of them standing there surrounded by several bundles and a basket, his sons in clean knee britches and long socks and matching shirts with round collars. Then suddenly the look upon Tía Elena's face registered, and the amusement died away.

His aunt raised her chin, her eyes gleaming with the pleasure of censure, and he knew that he had somehow given reason for offense, for she was very sure of herself, smug in her right to complain. But what had he done now? What was his crime this time? Before he could think, Rodolfo stepped forward, a cloth sack clutched in his little hands.

"Father," he said in Spanish, "will our mother welcome us, do you think?"

And then he knew what he had forgotten, and it seemed of a sudden that his prayers had been answered before he had said them. Of course! He should have known this would happen. Why hadn't he thought of this? Why hadn't he realized that as soon as he'd taken a wife and a decent honeymoon period had passed, his children would come home? Indeed, as they should have, as they must, as God and Tía Elena had ordained, his sons had come home.

Chapter Eleven

"It's really very simple," Rebecca whispered. "I'll just slip out every night after they're asleep and back in before they wake up."

"¡*Imposible!* You *loca* eef you t'ink dat work!"

"Don't shout!"

"I yam no' shouting! I whisper very loud, but I no' shout! An' I tell you Rodolfo will know. He ees a smart boy! De first time he open de door een de nigh' an' see me een bed alone, he will know! Wha' will he t'ink abou' dis? How long before he say to Lupé, 'Why my new modher no' sleep wit my fadher?' Rebecca, you got to stay here!" he concluded.

"And sleep where?" she wanted to know. "In the bed with you?"

"¡*Sí!*" He threw up his hands. "Ees dat no' where a wife shoul' sleep, next to her husban'?"

"But I'm *not* your wife!"

"You marry wit me!" he pointed out and winced, letting his voice grow too loud. She shushed him, craning her neck to look past him to the closed door of the nursery. How, she wondered, had this happened? Why hadn't they even realized it could? And how on earth were they going to get out of it?

"This is all your fault," she told him, satisfied the children were still sleeping next door. "Why didn't you just tell your sisters they had to keep the kids awhile longer?"

"Did I no' try? I beg dem for more time! But Tía Elena, she say de *luna de miel* ees over an' eet ees time for me to again be a fadher to my sons."

"Oh, I know exactly what Tía Elena thinks," Rebecca huffed. "And it doesn't have anything to do with the honeymoon being over! She thinks she'll make life difficult for me, that's what she thinks. And she's right, damn it!"

She turned away and walked across the room, leaning her shoulder against the wall next to one of the candle niches. The flame flickered. What a mess! How was she supposed to share a bed with Rodrigo and not... She couldn't even think about it without trembling. There had to be another option.

"Rebecca, I yam sorry," Rodrigo said, coming to stand before her. "I know I shou' have t'ought o' dis before we marry, but eet never came een my head dat my sons woul' come home."

"I know." She sighed. "Mine, either. We were thinking temporary, I guess, while everyone else was thinking permanent. But we have to do something, Rodrigo. Maybe if we take your aunt into our confidence like we did Padre Tomás."

"Rebecca! How do you say dis? Ees eet no' because o' Tía Elena dat we have done dis? She believe we were sleeping togedher *before* de padre marry us! She ees no' going to believe we sleep apar' now!"

He was right, of course, unfortunately. Rebecca put a hand to her forehead, trying to think, but every option seemed to have already presented itself. Her original idea had been to put the boys in one of the larger bedrooms, but she'd never even put that one to Rodrigo. Enrique was simply too small to be stuck in the back of the house, far from adult supervision and assistance. It came to her then that, as Rodolfo was the only one of them likely to notice if anything was amiss, he could be put in one of the larger rooms, while Enrique slept with his father and she stayed in the nursery. This they had actually discussed, but Rodrigo had pointed out that neither of the boys had ever slept a single night alone. Still, they had put it to Rodolfo—and watched his cherubic face fall, his eyes widen with dread. Rebecca herself had nixed the plan, guilt swamping her because she had been the one to suggest it. That left slipping out after the children were asleep or . . . She looked down, wondering how hard it would be to sleep on a stone floor.

"I'll just have to sneak out," she decided firmly, and Rodrigo rolled his eyes in dismay.

"Rebecca—"

A wail sounded from the other room, high, piercing, frightened. Little feet hit the floor and an instant later, the nursery door silently swung open.

"¿Padre?" Rodolfo rubbed his eyes with his fists, his baby brother crying in earnest now from the bed they shared.

Rodrigo shot Rebecca a look that said, "Didn't I tell you this would happen?" She curbed the impulse to stick her tongue out at him and went instead to the baby, gathering him up in her arms. He came readily, the middle finger of his left hand going into his mouth. She'd seen children suck their thumbs before but never their fingers, and by intuition she gently removed it from between his lips. He did not protest but laid his head upon her shoulder with a sigh. She knew what to do from practice with little Eustacia. While Rodrigo fetched a drink of water for Rodolfo, she gently rocked the baby, amazed by how naturally these things came to her once she'd relaxed.

By the time Rodolfo had had his drink and was once more settled upon the bed, the baby was snoozing on Rebecca's shoulder. Carefully, she leaned over the bed and placed the little one between his brother and the wall, then drew the covers up and tucked them into place, but as she started to withdraw, a small hand fell upon her neck.

"*Señora,*" Rodolfo said, his voice almost too soft to hear, "*Ya que es nuestra madre ahora, ¿me permite llamarle durante la noche si es que mi hermanito se despierta?*"

She didn't catch enough of it to understand and looked for help to Rodrigo, who was crouched beside the boy, smoothing his hair. He met her gaze evenly, his dark eyes seeming to probe her lighter ones, and translated.

"He wan's to know, now dat you are dheir modher, eef he can call you next time Enrique wakes."

Her heart swelled and shrunk all at once. To be accepted as Mother was one thing, to play house with Father was something else, and in this case, the former seemed predicated on the latter. Still, she wasn't about to tell this little boy that he would have to find himself a mother elsewhere. He would never understand.

So she smiled, leaned closer and whispered, "*Sí,* Rodolfo." Then she kissed him good-night. He smiled that beatific smile, making her think, not for the first time, that he was a sweet and adorable child. Rodrigo ruffled his hair and stood. Apparently content, the boy turned onto his side, tucked his hands beneath his chin and closed his eyes. Silently, Rodrigo and Rebecca stole from the room and oh-so-carefully closed the door.

"You see?" Don Rigo whispered as he ushered her away from the door. "We have no choice, Rebecca. We mus' sleep in dat bed togedher." He jerked his head toward the big four-poster dominating the room and slipped his fingertips into the waistband of his jeans, sucking in his lean middle as if to make room for them. "Dey are children, Rebecca. Even eef we tell dem no' to open dat door, one or de odher will! Eet ees—" He struggled for the right word and settled for "witou' doubt."

Reluctantly, Rebecca admitted to herself that he was right, but that didn't mean she could just agree without another word. She sighed and licked her lips, trying to find a diplomatic way of saying what she felt she must.

"Rodrigo," she began, "it's not sleeping in that bed that I'm worried about, it's . . . you know."

He glared at her. "Rebecca, eef you t'ink I woul' force myse'f on you—"

"I didn't say that! I just want it understood that we aren't . . . that we won't . . ." This was the most difficult conversation she'd ever tried to havé, bar none, and it seemed no easier for Rodrigo. He, in fact, chose not to have it.

Murmuring Spanish expletives under his breath, he marched away from her. Going to the side of the bed, he hopped around on one foot and then the other, getting his boots off. That done, he pulled his shirt up and over his head and threw it on the floor, still grumbling. Automatically, his hands went to the fly of his pants, and he'd freed two buttons before he realized what he was doing and stopped. Shooting her a thoroughly disgruntled glance, he lifted up the covers of the bed and slid beneath them, pants and all.

"I mus' sleep," he announced, keeping his voice low. "You can stan' dhere all nigh', or you can come to bed." He lifted his head from the pillow and glared at her. "Eidher way, I will no' touch you!" With that, he laid his head back, folded his arms across his chest and closed his eyes, adding, "Put ou' de ligh's. *Por favor.*"

Rebecca just stood there for some time, staring. It was an awfully big bed, and he didn't take up nearly half of it. In that bed, two people ought to be able to sleep side by side comfortably without touching, unless, of course, they wanted to—which they didn't, she reminded herself sternly. Besides, there really wasn't much choice. *And* he had as good as promised not to start anything. *And* she was tired. *And* she was just putting off the inevitable anyway.

At last, she went to blow out the flames, one by one. In the dark, she slipped off her sandals and gave her eyes time to adjust before she padded silently to her side of the bed and got in, fully clothed.

"Rodrigo," she whispered, wanting to say that she was sorry or that he shouldn't be angry or even, to repeat her old standby one more time, that all would be well. But Rodrigo never answered, so after a while, she shut her eyes and her mouth and concentrated on just getting through the night.

Rodrigo sat at the breakfast table, staring at his plate through bleary eyes. He had slept little the previous night, but then he hadn't really slept since the children had come home, and he was wondering now if he would ever learn to sleep with Rebecca in his bed. It was agony to lie there night after night, his body tense with the need to join with hers, his exhausted mind trying to think how to make her want to stay, for more than anything, he wanted her to stay, to live with him as his wife, his true wife. Yet, the time was coming when he would have to take her away, deliver her into the hands of her brother.

If what Padre Tomás had said was true, then Rodrigo had no reason to doubt that Rebecca's brother awaited her in San Benito. Of course, anything was possible. Matthew Harper had been accused of stealing, and he had run from that accusation like a guilty man, but Rodrigo was of no mind to label him one way or another. In truth, Rodrigo did not know what to make of the man. He had nothing by which to judge Matthew Harper except his sister, and Rebecca was a gentle, loving patient person who, nonetheless, possessed a certain fire at the core of her being. She was like his *luz roja,* beautiful and soft and glowing, but hot at the heart like the flame of the candle tip. How he would love to touch the source of that flame! But if it was not to be, then he must see her safely into her brother's care.

Meanwhile, he had no one to blame but himself if he suffered in body and heart because he had known from the beginning that it was unwise to allow himself to love and desire her. At least, he told himself, he need not suffer his soul. From that, he could still protect himself. He had thought that the marriage ceremony would protect him, but now he knew that was not so, for even if by some miracle this marriage should be consummated, he would never attempt to keep her against her will. He would lie to the good padre, if it came to that. He would give her his heart if only she would want it, but if the annullment was what she sought, she would have that, whatever it took. So it was better if he did not touch her, for if he did he would almost certainly have to lie to the padre, and he would not like to do that.

He should get her out of his bed, or get out of it himself, but never was a man so attached to his suffering. Still, it was time to at least think about being a man again instead of a lovesick groom. He should ride out with his vaqueros, those who had reported back, and make short work of this final stage of the roundup. Three or four nights on the trail ought to do it, and he decided again, as he had every morning this past week, that it had to be done—tomorrow.

Rebecca came in with a child on each hand. His sons were scrubbed clean and smiling, and his heart swelled at the sight of them. It was good to have them home again, to be a family again, even if having them here did make him suffer. He had forgotten what it was like to have his children in the house. They had been bound up in his heart with Sofía somehow, and he realized now that when he had lost her, he had considered the children lost, also. He had neglected them then, and yet here they were, climbing up to his table with smiles on their faces for him, adoration shining in their eyes.

He watched with pride as Rodolfo assumed responsibility for his younger brother, struggling to push his chair close to the table, capturing his eager hands as they reached too quickly for food and drink, whispering instruction. Rebecca, too, joined in schooling the child, removing things from his reach, shushing him when he squealed, placating him with a hunk of heavy bread torn from the flat round loaf on the table. Tolerably subdued, Enrique hunkered over his plate, both chubby elbows on the table, little heels swinging with muted clunks against his chair, drooling mouth busy with the oily bread. Beside him, Rodolfo spread his napkin in his lap as Rebecca had shown him. Ever solemn, he folded his fine hands and waited to be served.

The gloom that had cloaked Rodrigo since his rising suddenly lightened. He had not realized how he loved his children, how they enriched his life. It was time that he put some effort into teaching Rodolfo those things he would need to know when the responsibility of the rancho was his. He must make a point of it after the cattle were delivered. It would help to keep them close after the boy had returned to his aunts, after Rebecca had gone. Once more the gloom deepened, and he struggled to lift it.

"You are good wit de *niños,*" he told Rebecca as she filled Rodolfo's plate.

She smiled, but her eyes stayed with the boy. "Children used to make me nervous. Did you know I studied to be a teacher?"

He was surprised and pleased. "Why den did you change?"

"I told you, children used to make me nervous. I thought a teacher had to have a special understanding of them, a 'gift' for them."

"But ees eet no' so?"

She looked at him at last, the smile renewing itself. "Possibly, but it's amazing what a little practice can do. I can't even remember now what it was that frightened me about them." She looked to Rodolfo, who was listening intently though he understood not a word. "Eat, Rodolfo, *¡come!*"

"*Sí, Madre,*" the boy replied, dutifully doing as instructed.

Rodrigo's heart clinched in his chest. He would not be the only one to grieve when she left them.

"I mus' ride out wit de vaqueros soon," he mumbled. "Can you manage alone for a time?"

"I've already told you that I can," she reminded him. "Besides, I have Lupe. When are you going?"

He told himself that he should go at once, this very morning, but he heard himself say, "*Mañana,* perha's, or de day af'er."

She nodded, saying nothing more, but he imagined she was disappointed, even annoyed. He pushed his plate away, rising suddenly to reach for his hat and muttering about having much to do. He smoothed the hair of each of the boys as he passed them, striding toward the door, and then he let himself out into the blue light of early morning, unaware that behind him Rebecca's eyes were clouded with tears.

All day he sat astride El Pescado, moving from one gathering point to another, checking to see who had come in with how many cattle in what condition. At the same time, he tried to gauge what damage, if any, the cattle had done to the range for his goat herd, for the goats would remain the staple of the rancho. He worked hard, paying close attention to details, and yet his mind was not wholly about his business. Some part of him, it seemed, was ever with Rebecca, would ever be.

He slept in the shade of a rocky outcropping for a badly needed hour during the afternoon siesta and woke longing to be home again playing with his children and watching Rebecca as she tidied the room. The men were quick to pick up on his melancholy and teased him of being overly fond of his wife's skirts and what was under them. Usually, he took their ribbing good-naturedly, but today the need was too sharp, the moment of her departure looming too large, the lie too difficult to maintain. He cut short the siesta, ordering the men back to work though the sun blazed like a furnace still. He shamed himself by berating them and accusing them of laziness, and they were such good men, hard workers all, loyal, trusting. He fell into bitter silence, hat-ing himself for being unable to control his own emotions and in his misery, he began to think that perhaps it was not love at all that he felt for Rebecca but something else entirely.

It had not been like this with Sofía. No, indeed. From the moment her bold eyes had met his, all had seemed right and easy. The fires of love had built slowly, not flaring out of control all at once. He had not had to beat them back, and they had not burned him, but had warmed him slowly, invading every last cell of his body with their seductive heat. Why could it not be that way with Rebecca? But then Rebecca was not like Sofía, and wasn't that what had attracted him in the beginning? His life, he realized sadly, had become one big contradiction. Yet, as evening drew close and El Pescado's nose turned toward home, the longing sharpened and intensified, more distinct even than the weariness that lay over his body like a second skin, and when he flung open the door and stepped inside his own *casa,* it was to the bright, happy cries of his children. Even Rebecca smiled in welcome, and suddenly any price was worth paying just for the chance of having it always be like this.

So, holding himself rigid against the possibility of their bodies accidentally touching, he went to bed beside Rebecca in the soft, loose *pijamas* she had asked Lupe to make for him, the bottoms anyway. He could not abide the shirt; it twisted about him as he tossed and turned and seemed nearly to strangle him at times. The bottoms were good, though, for they kept him from sleeping in his pants and would seem more appropriate attire for a married man if he was suddenly shaken out in the middle of the night. As far as he knew, none of the other men wore them, but he was *el dueño* and expected to be different on occasion, especially with a gringa for a wife. Of course, had she really been his wife, he wouldn't have needed the *pijamas* or anything else for sleeping, but that was precisely the problem.

He could feel her tension, as deep as his own, and yet as he lay pretending sleep, it seemed to him that she had given in and actually slept. Snoozing as best he could, he lay waiting long into the night, for what he knew not, perhaps for the miracle that would make her truly his, perhaps for the unconsciousness of exhaustion. He seemed no closer to either when the distant ring of a pan being dropped on a stone floor came to him. Suddenly fully awake, he strained for a second sound, any clue that would tell him who or what had invaded his kitchen, and finally he had it. The door opened at the end of the hallway, and as a foot fell upon the stone there, he caught the lilt of a softly whistled tune.

Pacíno. Rodrigo smiled to himself. Doubtlessly the rough vaquero was unaware of *el jefe*'s newly achieved marital status. Pacíno was one of those single-minded, independent, impulsive and slightly careless unmarried men who would likely ever stay so. He had no interest in the Church, and only enough interest in women to make him seek out the less proper ones for an occasional dalliance. Likewise, he wanted no home other than the saddle of his horse, no roof more than the open sky, and he lived in horror at the idea of some hungry *niño* bearing his name. The far, solitary reaches were for Pacíno, and it was from just such a place that he had come, as was his custom, to report personally to *el jefe* and raid his larder. Woman's cooking, he liked to say, was the one talent for which he could not forgive God. Rodrigo rather fancied that the sticky caramels that Rebecca had helped Ochéa cook for the children were at that moment in imminent danger of being wiped out. It would serve Pacíno right if he embarrassed himself by walking unannounced into *el jefe*'s bedchamber, only to find his employer abed with his *esposa*. But for Rebecca, Rodrigo would have allowed it to happen. Instead, he whispered to warn her.

"Rebecca."

"Listen!" she whispered back, both relief and apprehension in her voice. So she had not slept, after all. That pleased him, and it pleased him also to have a reason to comfort her.

"Do no' fear," he said, rolling over to make himself more clearly understood and to offer her the protection of his arm should she desire it. But she, too, moved toward him, her hand reaching out to touch his hip as the footsteps drew near, and it was not his hip over which her hand glided, but the flat of his belly and the still partially engorged shaft of his desire that lay against it. He sucked in his breath with a gasp. Her hand jerked away as if it had touched an open flame, and in that very instant, the door swung wide.

"*¡Pacíno, eres un gran necio!*" Don Rigo barked, blindly groping for Rebecca's hand to prevent her attempt at bolting from the bed. He found it and clamped it tightly, dragging her down against his arm, which he wrapped around her. "Be calm, *mi esposa*. Dis ees jus' de *idiota* coming from de range." He ordered Pacíno to stay where he was and levered up onto his elbow. He pressed her to the bed, thankful for the near darkness and brought his face close to hers. "Ees no pro'lem, *querida*," Rodrigo told her softly. "Little accidents mean not'ing. Stay where you are, an' I will send de man away. He no' hear de news dat his *jefe* has marry an' so keep to his custom o' making my *casa* his *casa*. Eet will no' happen again, I promise. Now, for Pacíno's eyes..." And he kissed her lightly upon the lips. "Res' easy till I return."

She turned her head away, her hands knotting in the bed covers. Suddenly Rodrigo was angry: with her, with himself, with Pacíno, with everyone. Life had been good once, hard but good, and he had been master of his fate. Now, in the space of a few weeks, all had become lies—all he said, all he did, even the end results. Gritting his teeth, he threw back the covers and got out of the bed, moving quickly to the door. When he stepped into the hallway, pulling the door closed at his back, Pacíno's eyes widened in merry amazement and he began to chuckle both at *el jefe*'s attire and his appearance.

"Ho-ho," he said, his Spanish slurring around the last of the caramels, "my leader is a real man again! Who is the woman?"

Rodrigo scolded him, hissing in Spanish. "Shut up before you wake the children!"

"Children!" Pacíno gasped. "Here?" Clearly, he did not grasp the situation correctly as he could not quite believe the children were in residence at the same moment as the woman.

Rodrigo took him by the arm and steered him grimly toward the *sala.* "Of course, the children are here, and why not? Should a married man refuse his home to his sons?"

"Married!" Pacíno beamed his delight and, stopping near the dining table, threw both arms about his friend. "Ha-ha! Life goes on, does it not? I have great happiness for you. A man such as yourself needs a wife." The big vaquero held his *jefe* at arm's length. "But tell me, my friend, who is this woman? Would Glorieta make you a suitable wife?"

Rodrigo sighed. "As suitable as the one I have married, I am afraid."

"What is this?" The big man sobered, ready to play the part of confidant.

For a moment, Rodrigo toyed with the idea of confiding in the man, but then, for reasons he himself could not name, decided against it. Lies they might be, but he preferred them to the truth. He put on a smile.

"She is an American," he said, "a blonde, and I take back everything I've ever said about anglo women! *Aiii,* how love opens the eyes, eh?"

Pacíno grinned, reassured by his friend's playful declarations. "May heaven and earth smile on you, lucky man, and on this woman who has improved your vision! Does this new wife keep food in her house?"

"Glutton!" Rodrigo teased. "Is it not enough that you have eaten my children's sweets? Now you would have their breakfast, too?"

They laughed together as Rodrigo led Pacíno toward the kitchen. There they talked and laughed, comrades and friends as well as boss and employee. Rodrigo played the host as happy bridegroom so well that he almost convinced himself that he was a satisfied husband, and in the hour before dawn when he returned to his bed, he wanted nothing more than to hold his wife and whisper sweet words of love to her. He ached with the need to touch her, and as she lay sleeping, her lovely eyes hidden behind smooth, creamy lids studded with pale lashes, he watched and hardened again with desire.

What would she do, he wondered, now that she was aware of his desire for her? Would she leave him, sleep in the lane again outside the Espinozas' house, bathe surreptitiously in the fountain in the square? Would she prefer the dirt and the cold to his bed and his name? But it wouldn't come to that. He wouldn't allow it to come to that. Before he would let her go back to the Espinozas or anywhere else, he would sleep on the ground himself or take her immediately to her brother and end the charade. If only, he thought, it could work the other way, and his love would make her want him. He knew in his heart that he could please her as no other man, if only she would let him.

As he thought these things, he leaned close to her, adoring that pretty oval face with its enormous eyes and perfect nose and lush bow of a mouth. She looked so delicate in the soft pink light, yet her strength was there, too, in the prominence of cheekbones and the height of the forehead, with just a touch of stubbornness about the slightly pointed chin. Thoughtlessly, his hand moved beneath the cover and touched the sensitive flesh on the inside of her elbow. She jerked awake, eyes wide with alarm.

"What? Is he—"

"Shh, *querida*. All ees well."

She strained upward, her concern momentarily overwhelming her mental faculties, and in doing so, she brought her face close to his. His gaze went to her mouth, his fingers creeping up her arm, and it came to him suddenly that she might want this. Perhaps this was her answer to his desire of her. Perhaps... He closed his mind to further thought and covered her mouth with his. He might have been kissing his pillow, and deep inside himself he groaned, misery welling up.

All at once, her lips seemed to warm, parting beneath his, and he felt her hand upon his arm, tentative at first, then mindlessly kneading the muscle and finally sliding upward and over his shoulder to clamp about his neck. He could hardly believe it: she wanted him. She wanted him! Disappointment turned to hope. He thrust his tongue into her mouth, felt hers curl beneath it in welcome, and he exulted, hope blossoming into determination. She was his woman, his wife. He ripped away the covers between them and pressed against her with all the desperation of his cause.

She arched her back, flattening her breasts against his chest. He could feel her nipples hardening beneath the cool fabric of her gown and he pushed a knee between her legs, his tongue plunging into her mouth again and again. He wanted to rip away the gown, to bury himself in her body and spew his love into her flat, supple belly. They would be one, united in the eyes of man and God. Had not the padre said it was so? Was this not the law? Could tenderness and soft words be more important than the joining? He pulled up her skirt, his hand moving to the string at his waist. Never again would he wear *pijamas* or hold himself back. She would be his and he would be hers, partners in life and in pleasure.

She trembled beneath him, her hands clutching at his arms and shoulders, and he curled his fingers beneath the tiny strip of elastic that held up those slinky panties. She jerked and sucked in her stomach, her hands ceasing their restless wanderings. He peeled the strip of cloth back, spreading his fingers against the moist softness beneath them, and in his joy, he nearly wept. To think that he could know this again, the desire that surpassed even physical need, the love that made conquest incidental! He poised to thrust, ready to join, and it was then that he realized she was struggling, her mouth twisting away from him, legs scissoring, hands pushing where once they'd pulled. He lifted his weight from her, already sick at heart and wanting desperately to be mistaken. She was sliding her hands between them, tugging at her skirt, gasping.

"Dear God, what are we doing?"

He wanted to push her back and drive himself into her, but it was already too late. Still, he could not make himself move away. "On'y wha' ees our righ'" he whispered, attempting to nuzzle her ear. "Are we no' marry? Are we no' meant for dis?"

"Lovemaking without love?" she returned bitterly. He recoiled. She wanted him but she did not love him. The knowledge cut like a knife. Still, he wanted to declare that he would take what she could give and be satisfied, but he knew he would never be happy with only part of her. He did not want her body without her heart.

He turned away from her, rolling into a sitting position, his back to her. His head hung between his shoulders, a deep, dark misery coming over him, dwindling his desire. Beside him, she moved hastily to right her clothing, and he knew he should do the same, but somehow it didn't matter. He only wanted to be elsewhere.

"De sun rises soon," he heard himself say, and then he was up and moving across the floor. He let the *pijamas* fall away and stepped out of them into the legs of the first pair of pants that came to his hand. He slid his feet into his boots, took a pair of socks, a shirt and his hat, and moved to the door. "I will stay away a few days," he told her slowly, sighing. "De men need me on de range, an' I mus' check on dhose who keep wa'ch a' La Fuente Dos."

She said nothing for a long while, and then, "That seems best, yes."

He squeezed his eyes against the hurt of such words. "Eef you shoul' need somet'ing..." he began.

"I'll go to Fernando," she assured him quickly. "Don't worry about us."

Us. He wanted that word to mean family, wife and sons, but it named only the woman who lived with him and the children for whom she cared.

He went out and closed the door.

Chapter Twelve

"*¿Yo puedo ayudar, Madre?*"

Rodolfo's finely featured little face turned up at her, his mouth set exactly as his father's would have been. He seemed more and more like Rodrigo every day, as if that one's absence commanded it. Rebecca could almost see the thin line of an obsessively groomed mustache beginning to sprout on his smoothly chiseled upper lip. Or was it that she simply missed Rodrigo so much that she was projecting his image everywhere. She still expected to feel him roll out of bed every morning and slip about the room, quietly dressing as she pretended to sleep, and it was most puzzling that she seemed to sleep no better in his absence than she had in his presence.

Rodolfo tugged on her skirt insistently, bringing her back to the moment, and she sighed playfully, lips curling upward.

"I welcome your help, little man." Even to her own ears English seemed strange these days, yet Spanish remained an afterthought. She repeated her words for Rodolfo. *"Agra-desco tu ayuda."*

He cocked his head expectantly while Rebecca fished in the laundry basket balanced upon her hip. She found the heavy horsehair brush she used for scrubbing and delivered it into Rodolfo's hands. The boy looked down at it, a stubborn frown pinching his face. She watched the decision come to him, recognized the stiffening of his body, the drawing-up of his torso, the elongation of the spine. She had watched it with Rodrigo more than once.

Rodolfo turned and awarded the brush to his brother, who dropped to the ground and began to groom the dirt with broad, sandy swipes. When Rodolfo turned back to her, his features had adopted an implacable stubbornness. She'd seen that look, too, and she didn't know whether to be dismayed or amused, so she kept her expression carefully neutral as she bent and set the basket on the ground. Rodolfo hovered over it, carefully weighing the contents before taking out a bundle of pale linens. Tightening the loose knot in the sheet containing it, he grasped the ends and slung the bundle over his shoulder, giving her a look that clearly said, "Ready." Rebecca gently prodded the baby onto his feet, the dirty brush grasped in both of his pudgy hands, then picked up the basket again and followed Rodolfo down the lane toward the village square, Enrique toddling along behind.

They made slow progress with the baby stopping every ten feet to squat and brush the dirt. Both Rebecca and Rodolfo were constantly looking over their shoulders and urging him along with calls and feathery whistles. Finally, they reached the square. Everyone else was there ahead of them, and Rebecca cringed to see Tía Elena posed stiffly in a chair positioned near the washtubs. Ignoring the old woman's stern, censorious presence, Rebecca waved at Lupe, who came to sweep up the baby and hurry things along.

Rebecca smiled at the women as she moved among them, murmuring in stilted Spanish that she was sorry to have kept

them. She had tried on the last wash day to make it clear
that she did not want them to wait for her in order to begin
their washing. Their waiting was no doubt a sign of respect
for *La Doña,* as they now called her, but it made her extremely uncomfortable. It would have made her uncomfortable even if the circumstances of her marriage had been
different, but she couldn't expect them to understand that.
She couldn't, in fact, expect them to understand much of
anything beyond the most basic ideas, what with her sketchy
Spanish and their almost total lack of English. It was especially frustrating because they seemed to expect her to direct them, as if they hadn't been working together like this
long before she came.

She tried to avoid taking command this time by just setting to work herself, but it quickly became obvious that they
resented her silence. Reluctantly, her hands dripping with
soapy water, she assigned tubs and duties, making immediate changes whenever anyone showed the least chagrin or
displeasure. Finally, with everyone busy, she ignored Tía
Elena's sneer and plunged in herself, but she'd hardly gotten her hands wet again when the calls and cries of the children playing in the square suddenly elevated to alarming
shouts and screams.

Rebecca jerked her head up just in time to spot Rodolfo
as he struck another, bigger boy on the side of the head with
the flat of his fist. The boy came back slugging, and Rodolfo went down, but with his hands lashing out. The bigger boy toppled over on top of him, and they rolled together
in the dirt. Rebecca didn't even realize she was running until one of the other women bumped into her. Rebecca
grabbed her and together they ran, leading the others. As
soon as they reached the shouting mob of children, the other
woman broke away and went, as Rebecca had assumed she
would, to the bigger boy, while Rebecca got her hands on
Rodolfo and dragged him up.

"What is going on here? Are you hurt? Answer me!" She
realized in the same instant that his lip was bleeding and that

he didn't understand a word she was saying. She hugged him, then shook him. "*¿Por qué,* Rodolfo? *¿Por qué?*"

He wiped the blood from his lip and said nothing, but as the other boy sobbed out his replies to his angry mother, Rebecca caught the words gringa and *inglés.* She closed her eyes, understanding now that the fight had been about her. Oh, what was she to do? If she lashed out at that lout of a boy as she was inclined to do at the moment, there might well be further trouble, and she didn't want Rodolfo fighting. For his sake, he mustn't think that he was forever bound to defend her. She bit her lip, suddenly wondering what lay in store for Rodrigo and his sons once she was gone and the marriage annulled. Somehow, she had to do the right thing for everyone. A number of possibilities passed through her mind, but one stuck out among the others.

Grimly, she seized Rodolfo by the arm and marched him toward the other boy and his mother. She gave the mother a look meant to quell any protest, then determinedly shook fingers in both boys' faces, repeating over and over, "*¡No combatan! No peléen!*" After forcing agreement from each boy, she made them shake hands, taking their hands in hers and physically joining them. Afterward, she patted the other boy on the head to show that there were no hard feelings, then turned to Rodolfo. Gently, she touched his split lip and then kissed him on the cheek. Finally, she assumed her stern face once more and for good measure repeated, "*¡No combatan!*"

"*Sí,*" Rodolfo quietly said, and she smiled to let him know that it was forgotten.

As she sent him off to play again, the other woman sidled up next to her and whispered, "*Gracias,* Doña Becca."

Rebecca smiled and shrugged, communicating that it was a small thing, and linked her arm with the other woman's, walking her back toward the washtubs. Around them, the other women milled and commented with apparent approval, but Rebecca noticed that Tía Elena sniffed and frowned. So what else is new? she found herself thinking, and immediately dismissed the old woman, feeling a light touch on her arm.

She turned to find Clara at her elbow, but instead of speaking, the girl dropped her head and backed away. Rebecca was surprised. Clara had kept out of her way for a long time now, always hovering on the fringe of the group and never coming closer. Suddenly she seemed to want to speak to Rebecca but apparently lacked the courage. The girl turned as if to walk away, but Rebecca reached out a hand to stop her. After all, there was less reason than Clara even knew for the animosity between them.

"Clara?"

The girl darted a wary glance over her shoulder, then shook her bowed head.

"Clara, *por favor háblame.* Speak to me."

Shyly, slowly, the girl turned back. For a long time, she stood staring at the ground.

Rebecca sighed with both impatience and sympathy. "Clara, *mi amiga,*" she began, "I wish I knew how to tell you that all is forgiven." A big tear plopped into the dirt at Clara's feet. "No, no, no," Rebecca said, stepping forward to slip an arm about the girl. "Please don't cry." But suddenly Clara was sobbing on her shoulder. Rebecca didn't know what she should do. Everyone was looking at them. Tía Elena seemed about ready to fly to the girl's defense, poised as she was on the edge of her chair. Rebecca took a solid grip on the girl's upper arms and pushed her away a little, gently shaking her.

"Hush! No cry, uh, no..." She searched frantically for the proper Spanish word but didn't find it. "Clara," she began again, "Clara and Rebecca, friends. *Amigas.* Clara and Rebecca, *amigas,* uh..." She remembered the word for sisters. "*¡Hermanas! Clara y Rebecca, hermanas. ¿Sí?*"

The girl turned up an astonished face. "*¿Hermanas?*" she gasped. "*¡Sí! ¡Sí! ¡Hermanas!*" And then, before Rebecca could say another word, the girl dropped to the ground, throwing her arms around Rebecca's ankles! She was sobbing and rattling in incomprehensible Spanish. Rebecca was appalled.

"Stop it! Clara, no! Get . . ." But English wasn't going to accomplish a thing, and she didn't know or couldn't remember enough Spanish to get her message across. Gritting her teeth in frustration, she stooped and firmly dragged the girl's arms from about her feet, then bodily lifted her, struggling beneath her weight. She wished fervently that Rodrigo would come, but then a mental picture flashed before her.

For an instant, she clearly saw Rodrigo galloping his horse into the square and reining in, his face contorted with confusion as he stared at the scene before him. She realized suddenly how ridiculous they must look, wrestling there in the dust, and it came to her how insane the whole thing was: Clara bowing in the dirt like some grateful peon at the feet of the *patrona,* and her not even a common *señora,* let alone the wife of the *patrón!* Some wife she was! A baby-sitter, perhaps, a roommate, a maid and a laundress, but a wife? No. Clara would not have fallen at her feet if Clara knew how Rebecca's so-called husband had lain at her side night after night and controlled his manly desires in order to assure himself a proper annulment. How Clara would laugh if she knew! How they would all laugh! It was really terribly funny, so funny that Rebecca herself began to laugh. Within moments Clara was laughing, too, and that made it all the more funny to Rebecca, for Clara couldn't know what she was laughing at. They collapsed upon the ground, laughter building into howls.

It was, of course, incredibly undignified, a point Elena made when she stomped past them, her voluminous black skirt scattering dust. They took one look at her and shrieked like banshees, their arms draped about each other's shoulders. It was then that the giggles started among the others. Elena's already rigid back stiffened, lending a comical jerk to her gait. One of the women sputtered and erupted in laughter, then another, until finally everyone was joining in the joke, whatever it was. They laughed so loudly that the children came running and stood gawking and pointing as their mothers, aunts, sisters and grandmothers guffawed and held their sides and cackled and laughed all the more. Even Fernando came from his shop and stood and scratched his head, grinning uncertainly until Clara and Rebecca finally got up and dusted themselves off and, giggling still, went arm in arm to the washtubs. The frenzy eventually calmed, but for some time, isolated pockets of laughter sputtered to life and spent themselves, even after the children wandered back to their play. And the women were laughing still in little ways when, their arms filled with freshly laundered clothing, they began to return to their homes.

Rebecca hefted her own basket onto her hip and took the baby from Lupe, settling him on the other, then turned to look over the square. It had been a good day. Correction. It had been another good day. She could count Clara among her friends now, and she seemed to have gained respect from the others. She hated to think that she had caused Rodolfo to fight, but she was touched deeply that he cared enough to defend her honor. He was so like his father, gentle and fierce all at the same time. She would hate to leave him and the jolly baby on her hip, but she wasn't going to think of that just now. For once, she was just going to enjoy this place and these people and her part here with them.

Happy in a way she hadn't known possible, sad in another, she turned toward the lane. Enrique yawned and rubbed his face against her sleeve. It was siesta time, and he had played hard. His eyelids were already drooping. She would have to carry him this time along with the laundry. It would be no easy task, but she didn't mind. Then Rodolfo stepped up to take one handle of the basket, his big eyes peeping over its rim. She smiled at him—so like his father—and took the other handle, allowing the weight of the basket to slide from her hip. He just looked at her, his mouth lopsided with the swelling of his busted lip, and together they started home.

Rodrigo scoured his metal plate with a fistful of ash and sand from the edge of the fire ring. Rebecca had called it a pie tin once, and he'd wondered ever since just what that meant. He knew what a pie was, of course. It was a triangular piece of split crust filled sandwich-style with cooked fruit. What did that have to do with a round plate? Americans. Their ideas and expressions were so funny. He smiled, thinking about some of the things she was always saying. "That burns me," she would say, or, "Doesn't that take the cake?" And once she'd laughingly told him, "You're cracking me up!" It had frightened him at first, but then he had realized it was some sort of a nonsensical joke, and he had laughed without really understanding why. He chuckled to himself, remembering, and Pacíno joined him.

"A long while has passed since you last did that," his friend said in Spanish from the darkness. "You should do more of it, my chief."

Rodrigo tilted the plate and let the sand and ash dribble out. "One of life's great mysteries, Pacíno, is how a certain woman can make you laugh and gnash your teeth at the very same time." He dusted the plate on his knee, leaving a coat of pale gray ash on the denim. "This one," he observed wryly, "I am afraid will create much more gnashing than laughter." He stood, saying, "The worst part is that I'm without power to prevent it."

"Not so, old friend," insisted the other. "Not completely without power, I think. Between you is a certain... What? Natural attraction?"

Rodrigo scowled, regretting yet again that he had told Pacíno all. He had surely lowered himself in the eyes of a man he respected. How the men would gape if they knew their chief had yet to bed his own wife! Not that he feared Pacíno would tell the secret. He did not expect that at all.

Yet, he could not help a certain discomfort with Pacíno's knowledge of the situation.

"There is nothing *natural* between Rebecca and me," Rodrigo grumbled. "That is exactly the problem."

"Not so great a problem as you make it, I suspect," Pacíno told him boldly. "I have never seen a woman Don Rigo could not seduce. You think too much about her, this is all. Since when do you care what a woman thinks of you before you begin to work on her, eh? It is after that counts, is it not? And afterward, do not they all love you?"

"This time is different," Rodrigo said. "I do not want to seduce her! I want her to come to me willingly, happily!"

"All the more reason to seduce her," Pacíno said with a shrug, and he got up from the rock where he had sat hunkered over his plate. He dropped the empty plate in the sand and stretched.

He looked ten feet tall standing there in the shadows with his arms stretched over his head, and Rodrigo felt vaguely irritated by this. But then, he was irritated by everything these days and could fix his mind on nothing but Rebecca. Perhaps Pacíno was right. What had he to lose by trying? Perhaps it was time that he courted his wife. He had told her that he would not force himself on her, but that did not mean he would not try to make her want him. If she should come to want him badly enough, might she not come to love him, also? It was not as though she was unaware of him, after all. There was a physical attraction, if nothing else.

And what if she succumbed, allowed him to make love to her? Would it really change anything? Americans were notorious about disregarding their marriage vows when made in all sincerity. He could not expect that having sex with him would change her mind about the bargain they'd made and called a marriage. The most he could hope to acccomplish was to keep her legally bound to him, and he wasn't even certain that he could accomplish that. He shook his head dismally.

"A seduction would accomplish nothing," he said, "nothing at all."

Pacíno grunted, swinging his arms, and stepped forward. "Did the old don not teach you what could become of seduction, my friend? Did he never tell you how babies are made, then?"

The tone was bantering, but Don Rigo was astonished, nevertheless. "Are you suggesting I make a baby with this woman?"

"Why not?" Pacíno asked lightly. "Who better to make a baby with than your wife, eh?"

Who, indeed? Rodrigo found himself thinking, but the next instant he was berating himself as well as his man. "We are insane to think of these things!" he declared.

"And I say it is only reasonable," Pacíno argued. "Woo her, play the romantic, and do not think of the other if it plagues you too much, only do not think of preventing it. That way it is in God's hands, is it not?"

"Go away, you heretic," Rodrigo scolded. "I won't listen to you because you use God only when it suits you."

"Don't we all," Pacíno muttered. "And you will think about it, my friend, because you are a man in love." He turned and walked into the darkness, leaving his plate to be cleaned later.

Rodrigo kicked it, swiping it sideways toward the fire. He wanted to be angry at Pacíno or Rebecca or even himself. It would help to be angry, to rage until he was drained of all emotion, but he could not work up even a decent anger. His wanting of this woman overshadowed everything else, his whole life, his very being. He sighed and sat down on Pacíno's rock, the only sound that of the crackling fire, and in his mind he pictured a blue-eyed baby girl—or a son, perhaps. Could a man have too many sons? He thought of Rodolfo and Enrique and imagined Rebecca with her stomach swollen big with his child, and in some part of his mind, he began to hear the words he would say to her, to see the things he would do to win her. It occurred to him as he planned that this time he would mean every word and gesture from the very bottom of his heart.

Rebecca studied the finished product, biting her lower lip as she considered how best to judge the success or failure of this latest version of a homemade broom, while Clara waited breathlessly at one elbow and Fernando at the other. The horsehair stitching was straight and strong. The cut end of the brush was uniform and stiff to the touch. The other end was secured firmly to the notched stick with glue and leather bindings that had been wet and allowed to shrink tight in the sun. It looked good. The workmanship was excellent. It felt sturdy. Now for the performance test.

Rising from her chair at the dining table, she walked across the stone floor to a place just inside the door. Here the uneven flagstones were constantly gathering dust and sand tracked in on the feet of everyone who came to the *casa del dueño*. The old broom with its brush of unshredded palm leaves had done little more than scratch the uneven pits filled with dirt, as had two of three earlier versions of this particular design. This one looked most promising, however, and hopes were high as Rebecca lowered the brush of carefully shredded, grouped, glued, sewn and cut palm leaves. The finished product looked a great deal like the brooms Rebecca had purchased and used in Los Angeles. It was one of the things she could say she had truly missed about California and the good old U.S. of A. until now— she hoped. Squaring her shoulders, she made a determined sweep, saw the dust pile up, and made another and another and another, until the pile was a genuine mound of very fine dirt.

"*¿Es bueno, no?*" Fernando asked eagerly.

Rebecca laughed and held the unpainted broomstick out before her. "*¡Es muy bueno, sí. Muy, muy bueno!*" she gushed, and Clara laughed and clapped her hands together.

Clara had reason to be proud and happy. The girl had done the majority of the most tedious work in gathering, shredding, sizing and grouping the palm fronds. She also had come up with the idea of using wet leather stripping to secure the brush to the broomstick. Fernando had pronounced it a stroke of genius and had been suitably impressed with the design to help by fashioning a particularly smooth stick, cutting the notch around the end of it, stitching the brush head flat and cutting the brush evenly. The design, of course, had been Rebecca's, as well as the goal.

It was her hope that a more effective broom would inspire the women of the village to demand stone floors in their houses. Dirt floors, as Rebecca had discovered during her stay with the Espinozas, presented a variety of problems. It was impossible to keep clean a house with dirt floors, and very difficult to prepare and serve uncontaminated food. Moreover, it was Rebecca's guess that soot from the cookstoves mingled with the fine dust of the floor and was constantly circulated in the home by those who walked upon, played upon, slept upon, lived upon those dirt floors. She suspected that was the root of the cause for the coughs and runny noses plaguing many of the younger children. Then, of course, there was the convenience to be had with a tool that effectively and efficiently did what it was designed to do. Happily, she danced across the floor, sweeping up with single strokes what before she had been able only to blot with wet cloths.

"Perfect! Perfect! Perfect!" she sang. "Fernando, I want half a dozen of these right away!"

"Eh?" The old man cocked his head to the side curiously.

"Spanish, you fool," she muttered to herself. "Er, *seis escobas pronto, por favor. ¿Comprende?*"

The old man bobbed his gray and white head. "*¡Sí! ¡Sí! ¡Seis, siete, ocho, diez!*" He made wild hand gestures to Clara, who rushed from the house. A moment later she came in again, her arms wrapped around the sticks of a number of the new brooms.

"Oh, wonderful! Ah, *maravilloso. ¡Maravilloso!*"

Clara dropped them and went for more, while Rebecca quickly counted. There were ten altogether, counting the one she had personally tested and still held in her hand. She was overjoyed. Without thinking, she went to Fernando and placed an impulsive kiss upon his rough cheek. He blushed to the roots of his hair, a deep, dark wine-colored red.

"*Gracias,* Doña Becca, *gracias,*" he muttered, twisting his shirttail self-consciously.

Rebecca spun away. "Clara, summon, uh, uh, *convoca,* uh, *las mujeres en la…er, el…la plaza* before, umm, *antes* siesta." Whew! Rebecca wiped her brow, hoping she had communicated her intentions sufficiently. Apparently she had, because Clara skipped to the door, waved and disappeared, her pretty face wreathed in smiles. Fernando, too, took his leave, gathering up the brooms as he did so, all but the one Rebecca hugged to herself. He put on his hat, doffed it and left her, nodding his understanding as she instructed him to have the brooms in the square before siesta.

She was excited, but her enthusiasm paled beside Lupe's, who raved on and on about the new broom until Ochéa came to see what was the matter. Ochéa, too, was impressed. She carried the new tool to the kitchen and promptly swept the floor clean, displaying her approval by kissing the tip of the handle when she was done. Lupe came to inspect the floor on hands and knees, amazed at its cleanliness, and Rebecca seized the opportunity to explain to the two women in slow, painful hit-and-miss Spanish what she hoped to accomplish with this new broom. Ochéa was at first scandalized by the idea that every woman should have a stone floor in her house. Her feeling seemed to be that only the house of *el hidalgo* deserved real stone floors, but after a long while, during which she coughed for emphasis, Rebecca could see that the cook was changing her mind. She seemed quite taken with this wonder of straw, wood, leather, glue and horsehair.

Clara returned with the word that all the women would gather in the square just before siesta, as requested. She told her mother the details of her participation in the broom project that had taken place over the past three days and, it was obvious, spoke glowingly of Doña Becca's designs. As a result, Ochéa was firmly in Rebecca's corner by the time the four women started toward the square, a fact for which Rebecca gave silent thanks, as she was depending upon the woman's support.

By the time they reached the plaza, the village women were carefully examining the brooms, encouraged by Fernando, who proudly explained the construction and design. Clara joined him, and between the two of them, they made sure that Rebecca's all-important contribution was known by everyone. Rebecca made certain herself to present one of the brooms to Tía Elena, who snorted but then succumbed to examine the thing, albeit somewhat disdainfully.

As Rebecca had hoped, it was Ochéa who advised that anyone with such a broom should have a stone floor. Some of the women gasped. Others reacted with glee. More still were simply puzzled. It was then that Rebecca began a painstaking explanation of their children's coughs and the dust that permeated everything in the house from pots and pans to bed linens. Ochéa, too, was arguing for stone floors, as was Lupe and Clara and even Fernando, who would probably have to do the majority of the work that went with laying those floors. Suddenly, Tía Elena threw up her arms and loudly repudiated the plan. Slowly, deliberately, she drew herself up and eloquently invoked the specter of tradition. Never—from what Rebecca could ascertain—had the peasant women of El Rancho de Dos Fuentes aspired to rock floors. It was unthinkable, even—to use Elena's favorite word—*maligno,* evil.

Rebecca was so mad, she could spit. It was all she could do to keep from tossing the old bag into the fountain again, and to her absolute dismay, she hadn't the presence of mind to summon more than a few words of Spanish with which to express herself. Glorieta came to her rescue by pointing out that it was easy for Elena, who had a stone floor *and* someone to clean it, to speak of such questionable traditions as dirt floors. As for herself, Glorieta wanted to be the first to contract with Fernando for his services. She would trade many bundles of her finest herbs and *remedios* for a stone floor in her little house. Rebecca hugged her. Soon all the women were haggling with Fernando over the costs of such floors.

Rebecca was overjoyed, but even in the midst of her delight, she wondered if Don Rigo would approve of her meddling. It was not, after all, as if she were truly his *doña,* and God knew he had plenty to worry about as it was, without facing a horde of angry husbands whose wives had traded half of what they owned for stone floors. Still, she was certain she had done the right thing and assured herself that Rodrigo would understand once she explained her reasoning. At least with him, she could really explain. The fact that she couldn't do so with these others rankled terribly. It occurred to her that she would never have the upper hand with Tía Elena unless she developed a better grasp of the language. She thought instantly of a book she had found among those on Rodrigo's shelves, a Spanish-English dictionary, and she made up her mind to begin a study of it right away.

She made good on that decision that very evening and had worked her way through the first three letters of the alphabet before turning in. She dreamed in Spanish. *Abastecer,* to supply. *Ausencia,* absence. *Beldad,* beauty. *Boceto,* drawing. *Cabal,* perfect. *Concordia,* harmony. *Confiar,* to hope, to have trust... And on and on. The next morning, Clara found Rebecca at the breakfast table with her nose buried in the pages of the *diccionario,* and to Rebecca's everlasting surprise, the girl began to read from the cover.

"Para linguista, estudiante, y viajero. Completa pronunciación, auxilios especiales y prefacio."

"Clara! You read!"

"Sí. Mi abuela nos enseñó a mi madre y a mí. Una mujer debería leer por sí misma lo que dicen los libros."

Her grandmother had taught both Clara and Ochéa to read! How glad Rebecca was to have made a friend of Clara! Her mind was whirling. This girl, without even knowing it, was the new hope of her village. They could have a school! They didn't have to wait! Eagerly, she drew Clara down beside her and, with the help of the dictionary, engaged in a long conversation about the possibility of organizing and conducting a reading class.

There were problems to be overcome, of course, and Clara pointed them out firmly. They needed a meeting place and a few benches and, most importantly, books. Rebecca mentally added to that list a chalkboard of some kind, not to mention chalk, paper and pencils, for if they were to teach reading, they might as well teach spelling and writing. Rebecca realized right away that only one person could supply what she needed, what the children needed, and that was Don Rigo Avilés. It was up to her to convince him, for this must not wait on cattle sales or hired teachers or new priests or anything. The children would have a school. She meant to see to it, and with Clara's help, she would teach them herself. And after she was gone from this place, Clara and Ochéa could carry on. She would have that knowledge to comfort her during all the long, lonely nights to come.

Chapter Thirteen

Rebecca was sitting at the dining table with Lupe's sewing kit spread before her, its bits of thread wound neatly about several notched sticks, when Rodrigo opened the door and walked in.

"Don Rigo!" She rose from her chair, her needle dropping to the table, the stitches she had been practicing forgotten. His smile was dazzling, his bronze face lean but handsome. He had recently shaved, and his hair had been trimmed about his face and gathered at the nape and wrapped in leather. She quivered just at the sight of him.

"*Buenas tardes, señora,*" he said, striding forward and flourishing a small bouquet of ruffly yellow-and-red flowers. "Or shoul' I say, 'Doña Becca,' eh? I yam tol' de villagers call you dis as a sign o' respec'."

"I think it's more a sign of respect for you than me," she told him, taking the bouquet. A small, delicate sprig of violet blue had been tucked into its very center. "They're beautiful!" She smiled up at him. "Thank you for the flowers." She buried her nose in them, happily inhaling their fresh fragrance.

He made a bow. *"Flores para la belleza."*

Flowers for beauty. It was a gracious, charming compliment that she dared not take too seriously.

"They'll make a lovely centerpiece for the table," she said, pretending to visualize them as such. "I'll just get a vase from the kitchen. Uh, would you like something?"

He inclined his head and pulled out a chair. "A drink o' water, perha's?"

"All right." She moved away, and he gave a loud, exaggerated sigh as he settled into the chair. She halted at some distance and turned to look over her shoulder. "Anything wrong?" He stretched out his legs and crossed his ankles, his fingers laced over his belt buckle.

"No. Jus' glad to be home."

That, too, made her smile. She sniffed the flowers again, wanting to say how glad she was to have him here, but she didn't quite trust herself, so instead, she said, "The boys will be very happy to see you," and hurried away.

The kitchen was empty when she got there, but while she was poking around for a suitable container for the flowers, Ochéa came in from outside. Rebecca asked in easy Spanish if Lupe had also returned from the village with the boys, and received a positive answer before Ochéa started rattling pots and pans, all in a dither to prepare a special homecoming dinner for Don Rigo. She snatched up a clay bowl when Rebecca asked about a vase for the flowers and splashed water into it. Rebecca floated the posy in the bowl, decided it would do, and filled a cup for Rodrigo. She carried the bowl in one hand and the cup in the other on her trip back to the *sala*.

Giggles and rushed, excited Spanish greeted her even before she walked into the dining area of the big room to find Rodrigo bouncing baby Enrique upon his knee while Rodolfo poured out the story behind his scabbed lip. Lupe stood to the side, her hands pressed together indulgently, her lined face beaming. Her dark eyes danced as Rebecca moved to the table, reminding Rebecca that once again the whole village would be thinking of the romantic scenario that would normally be played out behind the closed door of Don Rigo's bedchamber.

Rebecca's insides already felt as if they were melting, and she was not yet closed behind that door with him. It occurred to her that perhaps she ought to insist that they not return to the old arrangement, but she reminded herself of the needed school supplies for which she intended to ask and decided to go carefully. Things had been awfully tense between them before Rodrigo left, and that was understandable, since she'd very nearly let him make love to her only to pull back at the last moment. A lot of men would label that teasing of the worst and most dangerous sort, but Rodrigo certainly seemed willing to let bygones be bygones now, and she was grateful for that. The problem was how to retain this amicable mood without going too far. It would help so much if she could just relax.

She made a concerted effort to shake off the physical tension. Keeping her movements smooth and measured, she placed the bowl in the center of the table and set the cup before Rodrigo. He rewarded her with a smile, his arm drawing Rodolfo to his side as Enrique attempted to climb up his chest on hands and knees.

"We ask your opinion," he said with a nod that included his elder son in the "we." "Ees a boy who figh's for de honor o' his modher ol' enou' to go witou' siesta for once an' ride to de range wit his fadher?"

His mother. She ignored the lump in her throat and smiled. "I think so." For Rodolfo's sake, she added, *"Sí. Bueno."*

The boy shook both fists in a gesture of triumph and delight. Rodrigo told him in Spanish to put on his chaps and boots and not to forget a hat, then suggested to Lupe that Enrique ought to be put down. He nuzzled the baby and promised him a surprise later on, cupping his little face in strong hands before sending him off. Lupe herded the boys out of the room, and Rodrigo settled back in his chair, cup in hand, to watch as Rebecca pulled and poked the flowers into a pleasing arrangement.

"Dey have become ver' fond o' you," he said, and she felt a genuine warmth.

"I'm very fond of them."

He took a drink from the cup. "Dey will miss you too much, I fear."

The reference to her leaving sent a chill through her, and the lump in her throat suddenly felt like a band tightening from the inside. She was walking a fine line, trying to remain upbeat while letting enough concern come through to make it believable.

"You're the center of their lives," she said. "They'll be all right, but maybe when the time comes, we should have a private word with them."

"An' esplain wha'?" he asked, waving the cup. "Dat we never inten'ed you to be dheir modher but preten'ed to for a while because eet was co'venient?"

He was clearly troubled, and she couldn't blame him. She sat down, her chin sinking onto the heel of her hand.

"We've made a real mess of this, haven't we?"

"Perha's no' so much," he answered softly. Leaning forward, he reached across the table and touched the inside of her elbow, his fingers sliding up her arm. Her breath stopped in her throat, her chin lifting from her hand. "Perha's," he went on, "we can fin' a way togedher to make t'ings righ'. I yam begin to t'ink, *querida,* dat—"

"Papá!"

Rebecca jerked back as Rodolfo ran into the room, her arm tingling where Don Rigo had touched her. His jaw clamped, a muscle flexing in the hollow of his cheek, but the next instant, he was smiling and getting to his feet. He tossed down the remaining water and placed the cup on the table, his gaze going back to Rebecca.

"We go now," he said, "but we will be back in time for dinner."

She nodded uncertainly, her fingers creeping over the spot where his had lain. "I—I'm sure Ochéa has something special planned."

His eyebrows drew together, and a finger traced the line of his mustache thoughtfully, first one side and then the other. For a second, he seemed about to speak, but then he just smiled and turned to walk toward the door, Rodolfo's hand in his.

"*¡Adiós!*" Rodolfo chimed happily, his leather chaps rubbing together as he strode beside his father.

"*Adiós, muchacho,*" Rebecca called, striving again for that carefree tone. Without thinking, she added in Spanish that he should be careful and received his *promesa* in return, evoking raised eyebrows and a pleased look from Don Rigo. She heard him say to Rodolfo as they left her that Doña Becca had improved her Spanish as well as their home, and for a moment, she wondered if he could be thinking what she had been thinking lately, that maybe she belonged here, after all. Was it really so crazy, she wondered, to think about staying? Perhaps, if it wasn't for Matthew, she might do it, but Matthew was her real family. She belonged with him, and she mustn't let herself forget that, however tempted she might be by Don Rigo and his sons.

The afternoon seemed to drag, so Rebecca didn't mind that the baby slept only fitfully and demanded more of her time than usual. She lay down with him for a little while, but found that she was too keyed-up to sleep. Just thinking about Don Rigo made her feel restless and expectant, but try as she might, she couldn't seem to keep from doing so, and Lupe certainly was of no help. Every glance she sent to Rebecca was loaded, every smile knowing. A part of her wanted to hide where the thoughts and expectations of others could not reach her, but another part, a stronger part, it seemed, wanted to be near Don Rigo. Besides, she had responsibilities now.

Others were dependent upon her for a change, including a fretting toddler. She rocked him upon her lap and sang every sweet ditty she could remember. He slept no more, but he seemed content, and she continued to lavish him with attention. It only seemed fair, after all. His brother was enjoying their father's treasured attention. Should not the baby enjoy the attention of his...mother? Funny how she'd never thought to put that word to herself before. Oh, but she was going to miss Enrique and Rodolfo! And Lupe and Clara and Glorieta and little Eustacia and Lura Espinoza. And Rodrigo. Everything always came back to Rodrigo.

Everyone was in a dither because Don Rigo had come home. Ochéa cooked right through siesta. Lupe swept the whole house with Doña Becca's broom and brought out new candles and fresh linens. She came into the bedchamber late in the day with a bucket of steaming water and hustled Rebecca into a bath. While Rebecca bathed, Lupe washed the baby and dressed him in freshly oiled sandals, black shorts and a white shirt with a flat, round collar. Afterward, he played quietly on the floor with a collection of smooth rocks painted with the images of various animals.

Lupe had laid out a simple white dress for her and Rebecca put it on while Lupe changed the bed. Full and gauzy with short, capped sleeves and a wide, scooped neckline trimmed in narrow, pale blue lace, the dress slipped on over the head and was belted with a pale blue sash that Rebecca tied in the front with a small, puffy bow. She stood before the mirror and fussed with the neckline, which seemed entirely too low and loose for safety's sake, but there seemed no solution. If she pulled the bodice tight by tugging on the skirt below the sash, the tops of her breasts were exposed, and if she loosened the bodice by tugging the skirt above the sash, the neckline gaped if she bent even slightly forward. It wouldn't do, she decided, but when she suggested a change, Lupe wouldn't hear of it and made all kinds of ex-

cuses. The green skirt and blouse had spots on them. A piece
of trim had been torn from the blue ones. The yellow had
faded unevenly, and somehow she had mislaid other things,
including Rebecca's jeans. Besides, the *señora* looked *muy
bella* in white with her golden skin and sleek hair, paled by
the sun, and the blue eyes of an angel.

"I think I have learned my Spanish too well," Rebecca
said, suddenly convinced that the white would do nicely if
she just held herself very straight and kept her shoulders
pressed back. Lupe merely smiled and offered another sug-
gestion.

Perhaps the *señor* would also like a bath before his evening meal. He had been many days and nights out-of-doors,
after all, and would not the warm water be very relaxing?
Rebecca narrowed her eyes suspiciously, but then it occurred to her that this situation might be turned to a wor-
thy purpose. She wanted to speak to Don Rigo about
supplies for the school. Perhaps assuring his good mood was
not such a bad idea, after all, especially as Lupe and Ochéa
were going to pamper him anyway. She made an instant decision. Lupe was to lay out clothes for the *señor* while Rebecca instructed Ochéa to heat the water. Also, it would be
wise to open a window and air out the place, and did Don
Rigo have a favorite wine stored in the cellar? Lupe told her
exactly where to find it and offered to keep an eye on the
baby.

Within an hour, all was prepared. The whole house waited
expectantly for Don Rigo to return with his son. Rebecca
could not prevent her own excitement from building, but
then the usual dinner hour came and went, and the minutes
continued to creep by while Don Rigo delayed his return.
Rebecca grew tense again, and again the baby responded
fretfully. He was hungry and sleepy, and the collar of his
shirt had chafed his little neck. Rebecca busied herself caring for him. There was no reason, after all, why he should
suffer. She fed him, exchanged the shirt and shorts for soft
bed clothes and kissed his tummy and tickled his toes until

he giggled. After a while, he drifted off to sleep in her lap, and she tucked him into his corner of the bed with special tenderness, for she was suddenly aware of how little time remained in which to play at being a mommy.

Ochéa had returned to her own house and the candles had burned low when at last Don Rigo returned. He came in quietly, carrying a sleeping Rodolfo, and Rebecca could see that he was tired and dirty himself from a long day in the saddle, yet he greeted her with a smile that made her forget the hours of waiting. She hurried ahead of him into the nursery and folded back the covers so he could lower the sleeping boy onto the bed. Carefully but quickly, they undressed him, slipped a nightshirt over his head and tucked him in beside his brother, who merely scratched an ear and snuggled deeper into the downy mattress.

"He wan'ed to eat wit de men," Rodrigo explained in a whisper as he led the way into the bedchamber next door. "I try to explain dat Ochéa ha' cook our dinner, but he plea'ed wit me, an' when I t'ink dat soon perha's he retur' to his aunt..." He left that and turned his attention to the tub waiting beside the bed. "*Ay,* I have dream o' a hot bat'!"

She looked up at him. "I'll reheat the water."

His hand skimmed her cheek. "You are good to come home to, Rebecca. *Gracias.*"

She bit her lip, but the smile shaped itself anyway. She turned and left him hurriedly, gliding out into the hall and along it to the covered walk and the kitchen beyond. There she found Lupe standing over an already steaming kettle. A large tray of food, complete with a carafe of wine, had been prepared and was waiting on the worktable behind her. Rebecca could only shake her head before taking the kettle from the stove. She returned to the bedchamber to find Rodrigo stripped to his pants. He took the kettle from her and slowly poured the steaming water into the cold water of the tub. She turned to leave, intending to go back to the kitchen for the food tray and linger there until he'd had ample time to bathe, but he quickly stopped her.

"Do no' go. We can talk, eh? Jus' keep your back turn a momen' longer." She could hear him shucking his jeans as he talked, and suddenly it was rather difficult to breathe. No way could she stay in that room while he sat naked in that tub.

"I—I have to get the, uh, food."

But when she opened the door, Lupe was already standing there with the tray, a mischievous gleam in her old eyes. She grinned and simply put the thing into Rebecca's hands before shuffling off toward the *sala*. Briefly Rebecca stared after her, but there wasn't much Rebecca could do without causing Lupe to wonder why a newlywed would abandon her recently returned husband when she ought to be pampering him. Gulping, she edged the door shut with her toe and backed warily toward the bed. Behind her, she could hear Rodrigo as he stepped into the tub.

"Aaaahhhh," he said, water lapping gently as he settled into the heated tub. "Jus' let me get de towel. *Bueno*. Come now. I yam decen', an' my nose has tol' my stomach dat Ochéa has cook a fine dinner for us. I fear eet will no' wait."

Rebecca closed her eyes and tried to still the trembling that softly rattled the dishes on the tray. Rodrigo hummed and soaped his hands. She thought about putting the tray down and walking out, but finally she turned. To her relief, he had draped a towel across the narrow tub, leaving only his naked chest exposed. He smiled sweetly and rinsed his hands before taking the tray from her. It was rather heavy, but he lowered it smoothly and placed it across the tub atop the towel.

"Sit," he told her, nodding toward the bed, "an' pour de wine while I try a tortilla, eh?"

He seemed fully preoccupied with the food, rolling the tortilla and using it to scoop up samples of first one dish then another. She sat and poured the wine. It was a fragrant red to which Ochéa had added chunks of oranges, limes and melon. Rodrigo drank his down in a single draught and asked for more, popping bits of *chorizo* into his mouth between words. He ate greedily, pausing to share with her only after the edge had been knocked off his hunger. She found that it was easier to relax if she talked, so while he savored the food and the wine and the bath, she snacked and sipped and chattered about all that had happened during his absence. Before too long, she worked her way around to the dictionary and the surprising revelation that Clara could read.

"Eet ees good you have made her a frien'," he said, his hunger sated at last. He had sunk down into the bath to soak his back, his long legs hanging over the sides at the other end, his wineglass in one hand. "I mus' get a bigger tub, eh? Dis one does no' let a man soak all de sore muscles a' once."

She tried to steer the conversation back onto the right course. "Actually, Clara's been more than merely a friend. She's really been a great help to me. She's the reason my Spanish has improved so much, and I was thinking, you know, that maybe she could help some of the children—"

Abruptly, he drew his legs in and pushed up into a sitting position again, water sloshing and his free hand going to the back of his neck. "Eet's really sore dhere," he said. "Eef you coul' jus' rub dhere a li'l, eh?"

Rebecca hesitated. "I, er, really want to talk about Clara and this idea we had."

"Ah," he said sheepishly. "I shoul' no' have ask. Eet ees o' no matter. You were saying?" His expression was one of benign interest, but his hand stayed on that sore muscle in his neck.

She feared it was a mistake even as she left the bed and moved to kneel beside the tub at his back. Setting her own glass upon the floor, she reasoned that he must not be distracted by a sore muscle or anything else while she put her idea to him. And if she could ease his pain, should she not do so? Carefully, she began to knead the muscles in the back of his neck with her fingertips. His skin warmed quickly to her touch, sending waves of heat up her arms through her palms.

"You are an angel," he murmured, slowly moving his head forward then back. "Umm, abou' Clara..." he prompted after a moment.

"Yes, Clara." Rebecca licked her lips. "As I said, I was, umm, pleased to find that Clara can read, and, well, we thought, Clara and I, that she could start a kind of reading class."

"A reading class?" He straightened and turned his head as if to hear better. Rebecca dropped her hands to her thighs, trying to let the tingles run out of them, but then he frowned, and she brought them back up again, tentatively working her thumbs against his spinal column as she tried to concentrate on what she must say.

"The children desperately need a school," she went on, "and reading is the foundation of education. Don't you agree?"

"*Sí.* Have I no' said de chil'ren mus' have a school?"

"Yes," she conceded, manipulating the joint at the base of his skull. "We just want to give them a beginning. It wouldn't take very much to do it, just a few supplies." She dropped her hands to his shoulders, feeling the muscles ripple beneath the skin, electric sparks shooting into her fingertips. For a second she couldn't speak. She swallowed, pushed on. "You know what I mean, a few books, some pencils and paper, maybe a chalkboard."

Her hands were beginning to tremble, and she moved them back to the base of his skull. They seemed safer there, somehow, than massaging those broad shoulders.

He mulled over what she'd said, sighing as she worked the knots out. Presently, he spoke up. "Clara ees on'y a chil' herse'f," he pointed out. "De chil'ren need a real teacher, someone to make discipline amongs' dem."

The thought Rebecca had been trying not to think for some time now fully jelled in her mind. *She* was a real teacher. *She* could "make discipline" in a classroom. But that would mean staying in La Fuente Uno, and she could only do that as Don Rigo's wife. But Don Rigo did not really want a wife. He had proved that with both Clara and Glorieta. Hadn't he? Of course, he could always change his mind, but even then he wasn't likely to choose a trouble-making gringa.

Her hands had worked their way back down to his shoulders again, and he was leaning forward, exposing the strong column of his spine and the muscles tapering toward his waist. She thought suddenly of other places her hands could touch, and heat rose all the way to her cheeks.

Besides, she told herself, there was always Matthew to consider. And she really wasn't a very good teacher, anyway. She decided to offer nothing, telling herself that she simply couldn't afford to.

"Just promise me that you'll think about it," she said, her thumbs sweeping along the curves of his shoulder blades.

"For you, Rebecca," he said softly, "I woul' promise anyt'ing."

She froze, keenly aware of the naked, masculine body that lay beneath her hands, aching to believe that he meant what he said. But it was just one of those innocent things nice people sometimes said without thinking, just one of those silly little catch phrases, just words, just...

"Somet'ing ees wrong, Rebecca?" he asked, twisting his upper body so quickly that water splashed over the rim of the tub into her lap. She gasped and fell back upon her heels. "Ah, no! Are you ver' wet?" He twisted in the other direction as if to see what damage he'd done, and his elbow sent a blade of water over her as high as her chest.

"Oh!"

"*¡Caramba!*" He snatched at the towel, pulling it around his hips as he stood. "I yam sorry, *querida*. I did no' mean—"

He broke off, staring down at her. The white gauze of her dress was plastered to her, translucent with water. Rebecca stared back, taking in all that wet brown skin, the sprinkles of crisp black hair, the molded muscles. For a long moment, neither moved while the air seemed to crackle and snap between them. Then, thankfully, as if steeling himself, he sucked in his breath, his already flat belly drawing tighter, and she was able to move her eyes away. He stepped from the tub and reached down a hand to her. She put her own in it, allowing him to pull her up and onto her feet, but when she would take her hand back, he tightened his grip.

"I yam a terr'ble liar," he said, stepping closer, and his free hand came up to pluck at her sleeve. She held herself tightly, afraid of the way her heart leapt when she looked at him. He fingered the delicate fabric. "I splash de water for a reason," he confessed, gently tugging at her sleeve. "I wan'ed to get you ou' o' your clo'hes." The dress slid off her shoulder, and his hand moved upward to bare flesh.

Rebecca felt herself swaying, her head going round and round on the inside. He wanted her! And if she moved, if she even looked at him . . .

His hand slid over her shoulder and up her neck, into her hair. "Eet ees too hard!" he whispered, his voice both sandpaper and velvet. "To wan' you, an' no' to touch you. To be so close, when I wan' on'y to be—" he swallowed "—inside!"

It was too much. She closed her eyes, all her strength draining away, and his mouth came to hers, his arm sliding around her. He was so hungry, so needful, and fire was spreading from the apex of her legs upward, from the pinnacle of her mouth downward. To be wanted so! She hadn't known she could be wanted like this, that any woman could elicit such passion.

His hands moved over her body, and it seemed that even her skin was hot now, the palms of her hands, the soles of her feet. She wouldn't have been surprised if steam had risen off her sodden clothing. But with all this heat, how could she tremble? How could she jerk and quiver when he broke apart their mouths, his hands sliding up to hold her face? It was against all reason, this burning and shivering, but still her skin prickled when his hands then moved to the sash at her waist, slipped the knot from the bow and let it fall away. Slowly, gently, he gathered the delicate gauze, lifting it up and up, her arms floating upward with it until it whispered over them, a cloud against her hair, and then was gone. Her arms drifted downward, but he met them and, with a single stroke of his fingertips, urged them to stay aloft a moment longer. Carefully, tenderly, he reached around her and un-hooked her bra. When she lowered her arms, it slid away and she found to her wonder that she no longer shook and the fire in her middle was liquid and throbbing, her body knowing with certainty what her mind was only beginning to understand.

She was meant to be wanted. She was made for this, and maybe, in some part of her, she had known it all along. She knew for certain only that she no longer had the will to fight it, if ever she had, and so became a partner to it, helpless to be otherwise. She thought no more of Matthew or tomorrow or what she had left behind, of children or schools or bargains made in desperation. She thought only of touching him, of sating every desire, filling every need. She touched his cheek, such a simple thing: an arm that bends, a hand that opens, fingers that extend, skin that meets skin. And now he trembled, a small wavering that became a great, racking shudder. Something in him seemed to break free. He ground his teeth, then swept her up into his arms, his head bending so his mouth could taste the curve of her neck, the tip of her chin, an earlobe.

He turned to the bed. One step, and he bent, sweeping away the clothing that had been laid out for him, ripping at the towel that cloaked him. She was on her back, her arms opened to him, and he was coming down to her. A hand took his weight on the mattress, an elbow. His brown eyes glittered red with reflected candlelight. His black hair set-tled about his lean face in damp, gleaming curls. His mouth parted, and she smiled in welcome.

Then a child screamed into the night. *"¡Mamá!"*

Not *"Papá"* but *"Mamá,"* and not the smooth, solemn tones of Rodolfo. Enrique screamed, wailed, his little voice a keen of pain and fear and need.

Rebecca's head turned automatically to the nursery door, and her heart contracted. He had called her *"Mamá,"* and something was terribly, horribly wrong. She looked at Rodrigo, unaware of the emotion written in raw, bold strokes upon her face. She said, "The baby!"

Already Rodrigo was pushing back, his arm straightening as he levered his weight away from the bed. She sat up, one leg jacknifing beneath the other, a hand to her hair. He threw his shirt at her, the shirt Lupe had laid out, and stepped into his pants. She fumbled with the shirt, pulling it on over her head and scrambling off the bed. He met her at the door, a single look conveying the sense of loss he felt, and together they stepped into the narrow room.

"¡Mamá! ¡Mamá!" Enrique sat up on the bed, his back to the wall, the plump fingers of his left hand working frantically at his ear. A shaken Rodolfo was trying to quiet him. Half lying, he patted the tear-streaked face with a wobbly hand. Rebecca gathered the child to her, feeling at once the hot, dry skin, the panic in that small body.

"Oh, God, he has a fever! Rodrigo, he's sick!"

Rodolfo blurted something and lurched toward the foot of the bed.

"No!" Rodrigo commanded, softening the bark with fatherly hands placed upon his son's shoulders. Rodolfo sat back on his heels. Rodrigo looked at the baby wailing against Rebecca's shoulder. His smooth brow wrinkled with worry. "I will go for Glorieta," he decided, and moved away.

Rebecca's hand shot out and found his wrist. "Put on a shirt!" she heard herself insisting, so surprised that she let him go again. He gaped at her, then a smile broke across his face and he bent to kiss her hard on the mouth.

"I go for Glorieta because she know de herbs an' *medicinas,"* he told her reassuringly, and he stroked first her cheek, then the baby's. "Beside, you wear my shirt." He grinned and ran out on bare feet. She knew then how much she loved him, but all else was confusion and fear as the baby wailed and rocked and wrapped his right hand in a pale lock of her hair.

"*Madre*," Rodolfo whimpered softly, "*yo no puedo ayudar.*" I cannot help.

She put her arm about him and kissed the top of his head. "*Puedes rezar*, Rodolfo," she whispered. "You can pray."

Chapter Fourteen

Rodrigo crouched beside the narrow bed and petted the sleepy child whose cheek lay against Rebecca's shoulder.

"Eet ees but a *furúnculo* een de *niño*'s ear," he said softly. "Painful, *sí*, but no' dangerous."

"I understand," Rebecca told him, pressing the warm cloth to the little one's aching ear, "but the fever worries me. The infection could go beyond the boil. I'll just feel better if I stay with him. Besides, Rodolfo's already asleep in your...our bed."

She glanced to where Glorieta stood with her back against the wall, remembering only then that the woman did not understand English. It was not the slip of tongue that really bothered her, however. She was jealous of the sultry woman, even though Glorieta had proven herself a friend and Don Rigo was quietly pleading with Rebecca to return to his bed. She didn't like herself for it, but the truth was that she hated the idea of Glorieta having shared Don Rigo's bed when she herself must not. Despite what had almost happened, Rebecca knew she must not get back in that bed. Rodrigo obviously did not share her conviction, however.

"Rodolfo will sleep better here wit his brodher," he was saying. Rebecca could see that he was wavering between anger and frustration.

She bit her lip, knowing it was cowardly of her to take this way out, but she'd had some time to think now, and she just wasn't sure what he was asking of her or on what basis she was willing to give. And there was the baby to consider. He had screamed so and fought with all his puny strength when Glorieta had first attempted to apply the heat to his ear. Only his *mamá* had been able to quiet him and eventually draw the poison from the boil. He slept now against her shoulder, and the powder Glorieta had given him from the infirmary had driven away his fever, but Rebecca was not convinced that such an awful experience could be over and done with so quickly. She could not leave him just now.

"We just can't be sure," she told Rodrigo, and watched his jaw clamp and flex, but then he gazed upon his son and his dark face softened.

"You will wan' anodher hot compress," he said, his voice thick with capitulation. "I will bring eet fro' de ki'chen."

She laid her hand against his cheek. "Thank you."

He merely nodded and rose to his feet. Glorieta came forward as he brushed past her, a tattered shawl clutched about her shoulders.

"*No te preocupes,*" she said gently, understanding enough to know that Rebecca was still worried for the child. "*El niño está bien. El médico estará aquí cuanto antes y él te puede decir.*"

"*El médico,*" Rebecca repeated dully. Had Glorieta just said that the doctor would come soon to reassure her? "*¿Un médico viene aquí?*"

"*Sí,*" Glorieta confirmed, going on to say again that the doctor would find the baby well when he came. The coming of a doctor to La Fuente Uno was a surprise to Rebecca, but now that she thought about it, it made sense. Why else would the village have built an infirmary, and who but a doctor could have trained Glorieta in the dispensing of medications? She was glad to know that Glorieta's expertise had some basis in genuine learning, and equally glad that the doctor would come shortly to confirm the woman's diagnosis, but Rebecca was curious, too. She asked for the doctor's name.

"Roberto," Glorieta answered idly, bending to straighten the contents of the herb basket she had set upon the bed earlier. "*Nosotros lo llamamos* Dr. Bob."

Bob? That made Rebecca tilt her head thoughtfully. Who ever heard of a Mexican called Bob? She watched Glorieta drape a checkered cloth over the basket.

"Glorieta," she queried, "*¿es este médico gringo?*"

"*Sí, un americano.*" Glorieta straightened and smiled at Rebecca, whose mouth was slowly falling open.

An American! An American doctor who traveled a circuit similar to that of Padre Tomás? It was possible, wasn't it? If it was true, he would know every American in the area, especially an American who lived in San Benito! He would know Matthew. He had to! Her heart was beating like a bass drum. Matthew was her haven, a safe port in a storm of confusion, and yet . . . What excuse would she have to stay once she'd found him? She tightened her arms about the baby. Would Rodrigo even try to keep her? Did he want her that much? She wanted to believe that a dissolution of the marriage would be out of the question if they slept together, that Rodrigo had no intention of deceiving Padre Tomás, but were they not already embroiled in a deception many times that magnitude? She didn't know what to think anymore.

Rodrigo came into the room, carrying a small metal basin that steamed with hot water. He set it carefully upon the bed and gingerly plucked out the cloth, wringing it as best he could, the hot water reddening the brown skin of his fingers.

"Cuidadosamente, querida," he said, trading cloths with her. "Eet ees ver' hot."

Gently she placed the warm, moist cloth over the baby's ear. He stirred but quieted again, sighing deeply. She smiled at his father. "Thank you."

He smiled back and stroked the little hand that lay against her arm. He seemed about to speak, but she didn't want to give him the chance to bring up their sleeping arrangements again, and she simply couldn't go on wondering.

"Rodrigo," she began, "Glorieta says there's an American doctor coming here in a few days."

The information seemed to take him off guard. He straightened, one hand going to his hip, the other smoothing back his hair, and he looked to Glorieta. She obviously didn't have a clue as to what was going on. He turned back to Rebecca with an expression of ambivalence on his face.

"I yam sure de boy will be well by de time he comes," he said.

"Then he is coming?" she pressed. "An American doctor is coming here?"

Rodrigo shrugged. "He come abou' ever' eigh' weeks."

"From where?"

He leveled his dark gaze and said carefully, "From San Benito."

Rebecca caught her breath. "He'll know Matthew," she stated flatly. "Rodrigo, he'll know Matthew. He's got to!" The baby stirred as her voice rose, and she made a concerted effort to relax, to keep her tone low and even. "Why didn't you think of this before? We could've contacted him."

He put a hand to his head, thumb and forefinger at his temples. "I—I do no' know," he said. "I . . . believe me, Rebecca, eef I had t'ought o' de doctor I woul' have send someone. I jus' did no' t'ink!" He seemed to have a sudden inspiration. "I will take you to him," he said. "We will no' wait for him to come. We will go to him! H-he alway' go firs' to La Fuente Dos. *Mañana* I take you dhere.' "

She was both appalled and elated. She was going to find Matthew, but Rodrigo didn't want her. It was as if he suddenly couldn't wait to be rid of her. She knew now what she had wanted to hear: that he couldn't bear to let her go, that he had no intention of losing her to Matthew or anyone else, that he wanted her for his wife in his heart as well as his bed. She felt perilously close to tears.

"Wh-what about the roundup?" she asked, rocking to and fro with the child.

"We can go dhere an' back before eet ees done," he said, "een two days eef we travel *rápidamente.*"

She could only stare, wondering which of them he was making this trip for, which he was trying to save, her or himself? She swallowed around a thickening in her throat.

"All right," she agreed softly. "If Enrique's okay tomorrow, then we'll go."

Rodrigo bowed his head, but whether from relief or something else she couldn't tell, and she wasn't even certain that she wanted to know. All that mattered now was finding Matthew, not that it had ever changed, really. It was just that for a moment, she had imagined it could.

"Get some sleep," Rodrigo muttered, turning away. "We all need some res'. I take Glorieta home an' return."

Rebecca nodded and looked at the toddler sleeping peacefully against her shoulder. Yes, they all needed peace and rest, but she knew in her heart that it would be a very long time before she could sleep like a baby again. A very long time.

Rodrigo clenched his fists and looked away. He couldn't bear to watch Rebecca bid the children goodbye. It was too much as if she would never return, and also, he was nervous that the doctor would arrive before he could get her away from the village. She would know then that he had lied, and it was very likely that she would hate him for it. But what was he to do? He had truly forgotten about the physician's impending visit. It was just routine, after all, and he'd had so much on his mind. Then suddenly Rebecca had asked him about the American doctor from San Benito, and he had realized that the doctor would undoubtedly know Matthew Harper, and if Matthew was in San Benito, then Rebecca would leave him before he had an opportunity to make her want to stay. This could be his last chance.

It was for this reason that he had ridden out at daybreak to ask Pacíno and Alonzo to accompany him and his wife to the small outpost called La Fuente Dos—Spring Two—where a handful of people, three families and a very old man, kept watch over the source of the rancho's lifeblood, the water that trickled from the ground. The doctor always visited there—on his way back to San Benito, *after* he had visited La Fuente Uno and the small Loma holdings to the northeast. By taking Rebecca there now, Rodrigo hoped to keep her from seeing the doctor at all, or at least until he could convince her that life with him could be good.

He wasn't fooling himself. He knew that he had nothing to offer her that could compare with Los Angeles, nothing except love and passion, the kind that seldom came twice in a lifetime. He had known it and knew how truly precious it was. Somehow he had to make her know it, too. He had to show her. And so he had lied and made a plan. It was a plan that would work, he told himself as he heard her footsteps coming toward him across the courtyard. He had to believe it would work.

Jaqueca, the mare, snickered as Rebecca drew near, and bobbed her shaggy head. Rodrigo pushed the mare's muzzle down and turned to give Rebecca his most casual smile and helped her up into the saddle. She was wearing jeans and a soft yellow T-shirt beneath an old serape of Lupe's. On her feet were the *teguas* Fernando had made for her, and

Paco's best hat, made of white straw in the cowboy style and banded with snakeskin, sat on the back of her head. She was very beautiful, more beautiful even than on their wedding day, and she had taken away his breath then and made an ache in his groin. He ached now. It seemed to him that he had ached in this way since the night he had found her.

She swung up into the saddle with more ease than he would have expected and leaned over to pat the skittish mare with her left hand, her right firmly gripping the reins. He let his own hand linger a moment upon her thigh before mounting El Pescado. He waved to his children, happy to see Enrique toddling about ahead of Clara, his sweet little self again. Even the illness of his child he had worked to his advantage, giving him an excuse to delay their departure for several hours, ostensibly to insure that the boy was well enough to be left behind, but in reality to guarantee that they would have to spend the night on the trail. Rebecca had been agreeable. In fact, her enthusiasm for the trip seemed to have waned, and he hoped that this was a good sign. He knew that she had come to care deeply for his sons, and he was not above using even this to keep her with him, but he wanted it to be more than that. He wanted her to love him. He wanted her to want him. Tonight, he told himself, looking around at the little party of travelers.

"We ride," he said, but his thoughts were of the night.

Rebecca stretched and squirmed, hoping to alleviate the stiffness in her back. All day she had been remembering the ride across the desert and how easy Don Rigo had made it for her. Of course, she hadn't thought so at the time, but she realized now that he had spared her every possible inconvenience. It had been easier riding double on El Pescado, almost in Don Rigo's lap, than on this spirited mare with her tendency to lunge at the other horses. The trail was very different, too, all rock and narrow, winding ledges slashed with odd sorts of vegetation and slides of broken shale. It was cooler than the desert, but the glare of the sun had been pitiless most of the day, forcing her to keep her head down and Paco's hat pulled forward while she hauled at the reins to control the mare, hence the strain on her back and the growing stiffness. But perhaps her discomfort was more than that. She didn't want to think of why she was making this trip or what might come of it or how Rodrigo could be so cheerful when she felt so troubled and disappointed.

It had been hard to say goodbye this morning. Rodolfo had asked over and over again when they were coming home and if he couldn't go along on the next trip, while Enrique had kept avoiding the hot compress now that the pain in his ear was no longer excruciating. He didn't even want to be held; he wanted to flirt and tease, peeking out from behind Clara's skirt, and be chased, squealing, across the courtyard. They had no idea, those precious ones, that their time with her was growing painfully short. How could she tell them that she had never meant to be their mother? She'd never meant to care so much about them or to miss them when she'd gone, and she'd never meant to love their father.

Don Rigo rode ahead on El Pescado, his back straight as a rod, and occasionally she heard him whistling. It seemed to her that they were just plodding along, and after the late start they'd gotten, too. Riding single file didn't exactly invite conversation, though, so she'd not been able to ask anybody how much farther the second village might be or when they might arrive. She felt vaguely irritated with the whole thing, and it didn't seem to help to remind herself that every clop of the horse's hooves was bringing her closer to Matthew. But Matthew was family and she belonged with him. She was telling herself—again—that everything would work out fine once she'd found Matt, when the trail suddenly rounded a curve and sloped steeply upward to a flat, wide bowl at the top of the mountain.

The riders behind her surged forward and sent their mounts scampering up the slope, joining Don Rigo. The little mare struggled along, with Rebecca hauling back on the reins lest her mount catch up with and butt one of the other horses, while up ahead, Don Rigo and his men seemed to be conferring. As soon as the mare gained a steady foothold at the top of the slope, Pacíno and Alonzo put their mounts into a canter and rode away, disappearing into a notch on the far side of the mountaintop depression.

"Where are they going?" Rebecca asked, riding up as Don Rigo was dismounting.

"Eh? Ah, dey wish to check some o' de range up dis way. Alonzo has a brodher who has no' repor'ed een some time, so dey t'ink to look for him."

"I see. So how long will we be here?"

"For de nigh'."

"The *night?*"

"*Sí.* We camp for de nigh'. Eet come pronto up here."

"But shouldn't we press on to La Fuente Dos?"

"An' ride een de dark o'er such rough groun' as dis?" he scoffed, loosening the cinch on his saddle. "No, *señora.* Eet ees better we stay here. Beside, you have no' seen de sky from dis place at nigh'. Eet ees a t'ing you will reme'ber all your life."

He lifted the saddle, bags, roll and all, from the horse's back and slung it to the ground, then quickly slid the bridle from El Pescado's head and sent him off with a whack on his rump. The proud animal whinnied and kicked up his hind legs as he galloped away, stopping nearby to crop at a tall clump of yellow grass.

"Won't he run?" she asked, but Don Rigo shook his head.

"Naw, he like de grass here. An' dis place ees a kin' o' nat'ral—how you say eet?—corral."

"That's how you say it," she muttered.

The mare blew impatiently, and Rebecca climbed down, though not completely resigned. Don Rigo flashed her a smile and moved in to begin uncinching her saddle. She was more stiff than she realized and began to stretch her muscles gingerly.

"You shoul' walk aroun'," he told her. "Go on. I can set up camp."

"You sure you don't mind?"

"Go on," he urged, working at that cinch. "Perha's you will pick up some de' wood, eh?"

"Okay. I'll take a look around."

She wandered off, her hands easing the pull in her back. It was a pretty place, a kind of a crater with a few small bushy trees poked in among the rocks and grasses waving over the sand. She found a secluded place behind a small hillock and emptied her bladder, surprised to find that this eased a good deal of her soreness, then wandered on, picking up twigs and small, dry branches for the fire. Her arms were full of spindly pieces of wood and the shadows were lengthening in a blue-gray fringe all around the lip of the hollow when she returned to Don Rigo.

He had chosen a sandy spot against the northern rim and laid a small ring of rocks in its center, with some bigger ones rolled nearby for sitting upon. He'd placed his hat atop one, and next to it he'd spread a large piece of hide, upon which he laid a frying pan, tin plates and several small unopened bundles, along with a canteen, a pair of metal cups and a coffeepot. He came to meet her, taking the dry twigs and branches from her arms despite her protest that they weren't heavy.

"You did good," he said, leading her back to the fire ring. "Sit down. I make us some food, eh?"

"Don't be silly. I can do that," she replied, but he wasn't having any of it. He dropped the wood and physically urged her to follow his instructions, his hands placed upon her upper arms.

"I wan' to do eet," he declared, guiding her into a sitting position upon the nearest rock. He seemed very tall, standing over her there, and she felt that familiar heat building inside her again. He seemed to sense it, for he quickly moved away, going to the hide mat and squatting beside it. "Le's see wha' Lupe pack for us, eh?"

He uncovered bacon and a yellow squash, an onion, a can of beans and some pickled eggs, cornmeal, coffee, mashed peas, a sliced *jícama,* a potatolike vegetable tasting something like a tart apple, wrapped in lettuce leaves, and several peeled *nopalitos*—cactus pieces—swimming in a vinegary dressing. And, of course, there were tortillas and oranges, but the real treat was two bottles of commercial beer. Don Rigo exclaimed over those as he set them aside in a cool place, blessing Lupe for her thoughtfulness.

He went to work, making idle conversation as he put together a salad and cut up pieces of bacon and onion to cook with the beans. Soon he'd made a proper meal and pried the tops from the beer bottles with his knife. He sat with Rebecca before the fire, their plates on their knees, and they both ate heartily as the night gathered gently around them. It was a quiet, easy time marked by good but simple food and effortless talk.

Afterward, at Don Rigo's insistence, Rebecca sat on her rock, one knee drawn up and her hands clasped about it, and stared at the breathtaking canvas of the night sky while he cleaned up. It was, indeed, a stirring sight. The sky seemed endless, flung with brilliant stars whose light was unimpeded by cloud or artificial light, and when the moon rose over the rim of their little valley, it was huge and oval and the color of milk. She felt as though she could reach out and touch it or step off onto its mottled surface and ride it high into the sky.

"Ees eet no' *bello?* Rodrigo asked, coming to spread a blanket on the sand beside her.

"*Encantador,*" she agreed. "Absolutely enchanting."

He sat beside her and drew up his knees, forearms balanced atop them. "I wan'ed to bring you here," he said. "Eet ees a special place. De Indians call eet Lo Más Alto del Mundo, de Top o' de Worl'."

It occurred to her suddenly that they were alone here in this beautiful place, and though he had not touched her, the skin on her arm seemed to crawl with anticipated feeling. She thought she'd done enough stargazing for a while.

"Uh, listen, when are the others coming back?" she asked as casually as possible.

"Ah." He shifted position and began to pull off his boots. "De odhers are no' coming back," he said evenly.

"Not coming back! But why?"

He set his boots aside and lay back upon the blanket, his arms folded behind his head. "I ask dem no' to," he admitted lightly.

"You . . ." She twisted around, dumbfounded. "Why?"

His dark eyes met hers. "Because," he said softly, "I canno' let you go until we have made love."

She didn't say a word. She just got up and walked away. He got up and followed her.

"Eet mus' be, Rebecca," he said softly. "I coul' no' live my life wondering wha' eet woul' be like for us, an' I do no' believe dat you coul'."

"Well, you just don't know me very well, then!" she retorted, hugging herself.

He stepped closer and swept the hat from her head, tossing it away. Her hand went automatically to her hair, but before she had time for further reaction, he took her face in his hands, tilted it back and kissed her. She thought she'd collapse, just fall to pieces right there, but he suddenly released her and ripped open his shirt, peeling it off and letting it fall to the ground.

"I know you wan' me," he said, sliding his hands down her arms. "An' I have thought o' not'ing else since de nigh' I foun' you." He moved his hands to her shoulders, lifted the serape over her head and dropped it. She was having trouble breathing, and her heart was pounding so hard that it hurt, but she brushed at her hair and attempted to move away. He followed, and when she stopped, he took her in his arms.

"Rodrigo, please..." she began. "We said we wouldn't..."

"I know," he whispered, nuzzling her cheek, "but, Rebecca, I have try no' to feel dese t'ings, jus' as you have, an' eet ees no good. I lis'en een my head to all de reasons why I shoul' no' touch you, but I can no' make me believe dem. I know you will leave me soon. I will no' keep you agains' your will, but I canno' bear to le' you go like dis." He placed a kiss beside her mouth and another against her ear and a third in her hair. "We are alone a' de top o' de worl', *mi vida,* an' eef we do no' take dis momen', eet may never come again. Can you live wit dat? Because I canno'!"

He took her mouth again, carefully parting her lips and sliding his tongue between them, and she felt that heat spreading inside of her, growing hotter by the moment. She told herself she had to get away from him, but his tongue was pressing insistently against her teeth, and she could not resist parting them for him and feeling his tongue slide into the wet sheath of her mouth. Her hands wandered upward, stroked his hair, moved downward, coming to rest at his nape, and for an instant, it seemed to her that her knees had buckled, but then she realized that his strong arms were bearing her up, carrying her back to the blanket spread upon the soft sand. She ran her hands over his back, feeling the heat rise from his bare skin, delighting in the passion that stoked it. He was her husband, her love. Why shouldn't she give herself to him? Perhaps if she did, he would not let her go at all. But if she had to leave him, was it so wrong to have this one night, this one joining?

He set her back on her feet, breaking the kiss, and with great concentration he peeled the T-shirt up and over her head. His hands manacled her wrists and slid down her arms, his mouth finding hers again. She let her arms come down around his neck and leaned into him. He pushed her away, bending to trail his mouth over her chin and neck as his hands worked behind her. She felt the band of her bra go suddenly slack and his hands sliding the straps from her shoulders. She withdrew her arms and dropped the bra upon the rock where she had sat earlier, while he went down on his knees. An instant later, she sucked in her breath and caught her lip between her teeth as his mouth teased first one swollen breast then the other, while his hands journeyed to the waistband of her jeans, parting the snap and sliding the zipper open. He breathed fire into her navel and put it out with his tongue before settling down to slip her shoes from her feet, his hands coming back up to tug at her jeans, his mouth exploring every newly exposed inch of flesh until she gasped and convulsed, her fingers pushing into his hair.

He shoved her jeans down around her ankles, and she stepped out of them as he peeled her panties down, then slowly rose to his feet. He kissed her, running his hands over her body from her waist downward, between her legs and up again, to cup the fullness of each breast and move on to her face before falling away. He nipped at her lips with his teeth, sucked her tongue into his mouth and splayed his hands over her buttocks, crushing her hard against his thrusting pelvis, only to break away again and swiftly unbutton his own jeans, shucking them in one fluid movement. Finally they stood together, as naked as at birth, and he took her hands into his.

"Touch me," he said, guiding her. She felt the sharp intake of his breath as her hands closed around him, then he was sagging, his arms pulling her down with him until they lay side by side upon the blanket, their hands exploring each other's bodies. It was too late to go back, even if she had wanted to. It simply didn't matter anymore why this shouldn't be happening, and so she not only let it happen but made it happen, giving of herself in a way she had never done before.

Later, much later, she lay on her back, feeling his weight atop her as he thrust into her, joining their bodies yet again. That wonderful, heady ecstasy was building once more, and in her exhaustion, she seemed to be floating. She turned her face up to the incredibly vast sky, her eyelids shuttering as the first of a deliciously long chain of dizzying waves flowed over her, and when she lifted them again, it seemed to her that she was there among the stars, floating dreamily above the top of the earth. Only dimly did she hear him cry out, and the shuddering that followed seemed distant though she clasped him in her arms.

Then from a faraway place came the words, whispers in a sultry wind. "Rebecca. *Mi esposa. Mi amor.*" My wife. My love.

She woke in the morning to the patient blowing of horses and the pleasant weight of Rodrigo's arm and leg enveloping her body as they lay together, nestled like spoons. He had risen in the night and covered them with a second blanket, and it was lovely and warm there beneath it with the steady rise and fall of his chest rocking her gently. She hated to get up, but she was aching in certain parts of her body, and the brilliant, crystalline sun was already peeking over the rim of the top of the world. It was time.

She slipped from his embrace into the clean morning air and quickly dressed, at peace with her world and bubbling inside. She was sore, but it was a lovely kind of soreness she had never known before, and she hugged herself, happy with it. Silently, she went about her morning ablutions, then made coffee, cooked bacon and fried squaw bread in the grease. She didn't even know he was awake until he sat up and extended a hand to her.

"Come back to bed," he urged, and she was tempted, very tempted, but the sun was throwing its blinding rays into the bowl at the top of the world, and she knew that if she went back to bed she wouldn't get up again for many hours. She shook her head, smiling, and tended her skillet.

"You have a rancho to run, *señor.*"

He groaned and threw off the blanket, getting to his feet, naked as the day. She averted her eyes, remembering the hard, rugged planes of his body.

"I a'mire your streng'h o' will, my wife," he told her teasingly, pulling on his jeans. "I coul' no' have resis'ed such a' inv'tation from you. Were I no' wearing your scratches and deaf een my ear from your cries, I woul' t'ink I had no' please you."

She flipped a hot lump of corn bread at him. He caught it, baubled it and popped it into his mouth, then came to squat behind her and wrap her in his arms, kissing the back of her neck.

"I will dream o' las' nigh' all de res' o' my life," he whispered, and she put her head back to let him have her mouth.

"You pleased me very much," she admitted, and he chuckled into her ear.

"I woul' like to please you ver' much again righ' now, but . . ." He sighed. "I have a rancho to run, an' dey will be ezpec'ing us een La Fuente Dos. Later, eh?"

He got up and moved away, returning later to help himself to coffee, bread and oranges. Afterward, he saddled the horses while she rolled up and bundled their goods. They mounted up and rode through the break in the rim in the bowl at the top of the world, winding downward to a small valley below.

The sun was high when they dismounted at the little spring. Pacíno and Alonzo had arrived ahead of them and stood nearby, accompanied by three men and two women. A number of small children darted in and out of the four small buildings that comprised the community. A very old man came forward, his hat in his hand.

"Welcome, Don Rigo." He grinned at Rebecca and bobbed a stiff bow. "Welcome, *señora.*"

"*Gracias,*" she returned, and Don Rigo slipped an arm about her shoulders, remarking in Spanish that he and his wife were pleased to visit them. Suddenly everyone was talking. One woman exclaimed over the color of Rebecca's hair and the other came forward to offer a drink from the spring, while their husbands crowded around with various comments of their own. The old man said how the people of La Fuente Dos were saddened not to have been invited to the wedding, but Don Rigo only laughed and said something about impatience. Then he moved behind Rebecca and slid his arms about her waist.

"You will definitely be invited to the baptism of our first child," he said in rapid Spanish.

It struck her then that she could, indeed, be carrying his baby, and her own rashness stunned her, but no more than his calm acceptance of this possibility. She was truly his wife, then. The game had become reality, after all. She wanted to take his face in her hands and tell him how very much she loved him, wondering why she had not done so before. Instead, she smiled and thought of what later would bring.

Pacíno excused himself and pushed into the group to gain his *jefe*'s ear. Rebecca caught none of it, but she saw Alonzo mount up, and turned inquiring eyes on her husband. He frowned and sighed.

"I yam sorry, *querida,*" he said softly, his gaze dropping away. "De doctor has come and gone. We have miss him."

"It's all right," she said, touching his face to show him that she understood. "We'll find Matthew one day." He turned his lips into her palm before giving his attention once more to their hosts.

Rebecca stood at his side, her hand in his, and smiled. They would find Matthew one day, and when they did, she would introduce him to her husband, her wonderful, charming, enchanting, romantic husband. She hoped, wherever he was, that Matthew was as happy at that moment as she was.

Chapter Fifteen

It was dusk when they rode into the courtyard of the *casa,* and already a light burned in the window of the *sala.* They dismounted and walked hand in hand into the house.

"*Padre!*" Rodolfo cried, flinging himself down from the table. "*Madre!*" But instead of flying to them, he ran away, calling out for Lupe, and instead of Lupe, Clara appeared, fresh tears starting from her eyes.

She fell upon Rebecca's neck, crying, "*¡Gracias a Dios!*" And then, before Rodrigo could stop her, she seized Rebecca's hands and gasped, "*¡Tu hermano ha sido apuñalado!*"

Rebecca reeled backward, crying out, a hand flying to her cheek. Matthew had been stabbed! She felt Rodrigo's arms go about her and heard him sharply rebuke poor, dramatic Clara, demanding her silence, but the news had rendered Rebecca numb, and it all passed by in a fog. She could only think how desperately she had wanted news of Matthew, but not this. She looked at Clara and thought that it couldn't be true. What could that girl know of Matthew Harper? And yet, somehow, she did know. Rebecca could see it in her dark, troubled eyes. She swayed, feeling dizzy, and sat down hard on the chair Don Rigo pulled out for her.

Matthew had been stabbed! Her head was reeling. Was he dead, then? Oh, God, don't let him be dead! Where had it happened, anyway? And why? And how had Clara come by the news? She realized suddenly that if Don Rigo sent the girl away, as he was trying to do even then, her questions would go unanswered, and she couldn't bear that. She got a hold of herself, curling her fingers into her palm, and lifted her chin.

"Rodrigo, leave that child alone," she commanded, her voice shrill and hard. She saw him go rigid, saw his hands balling into fists, his head coming up sharply. But then his tension seemed to dwindle and he relaxed. When he turned to her, his expression was warm and mobile.

"Rebecca," he began, all reason and concern and patience, "you shou' res' now. You are tire, an' de chi'd knows no' o' what she speaks."

"But I have to know about my brother," she insisted.

"Let me do dis," he said, spreading his hands expansively. "Do no' trouble yourse'f. Eet ees pro'ably all wron'. You know how Clara ees. I will ask her an' see eef she ees perha's co'fused, eh?"

He smiled indulgently, too indulgently, so indulgently that it had a shade of panic about it, and the longer she held his gaze, the more panicked he became. It struck her suddenly that Rodrigo knew more than he was saying, but what? She turned it over in her mind, and came up with a question. How, she asked herself, had Clara come by news of her brother? And then she knew, but it couldn't be because Don Rigo had said the doctor would be in La Fuente Dos. He had taken her there to meet the gringo doctor. Or had he? She cocked her head to one side, trying to gauge his reaction very carefully.

"Clara, listen," she said in Spanish, her eyes never leaving Rodrigo's face, "how do you know about my brother?" Rodrigo bowed his head as Clara confirmed that she had spoken to the doctor only that afternoon, shortly before he had left. Rebecca sat back in her chair, her heart pounding with dread. "Clara," she asked, "does the doctor usually go to La Fuente Dos before or after he visits here?"

The girl was truly puzzled. She twisted her fingers together as she made her reply. "The doctor comes from the south," she said, "so, of course, he comes here first. Then naturally he goes to the Loma ranch and after that to the village of the second spring."

Rodrigo ground his teeth and walked away. Rebecca slumped in her chair, her thoughts too heavy, and tried to retain control of her trembling body. He had lied. Don Rigo had lied. He had taken her to the Top of the World knowing that the doctor would come and go in their absence. But why? Only to seduce her? He need not have cost her news of Matthew for that. Matthew. She fixed her thoughts on Matthew, her anchor still. Mechanically, she pulled the whole story from the girl, who fidgeted as she spoke, uncertain what was happening here.

Nearly four months earlier, the gringo doctor had treated Matthew Harper for a stab wound in San Benito. The wound had been a nasty one, very close to the heart, and the doctor had been quite concerned, for the patient had balked at the idea of going to the Little Sisters of Charity for the proper nursing care. He had wandered off into the night after only a few hours rest with an obviously inebriated young woman. The doctor had not seen Matthew Harper since but supposed that he still lived in San Benito, for the simple reason that he had not heard rumors of a gringo's death. Not yet.

Horrified to the point of tears, Rebecca nevertheless thanked Clara and sent the girl home. When the bewildered girl had gone, she lifted her gaze to Don Rigo.

"I must go to San Benito at once," she said briskly, her voice shaking.

Don Rigo turned, his face inscrutable, the pronounced rise and fall of his chest the only indication of his mood. He looked her straight in the eye and said, "No."

The word rocked her. First lies, and now a refusal. How dare he! "I have to go!" she insisted. "He's been hurt! He could be dead—or dying!"

"I can no' take you to San Benito now," he ground out. "I will no'!"

She squared her shoulders. "I'll go without you, then."

Suddenly he was there, bending over her, his arms trapping her in the chair. "No!" he shouted. "You can no' go! I will no' allow eet!"

"Allow?" Her mouth dropped open, anger surging through her. She pushed up to her feet, fighting him for room to stand, shoving him backward. "How dare you! And after what you've done! How dare you say I cannot go!"

"Because I yam your husban'!"

It seemed they were both stunned by what had tumbled out of his mouth. They just looked at each other, and for an instant she felt joy struggling to rise in her chest. Did he love her, then? Was that what this was about? He seemed to be expecting her to speak, but to say what? Her brow furrowed with confusion, and his face hardened, his jaw clamping stubbornly. It was the look of a man ready to bully another to have what he wanted, and suddenly she was angry again, words flowing out of her like water through a spigot.

"If you think just because I slept with you that you can suddenly tell me if and what I can do, then you'd better think again, because—"

She never finished. He wheeled and strode to the door, yanking it open with such force the hinges rattled. He glared at her, his hand on the latch, and she put her hands to her head, so confused and angry and frightened that she didn't know which way to turn or which emotion to give precedence. The man on whom she had depended for so many weeks now, the man who had come to mean so much to her was walking out, and she didn't know whether to run after him or to let him go. She stood rooted, frozen by indecision, and he turned to her a face so angry and wounded that her heart seemed to stop.

"Then I yam no' your husban'," he vowed raggedly, "an' you are no' my wife—an' las' nigh' never happen at all!"

The door slammed at his back, the sound reverberating throughout the silent house, and still she was frozen in place, until finally it came to her that he had actually gone.

It was a long, miserable night. Rebecca sobbed, alternating between anger and dread and a sense of great loss, worrying first about Matthew and whether or not he had died of that stab wound and how it had all happened to begin with, and next about Rodrigo and what had driven him to deceive her and ruin the memory of his lovemaking and, worst of all, dash the hope she had nurtured from the moment she had lain down with him. She sobbed and gave disjointed snippets of the mess to Lupe, who tried to comfort her and wound up shedding tears herself and finally went, near daybreak, for Clara in hopes of cheering *La Doña*.

Clara succeeded somewhat in putting many of Rebecca's worst fears to rest. It was reasonable, was it not, to assume that Señor Matthew had survived the knife wound which, by the way, he had probably acquired through no fault of his own. In a little town like San Benito, everyone would know about something like that. A gringo could not die in such a place without the *policía* looking in to ask why and an *alcalde* to sign the death certificate and a priest to give solace to the mourners. He could not even be very sick without all those people! But had Don Rigo's man been told such things? No! True, she admitted, it was all very confusing, but not something about which to worry so much. Don Rigo, it seemed, was another matter.

Here Clara was of little help. Indeed, she may even have made matters worse, for as the day stretched into evening and still Don Rigo had not returned, she could not help speculating where he might have gone, which was what nearly everyone in the village was doing once word leaked out. That, too, could be laid at Clara's door, for like most girls, Clara naturally voiced her speculations to her mother, who naturally voiced those same speculations to her neighbor, who naturally passed the word to her best friend—who happened to be Don Rigo's sister Beatriz, who wasted no time in delivering the news to her revered aunt, who was only too happy to receive it.

Tía Elena, of course, beat a path straight to the *casa del hidalgo,* where she baited his young wife for her shrewishness. Rebecca was not in the mood. In front of the children, with smooth if limited Spanish, she told the old hag to mind her own business and still her gossiping tongue, warning that if she failed to do so, she, Doña Becca, the *dueña,* would have her confined to her bat cave of a house for the rest of her miserable life! It was an empty threat, of course, but delivered with such forcefulness and solemnity that no one hearing it deemed it so. Elena, in fact, seemed quite shaken, but she managed to find the courage for a final attack.

"It will serve you fairly," the old woman told her, "if he has gone back to the whore as they are saying, but just look what you have done to our people by driving him away! A husband who publicly breaks his marriage vow cannot be respected!"

Rebecca had never felt such rage. She demanded to know who was saying such things, and a mere glance at Clara's face gave her one name. Then they were all saying it. And it might even be true! She thought she would choke on the hot bile that rose to her throat. Jealousy shook her, and for a moment she could think of nothing but Rodrigo in Glorieta's bed. But he would not have gone from her bed back to Glorieta's, would he? She thought of the night they had spent at the Top of the World, then she remembered how angry and hurt he had looked before he'd walked out, and knew that she must look very like that now. She had to ask herself what would become of them all if it was true, and the answer was catastrophic.

Already it was coming apart, every last shred of what she had thought to have accomplished. Then it had all been for nothing. Her time here, her struggle, her hope to give back something of value—finally, it had come to this. Glorieta was still the whore, and Rebecca was still the outsider, and the children still could not read, and Tía Elena was still trying to mold this world along the same pattern of the last, and Don Rigo... She couldn't bear to think where he might be, what regrets he might have because of her, but she'd be damned if she'd let it all end this way. Maybe it was too late for her and Rodrigo, but she still had a thing or two to give.

Drawing herself up, she sent Rodolfo to the village to call out the women, and dispensed Lupe to the nursery with the baby. She then strolled casually toward her aunt-by-marriage and deliberately yanked the rosary beads from her hand. Ignoring the old woman's cries of outrage, she dragged Clara forward by her hair, then quite literally drove the pair of them into the village. After ordering Rodolfo back home and seeing he had gone a good distance down the lane, she put herself in the center of the women and glared down every one.

"You are all bad!" she told them, not knowing the Spanish equivalent of a hypocrite. "It is no more right for Don Rigo to go to a woman who is not his wife now than it was before! And the woman is no more wrong than he is! But he has been a good landlord and a good leader, and if he has troubles, you should help him, not judge him! A good man makes mistakes, and a good woman does, too, but that does not make him or her a bad person. And who is to say that Don Rigo has made this mistake! You do not know!"

"Then someone should find out!" Tía Elena challenged. "You should find out! You are the one who shouted at him and made him go away!"

Rebecca lifted her chin regally. "Then I will find out!" Without another word, she turned and pushed her way through the crowd, marching resolutely toward Glorieta's little house on the lane with all the flowering shrubs. She was shaking, and there were tears burning the backs of her eyes, and she was beginning to think that she had been stupid to do this, but she had to know for her own sake. She half feared the women would follow her, but to her relief, they did not.

She was alone, very much alone, when she stopped at Glorieta's door. It was dark inside, but she didn't let herself think too much about what might be happening there in the dark. Instead, she gritted her teeth and rapped her knuckles hard against the door. Something clinked, and then came a scraping sound, followed quickly by a series of bumps against the door. An instant later, the door swung open. Glorieta hugged her shawl tightly over her nightdress.

"How are you, *doña?*" she said, surprise in her voice.

Rebecca answered in Spanish. "So-so. Do you know why I am here?"

Glorieta shrugged. "Should I?"

Rebecca wondered if Glorieta was simply trying to humiliate her by making her ask or if it was possible that she really didn't know what everyone was saying. She hoped with all her heart that it was the latter, and that hope gave her the courage to ask, "Is my husband here?"

"No!"

"Has he been here?"

The look on Glorieta's face was answer enough to spill tears of relief down Rebecca's cheeks.

"You should come in," Glorieta told her, reaching out her hand. Rebecca stepped into her small house, thankful for the shadows that gave her a moment to calm herself while Glorieta lit the little gas lantern she used. "You had better tell me everything," she said, trimming the wick and pushing the lantern to the center of the table.

Rebecca looked around her. The house consisted of a single room. A narrow bed, unmade, set against the far wall. The table was flanked by two chairs painted gaily with flowers and vines. A makeshift stove crafted from bent pieces of metal filled what had once been a fireplace. Beside it sat a bucket, and beside that was a tall, narrow chest over which hung a foggy mirror. The only other furnishings in the house were a pair of rugs woven from fabric scraps and some rough shelves, upon which were arranged dishes and pretty rocks and a few potted herbs. Though poor, it was neat and clean and cozy, a real home, with a friendly feel about it.

Glorieta pulled a chair out for her, and Rebecca sat down, the whole sorry story suddenly spilling out of her. She told it all, not just about the scene in the square or the conflict with Tía Elena, not just about the argument or the false search for the doctor, but everything. She told how she had come to be there in the first place and how Don Rigo had been kind to her and the circumstances of the marriage and how hard it had been to stick to the bargain until finally, at the Top of the World, they seemed to have broken it for good, and then how Clara had upset everything with her news about Matthew.

"I was so ugly to him," she said, lapsing into English.

"*Español, amiga,*" Glorieta reminded her, and so she repeated it, substituting the Spanish word for *bad* in place of *ugly* because she couldn't recall the Spanish equivalent. Finally, she had to say that Don Rigo no longer considered himself her husband—if ever he had—and when she had done with it, Glorieta sat back, folded her arms and shook her head.

"Little fool," she said, "the Don Rigo I know would not marry merely for convenience, and once married, he would not give away his vows through his own choice. Think of it, Doña Becca, he has not come to me since he went away and found you, though he has had the opportunity and, from what you tell me, the need. More than this, he has expended great effort to keep you with him, riding away to prevent you from learning news of your brother at a time when he was needed here. Ask yourself why Don Rigo would do these things, and remember the answer when he comes home again!"

"But what if he does not come home?" was Rebecca's tearful rejoinder.

Glorieta got up and came around the table to put her arm about Rebecca's shoulder. "He will come home again," she assured Rebecca. "He has driven the cattle to the sea! After that, he will come home."

Rebecca took hold of her hand. "How do you know this? The truth, please."

Glorieta sent a look over her shoulder at the unmade bed. "Alonzo came to say goodbye. He said that Don Rigo had come down off the mountain late today and told all the vaqueros there—those who keep watch, the ones without wives to go home to at night—that they were driving the cattle to the sea. Alonzo asked for permission to return to the village. Don Rigo knows about us, so he let him go, told him to catch up later." Her cheeks were scarlet, but she kept her chin aloft. "Afterward, I fell asleep. It could not have been more than an hour since Alonzo left me!"

Alonzo and Glorieta! Rebecca didn't know whether to laugh with her friend or scold her. She did both, reminding Glorieta that she would be outcast again if the relationship became known. Glorieta smiled secretively.

"It is of no matter. I am to be a wife again, soon! Alonzo says we will not wait for the priest to come but will go to San Benito and the church there."

Rebecca was truly happy for her—and a little envious. But there was no reason to burden Glorieta with any more of her foolishness, so she wished her friend well and said goodbye.

When she returned to the square, many of the women were still there, talking among themselves. She told them proudly that they were mistaken about Don Rigo and that they should be ashamed for saying bad things about him and poor Glorieta. Then she told them that what they thought of her did not matter so long as they retained their faith in Don Rigo, for he was a good landlord and a good leader and a good husband. Then she went home—to wait.

Don Rigo returned on the fourth evening so exhausted that he didn't bathe or even speak very much before falling asleep. Rebecca removed his boots but left the saddlebags where they lay, thinking to herself how different this homecoming was than the first she had experienced. She smiled to herself, remembering the *hidalgo*'s costume he had donned by the pool in the orange grove, all black, silver and gold, his hair bound beneath his hat. He had come home victorious, he had told her, because he had made a "beeg deal." Well, this was all part of that big deal, the end of it, in fact, and there in those saddlebags was the fruit of his labors, the money for the school and the teacher and only he knew what else. But he was not the returning victor he should have been this time, either. Twice now she had robbed him of his victory, of the praise and respect that was his due. She felt small inside herself and ashamed.

She did not lie down beside him. What was the use? It was nearly over now. Soon everyone would know that the marriage had been a farce or, anyway, that it was over. Everyone knew already that they had fought, that he had left in anger. She wondered how he would manage the annulment or if he would even try. She would tell him, she decided, that no one needed to know what had happened between them at the Top of the World. If he wanted, she would even lie to the padre. It was not so great a sin—not when compared to what she had done to Don Rigo himself. She had been so much trouble. If once he had wanted her, surely he thought better of it now.

She went into the *sala* and lay down upon the cushions to sleep, but Don Rigo so filled her thoughts and consciousness that she lay awake late into the night. She tried to make her mind a blank, and when that did not work, tried to put her mind on Matthew, but for the first time, she had no real desire for it. What difference did it make, anyway? What could she do for Matthew? And what could he do for her? Even giving up her claim to their father's company had failed to benefit Matthew, for he had never known and she could not be certain now that he ever would. Likewise, Matthew could not give her the husband she so desired. They should have done for themselves, she realized, and suddenly she was angry with Matthew because he had not stayed in L.A. and fought for his freedom and his inheritance. Instead, he had frittered away his share of the company and then had buckled beneath their stepfather's accusations and had run. Had he not, they might both be in Los Angeles now, working together, making their lives count for something—as Don Rigo had done and would do again. Somehow, it always came back to Don Rigo. She feared it always would.

He woke her late, having already bathed and shaved and dressed. She could hear the children playing in the court-yard, and the clink of dishes being gathered from the table. He laid a plate before her, bacon and tortillas and a potato cake cooked with egg and onion and chilies.

"Eat," he said, "an' dress an' pack your t'ings. We ride to San Benito."

She watched him walk away and go out the door, heard him call to the children. It was over then, done. She pushed the plate away and got up, smiling feebly at Lupe as she walked to their—his—room. She made short work of it, dressing in jeans and her pink T-shirt, socks and athletic shoes, keeping her toilet to the minimum, taking only those things she had brought with her and rolling them into a tight bundle. When she went back out, Lupe was waiting for her, her gnarled hands wringing a large, square scarf all purples and greens and yellows. She folded the scarf and put it around Rebecca's head, tying it loosely beneath her chin.

"Dios vaya contigo, mi hija," she said. Rebecca fixed the words in her heart—God go with you, my daughter—and hugged the old woman quickly before she hurried away, unable to speak.

The children were gone when she stepped out into the courtyard. It was better, she thought. She didn't want to cry in front of them, hear them call her *Mamá*. Only Don Rigo and Paco and Luca were there with the horses. She supposed it was fitting. These three had brought her here; now they would take her away. Don Rigo lifted her up into the saddle, but his eyes never met hers and his mouth was set in a grim, thin line.

"Rodrigo," she said, looking down at him. "It doesn't have to be today. We could wait until you've rested and..." But he shook his head and moved away, swinging up onto El Pescado's back with practiced ease. The sooner the better, then, as far as she was concerned, and she hauled on the reins, turning the reluctant mare toward the gate.

They journeyed all through the day, a silent party of four riding single file over twisting trails and rocky slopes, making their way carefully down the mountainside. All along the way there were signs of the herd that had passed only days before. Boulders had fallen in places, and grasses were crushed flat in others. Here and there the trail had crumbled away, leaving only the most precarious footing for the horses, and everywhere was the dung that had dried in the sun. She took pride in these things, for his sake, and said nothing about the way being rough.

They camped on a ledge that first night, where the ground was sandy and free of dung, and Rebecca lay on her blanket looking up at the sky, feeling Don Rigo beside her a mere arm's length away, but she took no joy in the vastness or the diamond light of the stars, and morning found her as tired as evening had. Don Rigo said little, but he brought her coffee and was there to tie her bedroll to the saddle skirt when she had lifted it to the mare's back. His eyes met hers then, sad and dull, but she held them as long as he allowed and was thankful.

About midday, she realized they were going up again, and that night, once more they made a place high above the desert floor. During the day it was hot here and as dusty as the desert below. It was Avilés land, so there was the occasional goat, and once, even a cow wandered by in the night, quietly foraging the dry grasses that grew only in scattered brown clumps. She placed her blanket close to Don Rigo's that night, and slept with her back to his, expecting at any moment to feel him move away, but when morning came, she found that she slept with her head on his arm. In their sleep, they had turned to each other. Might there be hope? she wondered, and she eased away, lest he wake and pull back from her.

Later, when they descended once more, the desert heat rising up to meet them, they stopped to take refuge from the sun and to rest the mounts. Luca and Paco went at once to drink in the shade, but Don Rigo unsaddled El Pescado, then moved routinely to the mare. Seeing her first opportunity in many days to speak privately with him, Rebecca quickly filled a cup with water from the canteen and carried it to him. He looked at her, stopped what he was doing and took the cup into his hands, his face guarded and stiff.

"*Gracias,*" he said, and drained the cup. "*Muy bien.*"

He gave it back to her and went on loosening the mare's girth.

Rebecca opened her mouth, but suddenly her tongue felt thick and unwieldy. She sought a drop of water from the cup and turned it up to her mouth, feeling the moisture but finding nothing, the small quantity of water evaporating even as she sought it. She lowered the cup to find him looking strangely at her, and something told her it was now or never.

"My husband," she said, gripping his wrist urgently, "things said in anger—"

"Are of'en t'ings dat need to be said," he finished for her softly.

"And often are not," she came back. "A-and sometimes, even when we mean them, we find later that we were wrong."

"An' which o' us was wrong, Rebecca?"

"Both of us! And neither."

He shook his head. "Eet canno' be two ways, *querida*, no' een my worl'. Dis ees de pro'lem, ees eet no'? Two diff'rent worl's, two diff'rent ways."

"But, Rodrigo," she said, "I don't care about that, not anymore. It was a struggle at first, I admit, but now I..." The words were on the tip of her tongue. I love you. I love you. But already she could see the doubt in his eyes, and the fear that he would turn away was very great. She swallowed the words and bowed her head, tears coming quickly.

"Ah, *querida*," he whispered, "do no' cry. Let us no' hurt one anodher more. Shh-shh." He took her in his arms and for a moment, all was well. She turned her face into his shirt front and felt safe for a time, but too soon he set her aside and as he lifted the saddle from the mare's back, she saw the pain in his eyes. Once more she had hurt him, and so she turned away, steeling herself for the distance that would only grow wider between them.

Yet, when evening came, he spread his blanket beside hers, and when they lay down, she felt his arms come around her, one a pillow for her head, the other to hold her safely through the night. She thought of Paco and Luca and knew what she would have done if not for their silent presence, but this was not the time, and she could only hope for another. Still, she slept as she had not done for many nights, only to wake that final morning and find San Benito waiting below.

From above, it looked like a place of square, pale roofs and dusty streets with old cars rusting in heaps between the houses. The people looked lethargic and disorganized. It was unfair to judge them, she knew, especially with the sun broiling everything to a crisp, but this place she had so struggled to reach now seemed to hold nothing for her. She shivered at the thought of what she might find, sparing her first thought for Matthew in days. She felt ashamed and frightened, but there was nothing she could do except follow along as they wound toward the little city below.

It was siesta when they reached the town, the hottest part of the day, but people of all sorts came to their doors as the riders made their way through the streets. Don Rigo stopped at a place where he was known and asked questions, receiving directions from a small, wizened old man who wore a strip of white cloth tied around his long gray hair. Don Rigo took the reins once more and led them at a walk through many turns and alleys and dusty lanes, stopping at last before a garishly painted adobe house with only a curtain for a door. Don Rigo called out, and another old man lifted the curtain, peering beneath it. After a moment, he stepped outside and sat down on the stoop, his hands shaking weakly. Rebecca got down off her horse and went to stand beside Don Rigo.

"I look for my brother," she told the old man in his own language. "An American with pale hair and blue eyes. His name is Matthew Harper, and his wife's name is Anita."

The old man nodded and began to cry. The whole ugly story was not told for some time, and when it was done, Rebecca was sick to her stomach and shamed all the more. Matthew, it seemed, had arrived in San Benito with Anita, the old man's granddaughter, and many American dollars. He had been angry when he saw the house, and angrier still as time passed. When it became obvious that Anita was pregnant, he had married her, but afterward he had drunk a good deal. Then, while his wife was big with child, he had begun to see another woman, Consuelo, and Consuelo's husband had stabbed him. They had feared he would die, but Consuelo had nursed him to health again. She and Matt had gone away together soon after Anita's daughter had been born. Within a few weeks Anita, too, disappeared with another rich *Americano* she had met in Santa Rosalía, where she had gone to work on the pleasure boats that came by way of the Sea of Cortés. She had left behind her little daughter, but the old man and his wife were unable to care for her, poor and ill as they were. The wife, he explained, no longer left her bed at all, and he himself was sick with old age and a tremor in his hands.

"Where is the child?" Rebecca asked, and he replied that she had been placed with the Sisters of Charity near the church on the far edge of the town.

Rebecca thanked him for the information and turned to Don Rigo. He held her close, saying nothing about the brother who had so disappointed her, while she dried her tears and tried to force her mind to tell her what to do next. In the end, though, it was Don Rigo who decided.

"I will take you to the sisters," he said. "You will want to see de *niño*."

"Yes, oh, yes!" she said. "She needs me, doesn't she? And I need her."

He nodded, scratching his chin speculatively, and said nothing more.

They rode on, finding the church and the little nunnery easily. The nuns welcomed them and quickly brought the baby, whom they had named Felicia, meaning blessed or happy. She was all coos and smiles, with skin the color of dried coriander, eyes that were deep pools of blue tinged with violet, and black hair curling softly about her plump face.

"She's beautiful!" Rebecca exclaimed, hearing the phrase repeated in Spanish as the men crowded around. The little one wiggled as if happy to see them, and the sister placed her in Rebecca's arms. The baby instantly latched on to a lock of Rebecca's hair, pulling it free of the scarf, and gurgled contentedly, making everyone laugh. Rebecca knew she would never let her go again nor have to, for Matthew would never come for her—just as he would never have come for her, his sister. The truth about Matthew Harper was that he was selfish and shallow and dishonest and, yes, even a thief. Deep down, she had always known it, but she could admit it now because he was not the only person in the world she had left to love, not by a long shot.

She thought of them: Rodolfo and Enrique and Lupe and Clara and Glorieta and little Eustacia and the other Espinozas and Teresa and Ana and María and Beatriz and Isabel and their respective families, and even Tía Elena, old crone that she was, but especially Rodrigo, whose arm was around her now, strong, steady, supportive. She looked up at him, all that she felt written on her face for him to read, but he only glanced at her and then back to the baby.

"She has your eyes," he said.

"And your hair!" she came back, laughing a little. He cocked his head to the side.

"She coul' be mine," he decided, "ours."

"Oh, Rodrigo," Rebecca said, "do you mean that? Could you possibly—"

"I t'ink we shoul' take her home wit us," he interrupted smoothly. "Perha's one day, she will have a brodher wit eyes like dat, eh? But eef no', dhere is a'ways Rodolfo and Enrique."

Rebecca felt her bottom lip begin to tremble and bit it, only to smile. She leaned against him, cradling the baby, and slipped her arm about his neck.

"I love you, you know," she whispered, "and I want to go home to my children!"

He put his arms around them both, Rebecca and the baby. *"Señora,"* he said, "I love my chil'ren as a fadher shou', but tonigh', my wife, we sleep alone."

"And from now on," she promised him happily. "Tonight and from now on."

"Two worl's no more?" he asked quietly.

"Oh, Rodrigo," she said, "I wouldn't want either one without you!"

He kissed her while the sisters laughed and Don Rigo's men grew red, their teeth showing in their faces, and the baby squirmed between them.

*   *   *   *   *

This April,
Silhouette *Special Edition* is pleased to present

ONCE IN A LIFETIME
by Ginna Gray

the long-awaited companion volume to her bestselling duo

Fools Rush In (#416)
Where Angels Fear (#468)

Ever since spitfire Erin Blaine and her angelic twin sister Elise stirred up double trouble and entangled their long-suffering brother David in some sticky hide-and-seek scenarios, readers clamored to hear more about dashing, debonair David himself.

Now that time has come, as straitlaced Abigail Stewart manages to invade the secrecy shrouding sardonic David Blaine's bachelor boat—and creates the kind of salty, saucy, swashbuckling romantic adventure that comes along only once in a lifetime!

Even if you missed the earlier novels,
you won't want to miss

ONCE IN A LIFETIME #661

Available this April, only in Silhouette *Special Edition*.　OL-1

IT'S A CELEBRATION OF MOTHERHOOD!

Following the success of BIRDS, BEES and BABIES, we are proud to announce our second collection of Mother's Day stories.

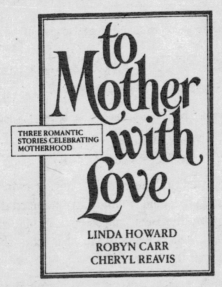

to **Mother** with **Love**

THREE ROMANTIC
STORIES CELEBRATING
MOTHERHOOD

LINDA HOWARD
ROBYN CARR
CHERYL REAVIS

Three stories in one volume, all by award-winning authors—stories especially selected to reflect the love all families share.

Available in May, TO MOTHER WITH LOVE is a perfect gift for yourself or a loved one to celebrate the joy of motherhood.

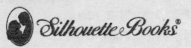

Silhouette Books®

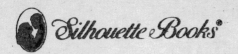 *Silhouette Books*

SILHOUETTE BOOKS ARE NOW AVAILABLE IN STORES AT THESE CONVENIENT TIMES EACH MONTH

Silhouette Desire and Silhouette Romance

> May titles: April 10
> June titles: May 8
> July titles: June 5
> August titles: July 10

Silhouette Intimate Moments and Silhouette Special Edition

> May titles: April 24
> June titles: May 22
> July titles: June 19
> August titles: July 24

We hope this new schedule is convenient for you. With only two trips each month to your local bookseller, you will always be sure not to miss any of your favorite authors!

Happy reading!

*Please note: There may be slight variations in on-sale dates in your area due to differences in shipping and handling.

SDATES-R

You'll flip . . . your pages won't!
Read paperbacks *hands-free* with

Book Mate · I

The perfect "mate" for all your romance paperbacks

Traveling • Vacationing • At Work • In Bed • Studying • Cooking • Eating

Perfect size for all standard paperbacks, this wonderful invention makes reading a pure pleasure! Ingenious design holds paperback books OPEN and FLAT so even wind can't ruffle pages – leaves your hands free to do other things. Reinforced, wipe-clean vinyl-covered holder flexes to let you turn pages without undoing the strap . . . supports paperbacks so well, they have the strength of hardcovers!

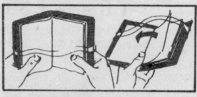

Pages turn WITHOUT opening the strap

SEE-THROUGH STRAP

Reinforced back stays flat

Built in bookmark

BOOK MARK

BACK COVER HOLDING STRIP

10 x 7¼ opened
Snaps closed for easy carrying, too

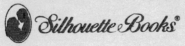